In *Confessions to a Stranger*, Danielle Grandinetti weaves a tale that is at once mysterious, suspenseful, romantic, and inspiring ... Filled with truths that made me ponder my own life, this novel is a lovely start to what is sure to be a wonderful series!

—Heidi Chiavaroli,
Carol Award-Winning Author of *The Orchard House*

Danielle Grandinetti has crafted a wonderful tale of suspense and romance that will keep you on the edge of your seat. With well-drawn characters authentic to the era, a gripping plot, and a strong message of hope, *Confessions to a Stranger* is a read I recommend!

—Misty M. Beller,
USA Today bestselling author of the Sisters of the Rockies

A Strike to the Heart is a compelling story. From the very first page, I was immersed into the thrilling action and remained gripped with intrigue until the satisfying ending. The romance escalated right along with the winding plot, creating a layered mystery that is sure to delight readers.

—Rachel Scott McDaniel,
Award-winning author of *The Mobster's Daughter*

Riveting from the first scene, *As Silent as the Night* offers a unique, edge-of-your-seat Christmas read ... A beautiful, gripping, and romantically suspenseful Christmas story you wouldn't be able to put down if you tried.

—Chautona Havig,
Author of *The Stars of New Cheltenham*

The Neighbor and the Gifts is a poignant tale that transforms a familiar carol into a stirring journey of faith, love, and danger ... For readers who love historical romance, mystery, and want a deeper meaning in their holiday stories—this one's for you.

—Natalie Walters,
bestselling and award-winning author of *Living Lies* and the *SNAP Agency* series

Refuge for the Archaeologist

**Discover the Foundation
of Danielle's Bookish World**

Harbored in Crow's Nest
Confessions to a Stranger
Refuge for the Archaeologist
Escape with the Prodigal
Relying on the Enemy
Sheltered by the Doctor
Investigation of a Journalist

Bridge: His Boss's Little Sister

Unexpected Protectors
To Stand in the Breach
A Strike to the Heart
As Silent as the Night

For a complete list, visit
daniellegrandinetti.com/books

Refuge for the Archaeologist

Danielle Grandinetti

Hearth Spot Press

REFUGE FOR THE ARCHAEOLOGIST
Published by Hearth Spot Press

Scripture quotations are taken from the King James Version of the Bible

Kindle Book ISBN: 978-1-956098-09-9
EPUB ISBN: 978-1-956098-22-8
Paperback ISBN: 978-1-956098-10-5

Cover Art: Roseanna White Designs
Author Picture: Abby Mae Tindal at Maeflower Photography
Editor: Denise Weimer

To my Readers,
who encourage and cheer me on with every story I write.

"God is our refuge and strength,
a very present help in trouble."
Psalm 46:1 (KJV)

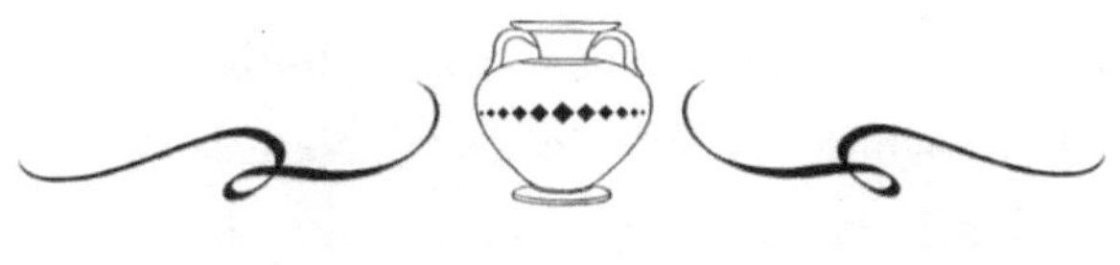

CHAPTER ONE

Tuesday, September 16, 1930
Crow's Nest, Wisconsin

Silas Ward hefted the newly built end table from the bed of his pickup. The solid piece of furniture had turned out well. Hopefully, Rose Wittlebush, the town's honorary grandmother, would like it, .

Thick heat pressed on his shoulders, causing sweat to trickle down his back. Though he was dressed in a simple cotton shirt with the sleeves rolled up, his suspenders created wet strips down his torso. Even the lake breeze was absent today.

Setting the end table down on the porch, he propped open the screen door with his hip and rapped on the wooden frame. The outgoing octogenarian lived in a farmhouse overlooking Lake Michigan. White railings, which could use a fresh coat of paint, surrounded the deep, wrap-around front porch. He mentally added it to his list of things to do before another Wisconsin winter chipped them even more.

Imagining the older lady's surprise, he pulled off the Stetson he wore despite the rolling farmland surrounding his hometown, not the rugged ranch land out west. Rose Wittlebush deserved every ounce of gallantry his father taught him, especially after losing both her seamstress shop and her assistant earlier this year. Widowed now for a decade, she had no family left, and he couldn't help but look out for her, same as his own mom. It's what neighbors did here in Crow's Nest.

He knocked again, and scuffling sounds came from behind the closed door, as if people were scrambling. Not the image that came to mind when he considered the white-haired lady who lived alone. Concern nipped at him like a cattle dog. He rapped harder.

More scrambling sounds, then a thump and a cry.

"Mrs. Wittlebush!" He jiggled the doorknob. Locked. She never locked it. "It's Silas Ward. Can you answer the door?"

He put his ear to the smooth plane of wood. He could barely hear through it and didn't like the hushed, hurried voices coming from inside. Rose had company. Not the good kind, considering she hadn't yet come to the door or assured him she was fine.

"Rose Wittlebush!" Another thirty seconds and he'd find an alternate entry point.

The door disappeared from in front of his face.

"Thank heavens." Mrs. Wittlebush grabbed his wrist with strong fingers and dragged him inside. A vinegary smell wrapped around him. Was she pickling vegetables today? "We need your help."

"I really don't." This frustrated statement came from a woman sitting on her haunches in the middle of Mrs. Whittlebush's front room. She had black curly hair—not tight corkscrews, but close—and the mass hung around her down-turned face like lamb's wool. From what he could tell from her hunched position, she was tall and slender. The deep olive brown of her arms stark against her white blouse, yet blending with her serviceable forest-green skirt.

He tossed his Stetson on the coat rack and bumped the front door closed with the heel of his boot. "What can I do?"

"Lift Cora to the couch." Mrs. Whittlebush gave his shoulder a firm shove.

The other woman—Cora—sighed as she grabbed a mass of curls away from her face, turning toward him. Her eyes were as blue as a mountain lake. He instinctively moved a step in front of Mrs. Whittlebush. Until he knew who this Cora was, he wouldn't let the older woman out of his sight. The danger she'd faced early this summer was enough for a lifetime. He wouldn't let Mrs. Whittlebush get caught up in any more.

"I just need a minute, and I'll be fine." Cora gave a smile, but her eyes seemed unfocused. It was a look he'd occasionally encountered from the ranch hands he used to work with—especially after they'd been thrown from a horse—but never in a lady.

Not that he'd ever seen this Cora around Crow's Nest before—and in such a small town, identifying strangers was easy—but Mrs. Whittlebush was known for her hospitality regardless of a person's background. What was it about the older women in this town taking in strays? He didn't know, but the last stranger to make herself at home in Crow's Nest nearly got herself killed, along with Silas's friend, David Martins. Speaking of Martins, Silas made a second mental note to mention Cora's arrival to David's uncle, Detective O'Connor.

"Water. That will help." Mrs. Whittlebush patted Silas's arm, then dashed for the kitchen as fast as her Mary Janes could carry her.

Time for answers.

As soon as Mrs. Whittlebush's steps faded, Silas crouched in front of Cora, one arm on his knee. "She can't hear you, so tell me the truth. Who are you really and what's going on?"

Her eyes narrowed at his command, then she cocked her head. "You said your name was Silas? You help her a lot, don't you?"

Not what he expected her to say, nor had he expected the gentle tone with which she spoke, as if Rose Wittlebush was this stranger's closest friend and simply saying her name required careful handling.

Cora squeezed his worked-roughened hand with fingers just as callused, and it touched something deep inside. "Thank you."

Two words that held a world of meaning he'd need a week to decipher. It set him off-kilter.

She offered a tired smile and clamped a hand on his shoulder, sending a protective streak shooting through him, then pushed to her feet. "Best not worry her more if I can help it." But she swayed as she stood upright.

Silas caught her elbow and led her straight to the couch. "Maybe I should take you to a doctor."

She waved him away as she sank to the sturdy cushions. "You're as bad as Tante." Another faded smile. "I'll be fine. And here she comes with water. Just what I need."

Tante? He squeezed his hand into a fist. *Tante* meant *aunt* and Mrs. Whittlebush had no family. What was this Cora woman up to? He refused to let the widow get taken advantage of—not on his watch. She'd lost too much already, and Silas owed her for taking care of his own family while he was out West.

"You need more than water, child." Mrs. Whittlebush handed the glass to Cora, then wiped her hands on the blue apron that covered her yellow house dress. As a seamstress, vibrant color always surrounded her. "Now put your feet up, and I'll tuck this blanket around you."

Silas leaned against the bookcase set against the north wall as Cora's cheeks grew a shade darker. Mrs. Whittlebush could be a fussbudget, but not a soul in Crow's Nest minded because she was always the one who turned up when a person needed help the most. But who helped her—besides David Martins and himself? Martins's grandmother and Silas's mother were Mrs. Whittlebush's closest friends. Could they know this Cora?

"Silas, dear." The older woman turned a cheery smile on him. "What brought you to my home today?"

The end table! "I brought you that furniture piece you commissioned last week."

"It's ready?" She followed him to the front door.

"Of course." It was the least he could do after the June tornado destroyed her business. He lifted the end table and carried it inside, only to catch Cora watching him before she glanced away. He had the strangest urge to show her just how strong he could be. Ridiculous. He had nothing to prove.

Mrs. Whittlebush squealed as if she were a little girl and he had brought her penny candy. "Silas, it's just what I imagined." She ran her hand over the piece. "Dark wood. Smooth lines. Oh Silas, you do wonderful work."

His turn to feel heat rising in his face. He shot a look at Cora. She was watching Mrs. Whittlebush with an expression of pure pleasure. Mrs. Whittlebush. Not him. Embarrassment turned the heat rising on his neck into a furnace. Thankfully, Mrs. Whittlebush waved him into motion.

"Carry it to the studio, would you?" She led the way through double doors to what used to be an unused formal room of sorts. Over the past few months, he'd helped her recreate a seamstress showroom with cushioned chairs for guests, a grand mirror, and a clean fireplace for winter. He set the table between the chairs, where he knew she intended it to go.

"Looks about finished." He looped his thumbs in his suspenders before remembering how damp his shirt had become. He quickly removed them, subtly wiping his hands down his pant legs. "We're going to be hard pressed to get customers to leave."

Instead of replying, she looked toward the stranger they'd left in the other room.

"Who is she, Mrs. Whittlebush?" He lowered his voice so it wouldn't carry.

"Cora Davis, a skilled archaeologist." Pride rang through her words.

"And?" Silas pressed. "Who is she to you?"

Her fingers wrapped themselves in her apron, and she bit her bottom lip as if fighting the urge to say more.

Silas wrapped an arm around Mrs. Whittlebush's well-cushioned shoulders, her gray hair barely reaching him mid-chest. "You can tell me."

"I have never wanted to tell someone the truth more than I do right now." She looked up at him, tears shimmering in her brown eyes. "But it is not my secret to tell."

His mind whirled with possibilities. Cora couldn't be a long-lost daughter. She appeared too young. Niece perhaps, since she called Mrs. Whittlebush *Tante*? But he hadn't heard the older lady speak of any siblings or extended family. No one came to help when she broke her ankle the summer before he went out West. Nor did anyone call while he took his turn beside her sickbed when she was laid up with influenza last winter, not long after his return to Crow's Nest. What game was Cora Davis playing?

Then again, why assume the worst? While the woman David's grandmother took in had brought danger with her, Martins had fallen in love with her—against Silas's advice. In the end, David and Adaleigh's situation turned out okay, but no way could lightning strike twice. Right? A deep frown pulled the muscles in his cheeks.

This Cora Davis better not be a con artist or a hobo planning to swindle a sweet old lady. He wouldn't stand for that, no matter how she tugged at his sympathies. He crossed his arms, letting his muscles bulge as he met Mrs. Whittlebush's gaze. "Do you feel safe with her?"

Mrs. Whittlebush laughed. "You fret too much."

"She's a stranger to me, Mrs. Whittlebush. I care about what happens to you."

"I know you do, Silas." She wove her arm around his waist as if he were a little boy and she wanted to be sure he listened to her words. "She's not a stranger to me."

Not a strange—

"Everything okay?" Cora gripped the doorframe as if holding herself upright. A fierce light in her eyes had him relaxing his posture so she didn't assume him to be the threat. Protector, yes, but not a danger unless she meant to harm Mrs. Whittlebush. She quirked her eyebrow and Silas took her measure.

She was as lithe as he'd guessed, like a strong, sinewy tree. Her skin was somehow pale as well as tanned and weathered. This woman spent long days in the sun. How unusual. He shook his head, pinning down his curiosity. Now wasn't the time for that.

"Please tell him, my dear," Mrs. Whittlebush pleaded with Cora. Clutching Silas's elbow, she pulled him closer to the woman.

"Tante." Her *T*s came out sharp, almost as if she lapsed into German, though she looked about as opposite a German woman as any he'd ever met.

Again, inquisitiveness rose against his better judgment, and it irritated him.

"Do it for me." Mrs. Whittlebush left Silas's side to cross the room and press her hands to Cora's cheeks. "I need someone else to know. And I trust him."

Silas's heart warmed at the older woman's words. Cora pursed her lips. Silas stood straighter in light of her appraisal of him. He had nothing to hide. In fact, better she know Mrs. Whittlebush had someone like him in her corner.

Cora moved to perch on the arm of one of the chairs. Closer to him and so informal it unsettled him. "Tante speaks of you often in her letters."

Didn't that just cause his brows to rise even more? "I don't recall her getting any from you."

Cora smirked, but Silas found he liked that look on her. Heaven help him.

"I do not share my correspondence with you." Mrs. Whittlebush swatted his arm.

"I get your mail more often than not," he grumbled. "None of the envelopes have her name on them."

"You've seen letters from a Davis Jones out of New York?" Cora paused, as if waiting for him to acknowledge that he'd seen such a return address. He had. Many times. "Since my male-dominated job takes me—a spinster—to volatile parts of the world, I set up a way to communicate that made my connection to Tante harder to track down."

"Okay." Silas spoke slowly, revealing the falseness of his acquiescence. Everything about this stranger screamed danger, and he didn't understand it at all. He was a simple man and he wanted straightforward answers. "But that doesn't tell me anything. Who are you? And more specifically, who are you to Mrs. Whittlebush?" He repeated the question he'd asked of the older woman.

Mrs. Whittlebush gave Cora a nod of encouragement.

"You're sure?" Cora asked her and Silas bristled. What had she to fear from him? Cora was the stranger.

"I'm very sure, dear." Mrs. Whittlebush waved a hand as if she could coax the answers from her visitor.

Cora released a breath and met Silas's gaze. "Tante is my great aunt."

Great aunt? Silas tried not to show too much confusion. Cora looked nothing like Mrs. Whittlebush. Where the older woman had a cheery, round face, Cora's was narrow and long. Mrs. Whittlebush had pleasant brown eyes. Cora had those sharp blue ones. And Mrs. Whittlebush's aged skin was much lighter than Cora's, a difference Silas supposed could be attributed to sun exposure or lack thereof. But what needled him most was him not knowing Rose Whittlebush had a living relative.

"Why is that such a secret?" Silas couldn't keep the irritation out of his voice. "A great aunt isn't someone to hide away so you can go on with your life." Especially not a caring older woman like Mrs. Whittlebush.

Cora threw up her chin. "I didn't need potential looters using my aunt as leverage to get me to help them. Best keep my private life a secret."

Looters! "You willingly go into dangerous places that have looters?" Silas couldn't get his mind wrapped around the implications. First, she was a woman and females deserved protection. Second, she was unmarried, gallivanting off to who-knows-where. And third, she left her aunt behind so she could go ... do what, exactly?

Cora crossed her arms. "In my work with the Corinvetter Foundation, I go wherever they allow a female archaeologist. If a dangerous place is where the digs are, the artifacts, the history, then I'm there, too."

"You willingly leave your great aunt with no relatives to take care of her, to go find *things*?" It boggled his mind!

"They aren't just *things*." The muscle along Cora's jaw clenched. "They are part of our world's history. Stories of people who lived centuries or millennia ago. Stories of real people. People who have voices that need to be heard. Finding what they left behind helps me tell their story. Gives them back their voice."

"But your great aunt!"

"Silas." Mrs. Whittlebush put her warm hand on his bare forearm, reminding him of her presence, and he sucked in a breath of air. "Why do you think I live in a small town? Am I a lonely old lady with no one to care for me? Not in Crow's Nest. Look at you, standing here trying to protect me."

"That's what family is supposed to do," Silas growled.

"So now that I have a family member present, you won't help me with my heavy furniture?" Mrs. Whittlebush narrowed her eyes in the same way Cora had earlier. "You're a better man than that, Silas Ward."

"That's not my point." Silas fought his exasperation. Why couldn't he get these two stubborn women to see what was so clear to him?

"And what is your point, Mr. Ward?" Cora glared, anger radiating off of her. "That I'm supposed to follow your rules and if I don't, you think me unfit? You have never met me before, and yet you put expectations on me just because you hear I'm someone's only living relative, and a female at that. Why do you think I have told no one about my connection to Tante? Why do you think I didn't want to—"

Cora stumbled off the arm of the couch, her hand going to her head, then her mouth.

"Sit, Cora." Mrs. Whittlebush was instantly by her side.

Cora shook her head, staggered as her eyes nearly rolled back. Silas bounded forward and caught Cora before she tumbled to the floor. Is this what happened when he knocked earlier?

Mrs. Whittlebush raced toward her kitchen as he carried Cora to the sofa in the living room. His heightened emotion mixed with concern for this stranger, creating a cauldron in his gut. How could he like the feel of her in his arms, want to take care of her, when only a moment ago he considered her someone from whom he needed to protect Mrs. Whittlebush?

"I'm fine, you know." Cora laid her head against the cushions as he settled her on the sofa, her voice weak. She appeared a shell of the fiery woman she'd been a moment ago as she sparred with him. "But can you ask Tante for a slice of toast?"

Silas pressed his lips together to keep from calling out her lie and nodded before heading to the kitchen, where he found Mrs. Whittlebush pacing before the wood stove. He delivered Cora's request as nausea swirled in his own stomach. He sank to a chair and buried his head in his hands. "She's sick, isn't she?"

"Yes," the older lady whispered.

"And I bashed her for her life choices. I'm an idiot, Mrs. Whittlebush."

She sliced a loaf of bread. "She arrived late last night and has been nauseous and unstable on her feet since. I'm worried. Very worried."

"She's seen a doctor?" He rested his forearms on his knees and looked at the older woman.

Mrs. Whittlebush dusted her hands on her apron. "She says she has."

"But?"

Mrs. Whittlebush buttered both slices of bread, then slid them into the oven. "You see her determination to keep up with her work? She's battled all sorts of illnesses without ever coming home. Whatever this is, it is enough to bring her back to me. That means she's worried, too."

Silas absorbed her meaning. "How long has it been since you've seen her?"

"Long enough." The kettle whistled, and she poured the steaming water into a cup. "I'm getting old, Silas. I don't think Cora wants to see that either. Staying away means remembering life as it was, not how it is."

Silas frowned. "What do you think I can do?"

"What you're doing right now, my boy."

Silas rose to wrap his arm around her shoulders and absorb her heartache. He didn't understand the separation—or the connection—between the older woman and her great niece, but he cared about Mrs. Whittlebush. She was like the grandmother he didn't have.

He closed his eyes as the feel of Cora in his arms came back to him. He had no room in his life for such things. His brother had loved married life. David Martins was moonstruck. Silas was too busy taking care of everyone to feel anything but annoyance with a woman who didn't take care of her own great aunt.

But Cora was sick, and Mrs. Whittlebush was worried.

Dragging Cora to a doctor wasn't the answer, as much as he wished it were since she obviously needed medical attention. However, he'd ruined any chance at speaking reason by condemning her. Maybe being nice would restore him to her good graces? Not that he wanted to be her friend. He'd do this for Mrs. Whittlebush.

Then again, what if he went a step further and offered Cora an olive branch? Just being nice might be too passive, especially after making such a gigantic fool of himself. Holding his tongue wasn't a strong suit of his, but for Mrs. Whittlebush, he'd try. Could he offer Cora a way to satisfy her treasure hunting by giving her *things* she could research?

He rubbed the scruff on his chin. No matter, he needed to apologize. Perhaps she would receive it better if he showed her he'd listened first.

"Maybe there's more I can do." Silas spoke carefully, the thought still forming in his mind. "Do you think Cora would like to see my family's curiosity shop?"

"Curiosity shop?" Cora reappeared in the doorway. She looked a few shades paler than before, if that was possible, but more focused. As though the few minutes of rest had allowed her to feel better. It eased his guilt. Some.

Silas reached his hands out as he crossed the room toward her. This was his first step toward an apology, and he needed to face it like the man his father raised him to be. "My family owns Crow's Nest Curiosities on the far south end of the wharf. I help run it." When he wasn't using his carpentry skills to build or fix things. They were having to depend on his skills more these past several months as money grew tighter and the store's profit shrank.

"What type of items do you sell?" She leaned against the door frame, expression blank. He had a mountain to climb in order to recover from his hasty words.

"All sorts of things that my mom finds—silver spoons and porcelain dishes, even old chests—as well as new and restored furniture." He motioned toward the seamstress room. "Like the side table."

"Silas does all the restoration himself." Mrs. Whittlebush set the plate of toast on the table.

He shrugged, self-conscious at the pride in the older woman's voice. He didn't deserve her defense of him. Not after how he'd treated her niece.

"And you want me to visit the shop ... why?" Cory studied him, as if she could discern his motives from his face. His heart pounded. Maybe she could.

"Silas is trying to be nice." Mrs. Whittlebush sounded too much like a referee. He needed to own up to his mistake.

He pulled on his ear. "I'm sorry for—"

"Stop." Cora held up a hand and marched forward until she was toe-to-toe with him. The top of her head barely reached his chin. The feminine scent of flowers contrasted with the confident woman it surrounded. "Do not apologize just because I got sick. Do not be nice because I'm not quite myself. If feeling sorry for me is the only reason you want to be nice, then I can do without it."

"Cora!" Mrs. Whittlebush scolded.

"She's right." Silas met Cora's gaze, the intensity of her eyes towing him in, loosening his tongue to once again speak the honest truth. "I'm not offering out of pity. The opposite, actually. Perhaps you'll find something that will make you feel at home. I judged you without reason, Cora, without first knowing you. I'm sorry and I hope you'll see this offer as the apology I mean it to be."

Cora's eyes widened.

He pressed a hand to his heart. "Will you forgive me?"

"I will, cowboy." Color returned to her cheeks. "I accept your apology and your offer. Tomorrow morning, Tante and I will come see what you have in that shop of yours." Her gaze darted away from his. "As long as you're the one to give us a tour."

She could bet her boots he would be there, but he squared his shoulders against the feeling and stuck out his hand to shake on it, as if they'd reached a bargain. It unnerved him to admit that her reaction to his idea had him looking forward to seeing her again. And that maybe he should be running the other way instead.

CHAPTER TWO

Wednesday, September 17

"How are you feeling?" Tante set a plate of pancakes in front of Cora as she had for breakfast at every one of Cora's visits as a little girl.

The kitchen smelled of flour and syrup. It was smaller than Tante's old house, but she still used the same blue-and-white Blue Willow plates set on the yellow tablecloth. The kerosene lap at the center reflected the morning sun in the shined glass chimney.

"Better." Cora gave her great aunt a brave smile.

She found she usually felt better in the morning, the one time of day when the world rarely spun. She couldn't remember when the dizziness started—the time between boarding a ship for Crow's Nest and the earthquake she survived while in Campania, Italy, two months ago was unnervingly blank—but she did remember when the dizziness caused her to lose her balance at the edge of a cliff, effectively sending her home, potentially for good.

"You sure you're ready to go calling?" Tante sat across from her. "Silas will understand if you want to wait another day."

She shoved away the fuzzy memories from that fateful day. Remembering caused the fluttering in her chest, not thoughts of Silas, right? "Silas, huh? You might have mentioned the man is a cowboy." A rather fit cowboy based on how easily he carried her yesterday. She fended off the heat that rose at recalling the muscles she'd felt as he held her. "Not something I expected to find in Wisconsin."

"Did I not mention that?" Tante took a bite of pancake, all feigned innocence.

Cora narrowed her eyes. Tante knew Cora had no place for a man in her life, especially a cowboy. She had the same weakness as her mother. Cowboys always threatened to turn her head, and that meant one thing—Tante had a reason for keeping that particular detail to herself. Cora needed to know what it was before she re-entered the presence of Silas Ward.

"Silas used to be a cowboy." Tante cut her pancake with a knife and fork. "He worked on a ranch out West until a year or so ago, when his brother died. Still wears the hat."

"Tante." Her aunt was skirting the truth.

"What?" Tante set down her silverware. "He's not technically a cowboy anymore, and I find it helpful to have a big, handsome man helping me around the house."

"Handsome!" She knew it. Tante was playing matchmaker. Not that Cora could deny the truth that Silas was incredibly handsome, with his scruffy, square jaw and solid shoulders ...

"Don't you think so?" Tante flashed those oh-so-innocent eyes. "Strong muscles, surely. And a kind and honest heart. Haven't I told you all of that in my letters?"

Most of that, yes, but Cora had taken little notice other than feeling reassured that Tante was being well-cared for by the people of Crow's

Nest. She certainly hadn't bothered picturing the *cowboy* who seemed to be the most helpful person in town.

Yesterday, she could barely tear her eyes away from the strength he exuded with his shirt sleeves rolled up. Then he'd actually carried her! Be still her heart. But when he challenged her as if he saw her as his equal and then humbly apologized, her heart wanted to run away with her. Her great uncle had been the only man she'd ever heard say the words *I'm sorry* and sincerely mean it. That she'd come across another man who did so ... a handsome cowboy at that?

Of course she had to go and flirt with Silas. Ugh. Usually she had a better grip on her feminine side. It had no place in her field. Not if she were to be taken seriously by her colleagues. She'd worked too hard to let herself slip now. A pain poked into her head. If only, just a moment, she could relax her guard. She fought for every inch of respect she earned, and weakness was a mark against her.

Some days, she considered giving up her dream, but there were just too many stories to unearth. Stories of once-living people with relatives who loved them. Stories begging to be freed from dirt and stone. No, she could not give in, give up. If only she could will the dizziness to end so she could prove herself healthy once again.

"Want to tell me what you're thinking?" Tante reached across the table to capture Cora's hand in both of hers. Worn hands wrapped in aged ones that had loved so well.

Tears pressed Cora's eyes. Silas's admonition roared in her ears. Had she been so focused on the dead that she forgot her only relative? "I've done right by you, haven't I, Tante? You're not lonely?"

"Don't you give it a second thought." Tante's smile seemed sad, but understanding. "I know you've needed to chase adventure. It's who you are. Like your mama. Your feet need to roam."

Not just roam. There was more to it, much more. She grasped Tante's hands in return and attempted to explain. "It's not about adventure, Tante, it's the stories. Stories formed from everyday items in a person's life. Like the pot a woman used to feed her family a thousand years ago. Or the spear of a man defending his home. The toys children used to play with. It's life trapped by layers of time. Life I get to be a part of bringing to the surface." Those feminine tears burned, but she refused to release them. She had to fight. If she didn't figure out what made her sick, she might never be able to go back.

"How much time off do you have?" Tante asked.

Cora's cheeks warmed with the truth. She stalled as she sifted through her words, not wanting to share the stark reality. Most of the time, her job of assessing cultural discoveries could be considered mundane—sweeping sand from jugs rarely sounded exciting—except she saw the story behind the jug along with the questions. Who had held the jug? Who crafted the clay? What had filled it? No, Cora would never consider that ordinary. However, because she was one of the very few female archaeologists in the world, and spent most of her time in the tumultuous regions around the Mediterranean Sea, it was far too dangerous for her to not be at her absolute best. Her tumble proved that.

"Cora?"

Her heart hammered as she remembered waking up at the bottom of the twenty-foot cliff, bruised, but somehow still alive thanks to the water she'd landed in, having missed the rocks nearby. God had been with her that day. And then she'd been unceremoniously placed on a ship back home like a discarded artifact. "They sent me home until a doctor deems me fit for work again," she told her aunt. The words tasted bitter, and failure tightened a noose around her neck.

Tante sucked in a breath. "What happened?"

If only she could remember. That's what scared her. She didn't know what she did to set off the dizziness that caused her fall. Her co-workers claimed they didn't see what happened. All her work, her history, her perfect track record meant nothing. All gone because she was a female with a dizzy spell. Now she simply had to wait, her life on hold, until a doctor allowed her to return—and even then, she might not be accepted back. It was like being trapped in the very rock in which she worked. It made her irritable and ornery, which was only exacerbated by her pain.

Of course she wouldn't tell Tante that. No reason to cause her to worry. Cora's presence alone did that.

Cora's silence must have gone on too long because Tante rose and picked up the dishes, including the one holding the pancake Cora had barely touched. "Well, the Wards keep quite the collection of trinkets," Tante said. "Elaine travels all around the area to curate the shop with all sorts of items from the last century. But since Silas returned home, the furniture they sell is getting a name for itself. Best we go now before he begins a new project."

And before Cora's body betrayed her again.

Tante drove them in her black Ford automobile and notably took streets other than the main one. Cora had visited Crow's Nest twice before. Once when she helped Tante purchase the home overlooking Lake Michigan and second when Tante moved in. One road leading in and out of town nestled the quaint fishing village in an arch of land bordered by the lake on one side and Crow's Nest Creek on the other. A boardwalk of shops lined the shoreline where many fishing boats docked. A block or so inland was Main Street, where Tante's seamstress shop used to be.

"Do you enjoy living in Crow's Nest?" Cora asked as they drove past a jailhouse.

"It's quite lovely." Tante kept her eyes on the road. "We look out for one another here. When the tornado destroyed my shop, Silas and David Martins salvaged everything they could. Even that young whippersnapper Buck Wilson helped by buying the property from me."

Cora glanced at Tante, worry snaking its way up her back. Tante had briefly told Cora about the destructive tornado that forced her to move her shop to her home. Cora sensed a larger story, but Tante had refused to tell it. What else wasn't her great aunt telling her?

"If you stay long, you'll hear all about Mr. Wilson. He's in charge of the Crow's Nest Conglomerate, which originally brought the fishermen together in a sort of organized union. But when Mr. Wilson took over, he welcomed all business owners into his Conglomerate. I'm grateful to be a member. Honestly, I'm not sure where I would be without those three men."

Had Cora not been listening closely, she might have missed that last muttered phrase. She tapped her thumb on her leg, her respiration increasing at the thought of these men helping her aunt. Silas had a point about how she should be the one to be here to help Tante, but she had a job to do elsewhere, which meant she should be grateful there were people who could help Tante. Still. Learning a strange man bought Tante's property set Cora's teeth on edge. If she'd been here, she could have helped look over the contract, made sure Tante wasn't being taken advantage of. But Silas was here, and he'd been ready to physically defend Tante against Cora yesterday. Maybe she needed to ask him about this Buck Wilson person.

"I think Adaleigh will be returning soon," Tante was saying. "You would get along with her."

"Who?" Cora scrambled to keep up with Tante's conversation.

"Adaleigh Sirland. She's from Chicago and fell in love with David earlier this summer. I'm planning to have tea with Marie—David's grandmother—this afternoon. You must join me. Tomorrow I need to can more vegetables from the garden, but all work and no play wears a body down. We will also have to stop at Sweetie's ice cream parlor and the Wharfside Cafe while you're here. Of course you'll come to church with me ..."

Cora's head spun at Tante's excitement. She never doubted it would thrill her aunt for her to visit, but the idea of all these social expectations made Cora feel physically ill. She came to recover, to lick her wounds until she'd regained enough strength to return to her work. She wanted to spend time with Tante, too, but not where all these strangers would ask her question after question. No, Cora needed solitude.

They pulled into an empty grass lot before Cora could formulate a way to express herself without offending her aunt. A white farmhouse stood beside a red barn. The large doors were open, and above them hung a painted sign that read *Crow's Nest Curiosities*. Tante parked and Cora hustled out, needing to keep a hand on the car as her equilibrium adjusted to the quick movement, but she didn't want Tante slipping on the dewy grass. No matter what Silas Ward thought of her, her motivation was pure. She really did desire to look out for her aunt.

"Take my arm?" Cora offered her elbow.

Tante gave her a look, then snatched a wooden cane from the back seat. "I reckon this stick is a mite sturdier than you at the moment."

Cora hid her embarrassment by adjusting the scarf around her neck. She'd been gifted it during a dig in Egypt a few years ago, and the memory of the Egyptian woman's kindness when she bestowed it gave Cora confidence when entering a new situation. She rubbed the cool fabric.

What she wouldn't give to have her hands covered in sand as she carefully extracted a household item from a long-forgotten ruin. Desert sun warming her skin. Excitement energizing her. And then the magical moment when the artifact broke free of the ground that encased it. For the first time in hundreds, maybe thousands of years, a human being was once again holding it in their hands.

Thinking about the last person to touch a discovery—a pitcher, a shield, a wooden horse—was enough to bring emotion to her eyes even now, half a world away. She pressed her eyes closed and breathed deeply, forcing herself to be fully in this moment, on this plot of ground. She'd learned early on how easily she could be transported elsewhere and forget herself. Had that caused her fall?

Another inhale and her senses kicked in. The fishy smell of water, the gurgle of waves, the clang of boats, the woody scent of grass.

"Cora?" Tante's worried voice broke through.

Cora slowly blinked open her eyes. "Sorry, Tante. Sometimes I need to take a moment to remember where I am at. Is Lake Michigan very close?"

Tante frowned and nodded. She pointed her cane toward the barn shop. "The wharf ends a stone's throw from the barn, and the lake is just beyond. Perhaps Silas can show you. Come now."

Cora ignored Tante's comment about Silas and followed her into the barn, immediately missing the warmth of the summer sun. It took a moment for her eyes to adjust to the dim interior.

"Rose!" A stout woman with graying brown hair whipped around the display counter to their right, hands extended toward Tante. "Such a delight to see you. How did the table turn out? Silas said he planned to drop it off. Is it exactly what you were hoping for?"

"Of course." Tante patted the woman's hands, then invited Cora over. "This is Silas's mother, Elaine Ward. This is Cora Davis. She's staying with me for a while."

"A pleasure, ma'am." Cora gave a slight nod.

"Any friend of Rose's is a friend of ours." Mrs. Ward pulled Cora into a tight hug.

Cora couldn't make sense of the emotions that shot through her at this warm embrace. She rarely liked to be touched by another person, but this felt as comforting as one of Tante's hugs.

"Welcome to our curiosity shop." A female voice brought her gaze up. It belonged to a lovely woman with long brown hair and a gorgeous smile. As she approached, her thinness gave the appearance of frailty despite her expressive brown eyes.

"Cora Davis, dear." Mrs. Ward kept her arm linked in Cora's. "She's a friend of Rose's and just the prettiest young woman, don't you think?"

The other woman laughed, removing several worry lines, and she offered Cora a handshake. "Wonderful to meet you, Cora. I'm Marian, Elaine's daughter-in-law. Make yourself comfortable and let us know if there's any way we can make your visit more pleasant."

"Did you sign up to make cookies for the church social on Sunday?" Tante pulled Mrs. Ward's attention. "I want to make sure we don't make the same kind."

Marian gave Cora a wink and grin, making Cora feel like she had a friend for life, even while a strange feeling wormed into her heart. If Marian was Mrs. Ward's daughter-in-law, did that make her Silas's wife? No, couldn't be, not with the way Tante was pushing them together. What did it matter, anyway? Cora had no room for a man in her life.

While talk of baking sweets distracted Tante and Mrs. Ward, and Marian disappeared, Cora thought to tour the shop before Silas realized they were there. Yesterday she'd wanted his company, but today she preferred to ignore the strange sensations that had been bombarding her ever since he knocked at the door yesterday afternoon.

She walked along a row of wooden furniture—chairs, tables, wardrobes—all covered with various items, from dishes to tea cups to lace doilies and tatted table runners. Farther down the aisle, a shelf displayed various china knickknacks. Cora ran her finger over a white dove. Whose grandmother had this on display half a century ago? Had it given a sense of hope through the Civil War? Maybe even the Great War?

The hum of untold stories drew her deeper into the dusty interior of the barn. A worn étagère, or whatnot, its open squares stuffed with rolls of fabric, yarn, and wooden knitting needles. Usually books and other items filled the spaces, but the brightly colored materials called her closer, reminding her of Tante. She picked up a narrow needle and imagined an expectant mother knitting a hat for her unborn baby.

"Do you knit?"

Cora spun at the question, pointing the needle like a sword.

"Whoa." Silas held up both hands as he took a step back. Again he dressed in rolled-up shirtsleeves and suspenders, though his hat was noticeably missing, giving him the look of an everyday man instead of a cowboy. She kind of missed the hat.

Cora exhaled and leaned against the étagère to regain her composure. "It's not nice to sneak up on people."

"It's not nice to stab people with knitting needles?" He offered the sentence like a question, as if he were unsure of her level of good humor.

Her lips quirked despite themselves. "I'm not mad at you." She replaced the needle, flushing at speaking so freely. What was it about Silas Ward that brought out the rawest parts of herself?

"Not sure I believe you."

More carefully this time, Cora turned to face him. He rested a shoulder against a wardrobe, blocking her escape, and studied her, projecting a confident air with his broad chest and muscled arms. Arms that had held her when she was at her weakest.

Ugh! These thoughts were not welcome.

Cora edged past him. "Did your ... mom find most of these antiques?" She ran her fingers over a pile of doilies sticking out of a dresser drawer across the aisle, her courage failing her to ask if Marian had found them.

"Yup. She and my sister-in-law do the collecting. These days, Marian seems to love it more than my mom, which is hard to believe."

Relief swept over her. Marian was his sister-in-law. Memory surfaced of Tante mentioning a deceased brother. She knocked on a pie safe sitting on a table beside the dresser. "You build and restore. Do you fix up every item before you sell it or only do so order by order?"

"Depends on how busy I am." Silas stepped beside her and rubbed a spot of dirt off the pie safe. "Mostly by order, but if I'm between projects, I'll pick an item I want to bring back to life."

"Bring back to life." She muttered the phrase as it gained purchase in her soul. That's what she did with the artifacts she discovered, which was exactly what she loved most about her work. Could Silas actually understand what she struggled to explain to most people?

"Did Mrs. Whittlebush come with you?" Silas asked.

The affection in his voice warmed her like the Mediterranean sun she missed so much. It was as if he viewed Tante as his own aunt. It swayed her to trust him just a little more. "Yes. She's over there talking to your mom."

"Are you feeling well enough to explore on your own, or shall I show you around?" Silas's inquiry brought her around too quickly. He steadied her with a hand to her shoulder, the question echoing in the worry lining his features.

"Is that why you're following me?" Her stomach flipped as she feared his answer. Did he only see her as a damsel in distress? A woman in need of saving? Or as a competent person with a minor health setback? Was it pity driving him or only his concern for Tante? Her heart pounded. What if he actually wanted to spend time with her?

His bearded cheek indented as he studied her, but he didn't move his hand from her arm. Maybe he didn't know the answer to her questions any more than she knew what he wanted to hear.

No, no, that wasn't right. She didn't want a relationship or the attentions of a man. If Silas thought there was any hope of attraction, she needed to put distance between them. She must focus on getting her health back so she could return to work. No man, even a handsome cowboy, would get in her way.

Cora turned slowly, losing the connection of his touch on her arm and immediately missing it. The world tipped, and she reached for the bookcase to steady herself. Her body was failing her when she needed it to show strength. She couldn't trust Silas to save her. Men were not dependable. Her lack of a father taught her that. If she could just make the straight walk back to the front counter, then Tante could take her home. That's all she needed right now.

Please, God.

But no matter how hard she focused on her destination, she staggered along the aisle. Silas kept a warm hand on her back, silently escorting her to the front of the barn. Her head felt like a balloon, and her body weighed her down. She wanted to lean into his strength, which was the last thing she could do. It wasn't fair to either of them, not when she needed to stand on her own two feet. Not when she didn't trust the male species.

Her weakness muddled her emotions. She needed to rest. Then she'd make sure to keep Silas Ward out of her life, no matter what Tante thought or the draw of the curiosities in his shop. Handsome cowboys and meddling aunts were not a welcome distraction right now. Nope. Not even one little bit.

CHAPTER THREE

Friday, September 19

"Where did your mom find this?" David Martins eased the bottom of the mahogany knee-hole desk off the bed of the Wards' truck. Silas had hoped to be finished unloading from his mom's excursion before noon, but the desk required help, so he'd had to wait for David to return from his morning catch, and now it was mid-afternoon.

"It was a man from Hawk's River's last attempt not to lose his house." Silas pushed the heavy monstrosity toward his friend, who grunted as he took more of the desk's weight. "Do you have a grip, Martins?"

"Yeah. Just hurry up." David stood with his feet spread, elbows bent, the lip of the desk's top resting in each palm. His cotton shirt hung limp and half untucked, looking as damp as Silas's own felt. Summer was hanging on with all its might, even as the maple in front of the house had tinges of color on its leaves. "Better put a blanket down or your ma'll have a fit."

David was right. The dirt would mar the beautiful wood. He snagged one of his mom's old quilts that he'd brought along. The crunching of tires drew his attention as he leapt over the wooden side of the truck bed. Mrs. Whittlebush's black car.

"That the woman staying with Mrs. Whittlebush?" David shifted his feet and Silas laid down the quilt.

Silas tipped up the rim of his Stetson enough to see whether David was right—he was—before climbing back into the truck, his mind whirling with possibilities, aided by the odd swirl in his gut at seeing her again.

Cora emerged, solo, from the car and seemed steadier on her feet today, thankfully, because with the way she'd looked when she left here the other day, he'd never have willingly let her get behind the wheel. He'd have driven her home himself. Which brought him back to the question that had nagged him since she asked it two days ago ... why did he want to help her? This woman who left her only family—an elderly widow, no less—to fend for herself. Family looked out for one another. Sacrificed for one another.

But Cora wasn't his family, so why did he want to look out for her too?

"Can I help?" Cora hurried over to them, her hair swept off her neck and wrapped with a yellow scarf. A blue scarf hung about her shoulders, but today she wore an adorable polka dot blouse and a yellow skirt that matched her headscarf. She set her handbag in the truck bed. "I'll keep it from tipping this way while you lower it."

"Lady's got a plan." The undercurrent in David's voice said Silas better hurry it up. No time to consider his questions, let alone worry whether he should let a woman help them with what would be considered men's work. Obviously, David didn't have a problem with it.

Silas made a quick introduction, then settled on his knees and met Cora's eyes. "You sure you have it?"

She planted her hands under the corner of the desk closest to the truck, using her body to support the back. "Go."

Somehow, they managed to get the thing off the truck and settled on its feet, adding no scratches to either the desk or themselves. Silas swiped off his Stetson, running his rolled-up sleeve over his forehead as he jumped from the truck bed. David wiped his face with a handkerchief, then stuffed his hands in his pockets as he studied Cora from under the brim of his flat cap. Silas watched him closely. Would David approve of Cora? Silas tucked his thumbs around his suspenders, not liking how much the answer to that question mattered to him.

I'm just looking out for Mrs. Whittlebush.

"This is a beautiful piece." Cora ignored them both as she ran her hands over the smooth wood, stepping past David as she moved to the front of the desk. "Mahogany wood. Knee-hole design. Claw-and-ball feet. I think this could be Chippendale. Unusual for one to show up in a small town in Wisconsin. Where'd your mom find it?"

Silas's breath caught when she looked at him with reverence in her eyes. He adjusted his Stetson to give himself a moment. Not fast enough, considering David's raised brow. The man saw entirely too much.

He cleared his throat before answering Cora's question. "The bank threatened to foreclose, so the owner had to sell off his property in an attempt to pay it back. It's how we're getting a lot of our furniture these days." It made him worry people would stop buying from the shop if they couldn't afford to hold on to their own homes. Then what would happen to his mom, sister-in-law, and nieces?

"I wonder ..." Cora dropped to the quilt, shimmying herself underneath the desk in a most unladylike fashion. "The dimensions are off." Cora offered the muttered statement by way of explanation.

David's other brow raised to match the first as he met Silas's glance. As if David Martins's sensitivities would be shocked. Ha! His girl rode a motorcycle. Silas shrugged before squatting to see what Cora was up to.

She ran her fingers along the inside edges of the desk. "If I can just find …" She trailed off, leapt to her feet to pull open the top right drawer. A click, a pop, and the middle dropped open to reveal a foot-by-foot square shelf.

"A secret compartment?" David lifted his flat cap to scratch his head. "How'd you know there'd be one?" Silas wanted to know the same thing.

Cora peered into the hidden space. "It's a common feature in Chippendale's work, so we may be looking at an original. Sometimes secret compartments like this remain undiscovered for decades, their contents left behind. Unfortunately, this one has already been emptied."

"That still doesn't answer—"

"She's an archaeologist." The defensiveness in Silas's voice surprised him. He forced himself to temper his tone as he explained. "It's her job. She's an expert at these things."

"Really?" David grinned. "Wouldn't Adaleigh love meeting you?"

She probably would.

"The drawer was really easy to find and in a common location." Cora dusted off her hands and skirt. "I'd be happy to examine the desk further. Sometimes they put in a decoy drawer—an obvious one, easy to find—like this one. That way, the real secret place, or places, remain overlooked."

"You must have supper with us once Adaleigh returns. She would find this fascinating." David cuffed Silas on the shoulder. "You should come along, too, Ward. You know my grandma makes plenty."

Silas tucked his cheek between his teeth. Just because the man was happy beyond belief didn't mean he needed to play matchmaker where he wasn't welcome. Silas had offered Cora a truce, but he still hadn't decided what he thought of her.

"I appreciate the gesture, but I hate to intrude." Cora smiled, but it didn't reach her eyes. "I'm happy to give Adaleigh a list of books if she's interested."

"Adaleigh loves her books. I'll make sure she can get that list from you." David moved to the side of the desk. "Let's get this put away. I have to meet Buck Wilson in half an hour, and I'd prefer not to be late."

"Everything okay?" Neither of them liked Buck Wilson, and David's uncle was investigating the man. But since both the Curiosity Shop and David's fishing business were part of the Conglomerate, they had to interact with him.

David glanced at Cora before saying, "I don't know. Buck asked me to meet."

David and Buck had history, so Silas dropped the topic until a better time. "I cleared a spot at the front of the store to show off this beauty."

"How can I help?" Cora clasped her hands at her waist.

Silas looked for something she could do. His gaze landed on her handbag, which lay in the truck's bed and had flopped open, allowing a letter with her name addressed on it to slip out. If she corresponded with her aunt under an assumed name, then why would she be receiving mail here under her actual name? Suspicion crept up, but he tucked it away for now and pointed to the quilt underneath the desk. "Can you fold up the quilt once we lift the desk?"

"Certainly. Then, I was hoping ... might I speak with you?"

The hesitation encouraged his curiosity. Perhaps he could ask after that letter, too. "Sure, we can talk after David leaves."

Cora agreed, and David counted off as they lifted the heavy piece of furniture. Silas's muscles strained, but he struggled to keep focused on his footing. His mind kept going back to the letter and what other secrets Cora Davis might be keeping.

Half an hour later, Cora followed Silas out a rear door of the curiosity shop, across a gravel patch, and into a narrow outbuilding. This one was covered in chipped gray paint, as if it were a forgotten place, which made Cora instantly love it. Stepping inside, Silas turned on an electric light, and Cora stopped to take in the twenty-by-twenty-foot room. Above them, the angled rafters showed the building stretched beyond the wall to the left.

The smell of sawdust, beeswax, and paint mingled with the fresh lake air, aggravating the ache in her head, but she came for a reason and wouldn't leave until she accomplished it. A large wooden table took up half the space. The other half held a workbench with a vise, a washstand, and a wall of tools. Beyond the workbench was another door, and behind the table was a large window. The view beyond showed where blue sky met blue water. Cora struggled to tear her eyes away. Tante's suggestion to ask Silas to show her the wharf repeated in her mind.

Cora pushed the idea away. "Is this your workshop?"

"Yup. My quarters are in the loft above the storage area." He pointed to the door by the workbench. "I do most of my work in this room or out back under the awning, depending on how much air I need."

"I imagine the sound of Lake Michigan could be a powerful draw."

Silas made a noncommittal sound that piqued her interest, then he pulled out a stool and snatched up a copy of the *Crow's Nest Gazette*—she'd read Tante's copy this morning—that lay open to the tragic story of a man stepping in front of a train, leaving his destitute widow and seven children behind. The reminder of the man's desperation threatened to overwhelm her, so she pushed thoughts of the tragedy away, turning her attention instead to her host.

She simultaneously wanted to ask him more questions and wished she could explore this space without an audience, because both would give her a better glimpse into the man who spent most of his day in this very building. But she had to remember that men, especially cowboys, were off limits or she risked derailing her life, just like what happened to her mother. Cowboys, especially, were untrustworthy. Her eyes drifted to Silas's muscled back as he replaced a wrench on his wall of tools. This cowboy was honest to a fault and so different from other men she'd met in her work.

Nope. Now wasn't the time, not with her health on the line.

"You're feeling better?" Silas sat on the stool beside her.

"I'm happy to say I've had over twenty-four good hours." She wanted to be ecstatic, but doubt crept in about how long it would last.

"That's good." He rested his thumbs and forefingers on his waistband.

Cora shrugged and looked out the window. "I suspect Tante's insistence on rest and her ability to ply me with food has much to do with it. Her garden is producing faster than I remember, so she's been working non-stop in the kitchen. After I dropped a jar of pickles, she won't let me help." Her cheeks heated. The apples in the northern part of the yard were just ripening, conjuring memories of helping with the apple harvest before Onkle died, and she wanted to be at her best so she could help.

"Cora." Silas bowed his head. "I didn't mean to make you feel ... No, that's not right. I'm sorry I made you feel guilt without regard for your situation, your health. I'm more than an idiot. I'm an absolute cad."

Cora couldn't stop a smile. "I appreciate that, but I actually came to apologize. I've not been myself. You know I'm fully capable of taking care of myself, right? I've lived on my own in a foreign country for years."

His ears reddened. "I didn't mean to imply—"

"I shouldn't need all this help." Right?

"We all need help, I imagine." Silas rested his forearms on his knees. His clasped hands were so close to her own knee.

She stared at the small space between them. "Is that why you're not a cowboy anymore?"

"Huh?" Silas's stunned question brought her head up. "What do you mean?"

"Tante said you came back to take care of your mom and sister-in-law and her kids. I'm sorry about your brother." She truly was. "I guess that's why you don't approve of me. You sacrificed everything to take care of your family and think I should have done the same."

Silas sat back. "That's honest of you."

Her cheeks heated like two suns. "Too honest?"

"I like honest." Silas grabbed his hat from the table, as if needing something in his hands. "Can a person be too honest when they're simply speaking the truth?"

A good question. "Perhaps the truth is more complicated. For both of us."

"Or maybe I shouldn't jump to hasty judgments?" Silas tapped the brim against his palm. "Cora, I'm so sorry. My words have been about me. Will you forgive me for not taking a moment to listen before scolding you for something I don't understand?"

"Forgiven." How could she not? "Silas, are you sorry you moved back to Wisconsin and gave up your dream, even if it was for family?"

"I ... Dream ... How did you know?" He sighed. "Maybe we understand each other more than we thought."

A tug, like an invisible lasso, pulled her toward him. She reached out, her fingers stretching ahead of their own accord, until she touched his hand. He stilled, the hat dangling.

"Silas?" Marian's voice crashed through the moment seconds before she entered the workroom. "Silas, have you seen Nettie?"

"Nettie?" Silas sounded as if he'd just awoken from a dream. That had to be exactly what transpired. Simply a figment of a buried hope Cora refused to give in to, not when her health and her work were at stake. Then why were butterflies swarming her stomach?

"She was supposed to be helping Mom in the shop while I settled Essie down for a rest after school. But when I passed through, she wasn't there."

Nettie and Essie? Marian's little girls? Cora had yet to meet them, but Tante had told her about them.

"Perhaps she's in the shop with a friend, like that one time?" Silas had an edge of hope in his voice.

Marian shook her head. "I looked through the barn and the house. She's not in either place. She didn't come in here, did she?"

"Not that I've seen." Silas stood and his fingers brushed Cora's arm. Purposeful or accidental? "Don't worry, Marian. She's here. We'll find her."

"Okay." Marian squeezed her eyes closed. "Mom's staying with Essie."

"You search the yard in front of the house and around the fields. I'll trek up to the wharf." He grabbed Marian's shoulders until she looked at him. "We'll find her, Marian. Don't worry."

We? He was right about that. Cora would force the dizziness to stay at bay because she wasn't about to let him search for his niece without her. Lake Michigan was not far away, and she didn't like the direction her thoughts took her.

"I'll be back." Silas turned to her once Marian left. "Nettie is an adventurous seven-year-old. I'm sure she's exploring somewhere Marian didn't look." He sounded like he was trying to convince himself more than her, and that only confirmed her resolve.

"I want to help." Cora carefully slid off the stool, hiding how the floor tilted beneath her feet.

Silas opened his mouth, closed it, then nodded as he stuffed his cowboy hat on his head.

"Where would Nettie go if she isn't in the house, barn, or workshop?" Cora asked. "Is there a place special to her? Somewhere she goes to feel safe?"

"That's it!" Silas cupped her face in his hands, and she thought he might kiss her square on the lips, but at the last moment, he detoured to kiss her forehead. Then he spun on his heels and ran out the door.

Cora blinked, the feeling of his lips on her skin like a branding iron. *He was simply grateful,* she tried to remind herself, then realized Silas was getting too far a head start. She hurried after him as he jogged toward the lake. A cool breeze blew in, and Cora adjusted the scarf around her neck as she followed Silas to the wharf, where he glanced over his shoulder, then stopped to wait for her.

He took her hand as she reached the wooden boards. Cora scanned the water, looking for any telltale sign that the little girl had fallen in, but Silas propelled them on. He must not think she fell in because his gaze remained straight ahead. The boardwalk curved as it came upon a red building called *The Barn*, with several tables and benches set outside. At one of the benches tucked in a little alcove corner, a woman sat beside a girl with brown hair plaited into two braids.

Silas squeezed Cora's hand, then relinquished his grip as he hurried over to the pair.

Cora stayed rooted to the boardwalk, tears pricking and worsening the pain behind her eyes. She'd once been as lost as Nettie appeared now. The world passing her by in bold colors and loud noises. Tante and Onkle had provided a light in Cora's darkness, a shelter from the confusion she faced as a child. Still, with her health in jeopardy and her job slipping away no matter how tightly she held on ... perhaps Nettie wasn't the only lost soul at the lake today.

"Mindy, thank you!" Silas greeted his childhood friend as she rose from the bench outside The Barn, where she rented a room on the second floor.

"I was coming home from work when I saw Nettie, and I couldn't let her sit all by herself." Melinda Zahn smiled down at his niece. Mindy was a waitress at the Wharfside Cafe and was the most cheerful person Silas knew, even at the end of a long shift. They had interacted little since he returned to Crow's Nest last year, but before he left for the ranch, he'd considered her a sister, like Marian. Someone to protect if she needed it. But he always thought David would end up marrying Mindy. Until Adaleigh came along. Adaleigh and Mindy were as different as the sun and moon, so just how well did he know his friends?

He tugged Mindy's arm to pull her away from Nettie, then lowered his voice. "Will you place a call to Marian? She's beside herself."

"Of course!" Mindy patted his hand, reminding him of her friendliness, yet he felt no connection with her. Not like when Cora touched his hand just a few moments ago. "Don't think any more on it. I'll just run right up to the house and make sure she knows you're with Nettie and not to worry."

"I'm in your debt, Mindy."

"Not at all, Silas. We have to help one another."

Silas bowed his head, unable to speak. Mindy patted him again, then waved at Nettie before heading up the wharf. Silas didn't miss Mindy going out of her way to say hello to Cora. He still couldn't believe he'd kissed Cora. And almost on the lips! Her idea, her willingness to help, and having just felt that connection with her, he'd reacted.

What if they'd lost Nettie? He puffed out a breath. He wouldn't think about it now. Nettie was here, safe. His heart finally slowed to a normal rhythm.

He lowered himself to the bench beside his niece. A seagull swept out of the blue sky. Ducks waddled nearby. Boats clanked along the wharf. "The lake is beautiful, isn't it?"

"Daddy loved it here," Nettie said, a catch in her voice.

Silas's gaze snagged on Cora where she stood at the edge of the wharf, watching them. She gave him a little nod, and the cold feeling that had clutched Silas's chest warmed. Nettie was right—his brother had loved Lake Michigan. They'd spent hours on the wharf together, just them or with friends like David Martins, fishing, bug catching, dreaming.

"I miss him." Nettie sniffed.

"I know, sweetie." Silas wrapped her in his arms. Her little body shuddered against him, breaking his heart into tiny pieces.

He could never replace her father—wouldn't try, for Zee was an amazing father—but Silas could be a caring presence in his niece's life. At least, he hoped that would be enough. That it would honor Zee enough. Honoring his brother's memory was his driving force since Zee died. Since their lives changed course and the world took on a different outlook. Since all the daydreams he'd created with his brother became mist, evaporated by the heat of grief.

"Your mom is worried about you."

Nettie pushed away. "She doesn't understand."

"What doesn't she understand?" Silas used his thumbs to wipe her tears from her cheeks, then handed her his handkerchief.

She wiped her nose. "There's going to be a dance at the end of the Harvest Festival in a couple weeks, and Christine King kept talking about how her dad would be there and how she milks their cows with him and helps him harvest their crops and drives their wagon."

"But you don't like those activities." Silas squinted at her. He'd tried inviting her along while he made deliveries or to sit with him while he worked in the workshop, but she always refused.

Nettie snapped her arms across her chest. "She didn't need to go on and on about them. She knows I don't have a dad. She just wanted me to know that she does."

Silas tugged his ear. He had no idea what to do. He glanced over at Cora and gave a slight nudge of his chin. Perhaps another woman's perspective would help.

"Hi, there." Cora gave a wary smile as she approached. Her head tilted slightly to one side—was she experiencing one of her episodes? She said she'd had a day of good health, but she hadn't appeared to expect that to last.

"Who are you?" Nettie palmed away any remnants of tears.

Perhaps this wasn't the right thing to do. Cora needed to get home, and Nettie had already talked with Mindy. What more could Cora do?

"I'm Cora. I'm staying with Mrs. Whittlebush."

"You know Mrs. Whittlebush?" Nettie shifted closer to Silas, giving a sliver of space for Cora to sit beside her on the bench. All right, he'd see where this went before he took Nettie home.

"I do." Cora sat slowly, as if a quick movement could startle Nettie. Or maybe because of the dizziness? "She's giving me a place to stay until I can go back to work."

Nettie nestled against Silas's side, under the arm he propped against the back of the bench. "What do you do?" Nettie asked.

"I'm an archaeologist." Cora smoothed her skirt. "That means I dig up old things."

"Dirt." Nettie scrunched her nose. "Gross."

Cora laughed and met Silas's gaze. He gave a subtle shrug, hoping she'd catch on that he didn't know what to do. By the twinkle in her eye, she got it all too well. Then she lowered her voice. "Girl trouble or boy trouble?"

Nettie shot a look at Silas, then leaned forward. "Christine King."

"Oh." Cora sounded as though everything was now explained, but Silas was as lost as ever. "What'd she do?"

"She would not stop talking about her dad."

"Sorry." Cora gave an exaggerated, sympathetic frown. "Not a friend, I take it."

"I thought she was." Nettie put a little hand on her hip. "Her dad is helping with the Harvest Festival Dance."

Now he remembered hearing an announcement at church on Sunday about the Harvest Festival. It was an annual, week-long event at the end of September. He'd returned to Crow's Nest after the event last year, but he remembered the girls talking about how the other children showed off their best animals, and the dance.

He opened his mouth to explain it to Cora, only to snap it shut when she squeezed the hand he rested on the back of the bench. He should have thought to volunteer for the Festival or at least make sure the women in his life knew he'd escort them to the dance, but he'd been distracted by how little money came in last week. The bank had limited his withdrawal so that he barely had enough to pay the electricity bill.

"I've never been to a dance." Cora turned to stare out at the lake. "Sounds fun."

"Christine said she's going to dress up real pretty. Her mom is making her a new dress."

"You like pretty dresses?" Cora glanced at Nettie.

"Who doesn't?"

"Me." Cora angled back toward the lake. "No one to take me to a dance, no need for a nice dress."

Silas frowned. Was Cora trying to connect with Nettie, or was there truth behind her words? The thought of no one asking her to attend a dance ... *he* wanted to take her to one, especially if that was true. And wasn't that weird? After he berated her over her choices?

Nettie sat up. "You don't have a daddy?"

Of course Nettie would make that assumption based on her own experience, but it surprised him when Cora shook her head.

"Did he ... die?" Nettie's voice quivered on that last word, knifing Silas's heart.

Cora adjusted her position on the bench so that she faced Nettie, one leg tucked underneath her other. "I don't know, Nettie. I never met my daddy."

"Never?" Nettie voiced what Silas wanted to ask.

"You know, I had a chance to go to a dance once." Cora cast a quick glance over Nettie's head to Silas. If only he could take her aside to ask her all the questions bubbling inside.

"No one would take you." Nettie's head sank to her chest. Why hadn't he offered to take her when he first heard about it on Sunday? Or even when she mentioned it just now? Did she think he didn't want to go with her?

"Actually, I did have someone," Cora said.

What?

Nettie's head shot up. "Then why didn't you go?"

Yes, why?

Again Cora cast him a glance before leaning close to whisper, "Because going with my uncle felt weird. All my friends were going with their daddy or mama, but I was going with a stand-in. I refused to go."

Silas swallowed, Cora's story offering a one-two punch. First, that Cora had no dad and no one to make her feel special, yet knowing Cora's uncle was likely Mrs. Whittlebush's late husband who had been gone a decade. Second, that he was Nettie's stand-in dad, and nothing he did would ever change that.

"I wish I did go with him." Cora smiled at Nettie, then held Silas's gaze. "My uncle was like a father to me, even if he wasn't the real thing."

Nettie looked over her shoulder at him. "I wanna go, Uncle Silas."

Cora squeezed Silas's wrist, the one he still had resting on the back of the bench. It was time to step up, to be the father figure he'd promised his brother he'd be. Cora had set the stage. Silas wouldn't fail Zee, Nettie, or Cora.

Chapter Four

Cora bit her lip to keep her emotions at bay as Silas lowered himself to one knee in front of his niece. It didn't help that the pressure continued to build behind her left eye and the nausea churned faster with the yeasty smell coming from The Barn. A tear escaped down Cora's cheek even as a spike of pain speared through her head. She'd been ignoring the ringing in her ears—a relatively new symptom—since she sat down beside Nettie, and she didn't want her body to interrupt what was happening here. Nettie needed this. Maybe Silas did, too.

"Miss Ward." Silas removed his cowboy hat as he spoke with stilted formality. Cora hid a smile behind her hand. "Would you do me the honor of allowing me to escort you to the Harvest Festival Dance?"

Nettie giggled.

"I shall wear my best Sunday clothes." Silas continued in his formal voice. "And shall escort you, m'lady, if you would do me the honor?"

A smile lit up Nettie's countenance. She threw her arms around Silas's neck, nearly knocking him backward. "Thank you, Uncle Silas. Thank you!"

"Of course, sweetie. I wouldn't miss it for the world." He held her tight, and Cora had to look away before her tears really started falling.

"I'm going to go tell Mom!" Nettie clapped ecstatically, then threw her arms around Cora's neck before dashing toward the boardwalk.

"Go straight there!" Silas called after her as he pushed to his feet. He looked down at Cora with a fond expression she never expected to be directed at her. "Thank you. I didn't know what to say, and you got her to open up about what was really going on. The Harvest Festival started after I left home, so I forgot it was coming up."

Cora brushed away any remnants of tears. He held out a hand. When she placed hers in it, he lifted her to her feet and didn't let go. His frame hedged her into the alcove so she could gather herself with no one seeing.

He brushed a curl from her forehead. "Is what you said true? About your dad and uncle?"

Cora nodded. She'd known Nettie needed to hear her story, but what would Silas think of her? She was the illegitimate daughter of an illegitimate daughter, with failing health and an unknown future. Then the image of Silas kneeling in front of Nettie popped into Cora's mind. The gallantry of the gesture and how he threw his whole self into showing his niece how valued she was to him—goodness. This cowboy had a sensitive side she hadn't seen coming, and it demolished the defenses she attempted to maintain around her heart.

She tugged him toward the boardwalk, unable to tell him more without being in motion. "My mother sent me to live with Tante when I became old enough to realize her job." Wait. Other daughters stayed and became saloon girls. Why had her mother ... She blinked up at Silas.

"What is it?"

"I think my mom saved me." Her head hurt to think, but the emotion of that thought barged through, regardless of her limitations. "She was born in a saloon out West after my grandmother—Tante's much younger sister—ran away from home. I never thought about why my mom followed in her mother's footsteps, but what if she didn't have a choice? What if sending me to live with Tante was her way of keeping me from being what she was? She died a year or so after I came to live with Tante, so I'll never know."

Silas stopped them on the boardwalk somewhere between The Barn and his house and lifted her chin. She found only compassion in his eyes. "I'm sorry, Cora."

The apology spread into her past, filling the empty places she'd locked away. Never had she thought any man, let alone a man she'd known less than a week, could utter three words and offer her the world. He spread his hand to cover her cheek, and she leaned into it. The safety and comfort eased the ache in her head and her heart. She had told no one the full story of her past, but she wanted to tell Silas.

"The only thing I know about my father is that he was a cowboy, like my grandfather." She depended on his touch for courage. "Nothing else, not even his name. Tante and Onkle filled the roles of mother and father, at least until Onkle passed away when I was at university. I wish you could have met him. He was a good man. Like you."

Silas scrubbed his face with his free hand and got them moving again, her hand wrapped around his arm. "I'm not as good as you think. I should have known what Nettie needed."

"Nonsense. Eloquence isn't as important as presence, Silas, especially for someone who has a hole in her heart from a missing loved one."

He looked away as he sucked in his cheek.

"Hey, remember, once you found out, you gave her the safe, loving response she needed." She slipped in front of him and placed a hand over his heart. Heat filled her face, but she had to finish her thought. He had to know what it would mean to Nettie. "You're the perfect person to escort Nettie in her beautiful dress. She'll remember this dance for the rest of her life."

"My brother was a better man than me. I'm trying to cover his loss, but I will never be him."

"No one expects you to be. What they need is for you to be there, just as you're doing."

"But am I enough?" His eyes turned into liquid pools of unguarded emotion that went straight to her heart.

"Oh, Silas." She lifted on her toes and pressed a light kiss on his cheek. "God is enough."

As a tear reached her lips—hers or his?—she pulled away. Her heart pounded in her chest, her head. The ringing in her ears shut out all other sounds. Nausea swirled her stomach.

"Cora." Silas tried to steady her, but she evaded him.

Panic at her overwhelming vulnerability squeezed her throat. She couldn't manage any more emotion. Not now. The planks of the boardwalk rocked beneath her feet. It was happening again. This was how she ended up falling off that cliff. This was what ended her job.

A memory sliced through the pain. She'd been emotional before falling. She'd been arguing with someone. Trying to persuade them to do the right thing. She could feel the emotion of that moment in her chest, but her mind couldn't latch onto the exact memory.

And then she was falling, and she could only hope the water would wake her before she drowned, as it did the last time.

Silas had a split second between Cora's face going white and her knees buckling. Instinct had him sweeping her into his arms. Whether or not she lost consciousness, she opened her eyes as he held her against his chest.

"I hate this." A tear slipped down her cheek.

So did he.

"Let me walk." She squirmed, and as loath as he was to release her, he gently lowered her feet to the ground. But kept his arm around her waist.

"Sturdy enough?"

"I have to be." She leaned into him as she stepped forward.

He wanted to point out the obvious—that she neither had to prove her strength to him, nor was she sturdy on her feet—but having already made a fool of himself when they first met, he kept his mouth closed.

"I remembered something." She trembled against him. "Something from when I fell. I need to get my handbag and read that letter. You know the one. I saw you notice it."

Embarrassment flashed through him. "Maybe you should recover first. You nearly fell into the lake. If I hadn't been here—"

"You don't need to tell me. But if I can't get this under control, then I can't go back." Her voice cracked.

Silas pinned his tongue between his molars. He had learned his lesson. He would not say a word about her work, her digging up *things*. If only he understood why she was so all-fired determined to run away from Mrs. Whittlebush and go back to the dangerous places she seemed to love so much.

"I know what you think," she grumbled. "But you tell me—was it really that easy to give up your dream? To leave that ranch and come back to Crow's Nest? You still wear the hat."

Silas dropped his chin.

"I'm not trying to judge."

He tightened his arm around her waist to assure her he didn't hold it against her. Man, she fit too perfectly there.

He'd let her go when they came in sight of the house, which would be just around this bend. Neither of his nieces needed to see him this close to a woman. But he wouldn't hurry. Cora needed support, and he liked being her physical pillar to lean on. Could he set aside his personal problems to be a rock for her? Then again, should he? If she was determined to leave, he'd eventually lose her because he sure wasn't going anywhere.

"I remembered I was having an emotional conversation with someone before I fell the first time." Her vulnerable tone captured his attention. "When I lost my balance just now, you caught me. That person didn't."

He stopped them, and she turned her crystal-blue eyes up at him. "What are you saying, Cora?"

"Was ... was I pushed over that cliff, Silas? Did one of my colleagues want me off the dig enough to risk killing me?"

He stared at her, the words reverberating through him like an echo in a canyon. He might not understand her motivations—or perhaps they hit too close to home—but how could someone want this beautiful soul ... dead? It sickened him, fired his anger, and ignited his protective streak.

"Silas, say something." She backed away from him. "You look upset. You don't think I'm right. You—"

"You're right, I'm upset." He grasped her upper arms. "And I promise you, no one is going to harm you. Not if I have anything to say about it. You're safe in this town. We'll tell Detective O'Connor. He helped keep David's Adaleigh safe. He can help us, too."

"You're not making sense. Why would I still be in danger? They succeeded in getting me off the dig. The letter back in your workshop probably says I'm not welcome back. They've won. What good will protection do here? And who is Detective O'Connor? And what does he and David's girl have to do with any of this?" She closed her eyes and pressed a hand to her head, a soft moan escaping.

He'd overreacted. Chalk it up to almost losing his niece—or thinking he had. He didn't need to scare Cora in the process. "I'm sorry. It seems I cannot manage a levelheaded conversation with you. Let's get you home."

She pressed her lips together. Because of her nausea or because she was exercising the self-restraint he failed at? He wrapped his arm around her shoulders—thankfully, she didn't shrug him off—and turned her toward his home. Until her steps faltered as they came in sight of his family. Marian waved her girls and Mindy toward the back door his mother held open.

Cora shifted away from him, but Silas tightened his hold, keeping her tucked against his side. No one was paying attention to them, and even if they were and demanded an explanation, Cora needed protection. The other women in his life had one another. Right now, Cora was alone.

She allowed him to help her back to his workshop, where he settled her on a stool. All the while, the air between them crackled with unsaid words. Silas needed to think this through before he said something that only made things worse.

But one thing he did know: Cora might not watch out for her family, but he wasn't about to desert her. It wasn't the way God made him.

Cora leaned her elbows on Silas's work table. If only she was back at Tante's house. She wanted to curl up in her bed with the covers over her head where she could hide from the light that hurt her eyes, the sounds that hurt her ears, and the kindness of Silas that pricked her conscience. She'd seen his mother, sister-in-law, and nieces. After Nettie's excitement, he needed to be inside with them, not coddling her out here.

Unshed tears clogged her nose, making the head pain worse. She must drive herself home. She had to try.

"Lean back and put this over your eyes." Silas's rumbly voice came from behind her. Then his hands tugged her shoulders so that she rested her back against his muscled chest. Before the heat could rise in her face, he laid a cool cloth over her forehead, blocking out the light. Instantly, the tension seeped from her neck, her shoulders, even her jaw.

When was the last time she felt so secure that she could allow herself to fully rest? Working on dig after dig, she always had to be alert to dangers, like cave-ins or thieves or threats particular to women. Even at Tante's house, she was always trying to help, to make up for her years away, to prove she was healthy enough to return to the dig. Yet here, with the warmth of Silas behind her, she didn't have to be strong.

Then she remembered his family. She tightened her muscles to straighten away from him, suddenly aware again of the impropriety of the situation, of the need for him to be inside with the niece who had just run off.

"Shh." He helped her sit up while keeping the cloth over her eyes. "Sit here while I tell Marian that I'm taking you home."

She wanted to protest, but Silas was gone before she found the words. Words. The letter.

Cora folded the cloth Silas had laid over her eyes and set it on the table, pushing aside the pain the light caused. She opened her handbag and slid out the letter. Her fate could be answered in this envelope. A fate already decided no matter what her health dictated. What would she do if she couldn't return to work? What would she do if they decided to not welcome her back to a dig?

Have you asked God?

The question stilled her hands. Had she? Or had she been so determined to follow in her own path that she didn't look for a change in God's direction? But how could he take away what she loved so much?

He took away Silas's dream.

Icy fear gripped her heart. Would God do that to her? Would the Corinvetter Foundation do that to her?

The envelope was addressed by two different hands. One had written her name, the other her address and her company's return designation. She slid a shaky finger under the seal, and another envelope slipped onto the table, along with a note from Signore Camposano, lead on her most recent dig. Fortunately, the man spoke both Italian and English and wrote his note in English.

Signorina Davis, Please find enclosed a letter from Signora Pimonte. I regret to inform you that Signora Pimonte has passed away. Upon finding the enclosed letter in her effects, I took the liberty of forwarding it to you through the Corinvetter Foundation. Saluti, Signore Camposano.

Cora read the note again, picturing the kindly older woman who had written her. Dead? She couldn't believe it. It seemed like yesterday that she was hale and hearty, making pasta while she shared stories with Cora. Cora pressed into her memory, irritated to find it so empty. Had Signora Pimonte not survived the earthquake? The cliff incident happened about a month afterward, and those few weeks in between were blank, except for a general sense of growing ill-health. She was fine prior to the earthquake, then the cliff episode, and then she was unceremoniously shipped home. Had she said goodbye to Signora Pimonte?

"Ready to go home?"

"What?" Cora pressed a hand to her chest. "Silas. You startled me."

Concern deepened the brown of his eyes. He removed his cowboy hat. "I'm sorry, Cora. I thought you'd be expecting me to return. I didn't mean for it to take so long. The girls were excited about the Harvest Festival and told me all about it."

"No apology necessary." She waved a hand. "You should stay and talk to them more. I'll get myself home. I'm feeling better already." Not a total lie. Honestly, the questions about Signora Pimonte had pushed some of the less distracting symptoms out of her mind. Her head still hurt, but if she didn't move quickly, she could manage everything else.

"I'm taking you home." Silas's tone brooked no argument. He glanced at the envelope. "Word on your job?"

Cora shook her head and regretted it. She pressed the heel of her palm to her temple.

Instantly, he was by her side. "You can tell me later. Let's get you home."

He put the letter in her handbag, slipped the handle over her arm so it hung in the crease of her elbow, and tucked that arm around his own before escorting her from his workshop. She couldn't get used to this cowboy's gallantry. It would spoil her. Eventually, she would need to stand on her own two feet, whether or not she had these headaches and whether or not she could ever return to her work.

She stayed silent, too much in her mind to express in words. What she witnessed between Silas and his niece, the question of whether she was pushed, Signora Pimonte's death. Silas's kiss. He helped her into Tante's car.

What had even brought her to the Ward's home in the first place? Right! Her desire to apologize for not being herself and her attempt at proving that she wasn't as fragile as her health made her appear. The thought was so hilarious, seeing that Silas had to drive her home, that a giggle escaped. And once it was past her lips, another slipped out, and another, until she was belly laughing.

"What's so funny?" Silas asked as he brought the car to a stop in front of Tante's house.

Cora rested her head against the seatback. "The irony in my day. I think myself so strong and then am reminded I'm not."

Silas didn't reply and hid his expression behind his hat.

"The letter is from a friend. She died and the dig leader forwarded it on."

"I'm sorry, Cora. It must have happened soon after you left for the letter to be here already."

Cora sat up, turning to him. "You're right. If she died before I left Italy, I would have had the letter in my belongings. But I've only been back for a short time, and she was in good health last I remember. That means she would have died right about the time I fell off that cliff."

Silas tipped his hat, revealing his concern. "Do you still think you may have been pushed?"

Nausea returned with a vengeance, and Cora pressed a hand to her stomach. "You think there could be a connection to my so-called accident and Signora Pimonte's death? She was such a lovely woman. I—" She clamped a hand over her mouth.

Silas jumped out and helped her out of the car, the fresh air from Lake Michigan calming her nausea—or was that the warmth of Silas's arm wrapped around her shoulders?

"Cora, dear!" Tante hurried out of the house. "Is she all right? Are you hurt?"

"She's fine, Mrs. Whittlebush," Silas said. Who'd have thought he'd lie for her? "She got some bad news and needs a rest. Perhaps a cup of tea?"

"Ginger and chamomile will calm the nerves." Tante spun on her Mary Janes and bustled right back into the house.

By the time the tea was ready, Silas had Cora settled on the sofa, a quilt across her lap, and a cool towel over her eyes. He sat in a chair nearby, silent, yet his presence relaxed the tension in Cora's shoulders, to the point where tears pricked her eyes. Other than the few years she spent with Tante and Onkle, how often had she ever experienced this type of care?

Even with Tante, her motherliness was almost smothering at times so that Cora wanted to prove to Tante she was fine. Not so with Silas. He'd seen her at her worst that very first day and had scolded her for her actions. Even so, here he sat when he should be home, taking care of the family for whom he left the ranch. It simultaneously shamed her for her selfishness and made her heart swell with gratefulness.

"Here we go." Tante entered the room. Cora swiped the towel from her head as Tante set the tea tray on a small table beside the sofa.

"Thank you, Tante."

Tante ignored her and poured three cups of tea. "Drink this and tell me what's really going on. I don't buy it for an instant that you're okay."

Cora reached for the handbag Silas had set beside the sofa. "I learned a friend of mine passed away." Might as well keep it simple.

"I'm so sorry, child."

Cora pulled out the letter from Signora Pimonte. "She wrote me a letter before she died."

No one spoke, and thank goodness Cora didn't have to ask Silas to stay. She wanted him to know what Signora Pimonte said in case it related to their other suspicions. The problem was, her throat clogged as she tore open the dear lady's letter. The mix of Italian and English words made her smile. They'd been teaching each other their own languages while Signora Pimonte told her stories. Cora translated as she read aloud.

"'My dear Cora, I heard of your accident yesterday and fear it is my fault. I ask too many questions. Forgive me.'"

Questions about what?

"'I meant to give you a gift before you finished the dig, but now I will send it. The story I told you of the statue of the mother and child that has been passed down from descendent to descendent is true, as is its value. That it is buried in the grotto with my ancestor is not true. It has been in my house.'"

Cora shared glances with Tante and Silas, who both had expressions of confusion that had to mirror her own.

"'I have no children to pass the statue on to, but you have been like a daughter to me.'" Cora's voice cracked, but she pressed on. "'A man I trust will help me send the statue to you. It is yours. When you see it, I hope you will remember me as I will always remember you. My dear girl—'"

Cora broke off, not wanting to share the rest of Signora's words. *You are loved. Remember Psalm 46:1,* God is our refuge and strength, a very present help in trouble. *Trust in Him, my daughter.*

"What does that mean?" Tante pulled Cora's attention from the letter. "What questions? And what is this statue?"

"Signora Pimonte called it the *Madre e Figlia* or *Mother and Daughter.*" A tear dropped onto the letter. Regardless of the monetary value of the statue, which was likely significant considering its provenance, it was now priceless because it was a gift from a woman who called Cora *daughter.*

CHAPTER FIVE

Sunday, September 21

"Will you manage the entire morning, child?" Tante eyed her over the carafe of coffee as she poured Cora a second cup. "We don't need to stay for the social after church."

Cora put on a brave smile. "I know how much you love those. I won't be the reason you miss it."

"Your health is more important."

"No pain this morning." Just the dratted dizziness. "I'll be fine."

Tante pursed her lips, adding a multitude of wrinkles around her mouth.

"I won't be coddled, Tante, so don't try." Cora took a sip of coffee. Its warmth spread through her body, giving energy and clearing her foggy mind. She'd stayed up too late last night re-reading Signora Pimonte's letter for the umpteenth time so that now she had it memorized. She also dug through her luggage, looking for her notes on Signora Pimonte's story. Had she recorded information about the statue? She'd brought all her notes with her from Italy, and her eyes were blurry with exhaustion by the time she sorted through everything and isolated the notes from her time with Signora Pimonte. She planned to read over it all again tonight.

"Fine, then," Tante said. "Service starts in twenty minutes, so eat up."

Cora had barely washed her plate before Tante shooed her toward the car. Crow's Nest boasted two large churches, a Catholic one and a Protestant one, one at either end of town. Tante attended the Protestant church on the north end of town, a walkable distance for a young, healthy person. But between Tante and Cora, neither fit that description.

Jitters plagued Cora through the whole service, destroying her concentration. Particularly after she realized the Ward clan attended Tante's church, as did David Martins, who sat between Mindy, the woman who helped Nettie, and another brown-haired woman. She should have been prepared to run into Silas and his family and friends, but the thought of seeing him after everything that transpired on Friday made her want to slip between the cracks of the wood-plank floor. What must he think of her now?

She stuck close to Tante as fellow church-goers spilled out of the service and into the churchyard. It was a perfect day with a bright blue sky and moderate temperatures. Cora had worn one of her straight line, short-sleeve dresses, a simple straw hat, and her blue scarf. The feminine clothes helped her feel as if she fit in, though social crowds like this made her uncomfortable. She much preferred one-on-one conversations, particularly when both she and her conversant were working on a project while they talked, as she often had with Signora Pimonte.

Then she spotted a singular cowboy hat. Tables were being arranged by none other than Silas and his friend David Martins. As soon as the pair had them placed, the tables were covered in food. On one of the dessert tables, Cora helped Tante find room for her cookie platter.

"Those look delicious." Mrs. Ward appeared across the table from them with a platter stacked high with chocolate cookies that smelled of molasses.

"I always think I make too many." Tante laughed. "But somehow, I never have any to take home."

"That's why I start with dessert." Mrs. Ward winked, looking a lot like Silas in that moment.

Cora drifted away. For as beautiful a day as it was, with the sun warm and the breeze cool, she couldn't overcome her discomfort. Everything seemed loud and bright. Maybe staying for the social was a bad idea. Surely, she could walk home. Tante wouldn't like it, but if Cora timed the disclosure for when her great-aunt was mid-meal and mid-conversation, Tante would have no choice but to let Cora go.

"You plotting an escape route?" Silas materialized beside her, stealing Cora's breath, not just by how handsome he looked in his cowboy hat and vest, but by his solid presence that drew her like a miner to gold dust.

"Hi, there." She gave him a smile to hide her nerves.

"Uncle Si!" A downy-haired girl in a grass-stained dress launched herself at Silas. He caught her and swung her high over his head.

"How's my favorite five-year-old?" He settled her on his hip.

"Uncle Silas!" Nettie bounded over, curls bouncing. "Miss Sirland brought us yo-yos!"

"Yo-yo!" The girl in Silas's arms bounced along with her words.

"Come on, Uncle Silas." Nettie grabbed his hand and tried to haul him away.

Silas laughed as his niece's efforts failed. "First say *hi* to Miss Davis."

Cora's cheeks grew warm.

"Hi!" Nettie threw her arms around Cora's waist, then looked up at her. "Come see the yo-yos, too."

Cora couldn't help but laugh. "Of course I will."

"This is Essie." Silas introduced the girl in his arms, who buried her face in his collar at the attention.

"Do you like to play in the dirt?" Cora smiled. "I do."

The right thing to say, considering Essie lit up like a mini sun. "I like dirt! But Mommy don't want me to get dirty."

"Yo-yo, Uncle Silas." Nettie took one of Silas's hands and one of Cora's and dragged them toward a small cluster of people at the far side of the yard, underneath a towering maple, which had turned a dark shade of purplish red.

Cora recognized David Martins and Mindy, but none of the others. Frankly, she would have avoided this knot of strangers, except that she couldn't disappoint Nettie. Then another woman—the brown-haired one she'd noticed earlier—joined the group. David immediately pulled her to his side. That must be his girl. Adaleigh. She wore a cream sweater and brown skirt, appearing as comfortable as could be in the understated clothes even though Cora didn't miss the sophisticated way she carried herself.

"There you are!" Adaleigh brightened when she spotted Nettie. Essie wiggled and Silas let her down. Adaleigh held out both hands, a yo-yo in each. "If you can't figure out how to use them, I have a third one. I know Mr. Martins or your uncle would love to show you how they work."

"Uncle Silas!" Nettie bounced. Adaleigh handed Nettie the third yo-yo, and before he and Cora had even reached the group, Nettie had shoved it into his hand.

Silas laughed. "All right, all right, I'll show you." He tugged the loop of string over his middle finger, resting the yo-yo in his palm, then he flipped his wrist and let the ball drop, only to give a yank, jerking it back into his hand. Nettie and Essie's eyes grew round.

"Do it again!" Nettie clapped.

Silas grinned.

"Come talk with the adults." Mindy tugged Cora's arm, leading her to the others. "This is David Martins and his sister Samantha and brother Patrick. Adaleigh Sirland. Kyle Docherty. Everyone, this is Cora Davis. She's staying with Mrs. Whittlebush."

As Cora accepted the greetings, she felt bad for deceiving these people. Tante was friends with Mrs. Martins. Shouldn't they know she was Tante's niece? Were her reasons for protecting Tante still valid? Memory of Signora Pimonte flashed across her mind. *Too many questions.* Yes. Protecting Tante was definitely worth the minor deception.

"I'm thrilled to meet you!" Adaleigh held out her hand. "David told me about meeting you the other day, and I cannot wait to learn more about your archaeology. Have you come from a recent dig?"

"In Italy."

"Oh, I loved Italy!" Adaleigh's eyes lit up. "I traveled mostly in the northern regions and, of course, France. But the food was heavenly and the art was incredible."

"You've been to Italy?" Cora clamped her mouth closed. How dare she assume that someone from a small little fishing village like Crow's Nest wouldn't have a relation or reason that could bring them to Europe? Look at Cora herself!

"I'm not from Crow's Nest." Adaleigh's excitement dimmed. "My parents were wealthy, so we did a European Tour at one time."

Were? "It is a wonderful country and the people are amazing." She cleared her throat as she thought of Signora Pimonte.

Adaleigh leaned close. "I'm so sorry for your loss. If you need to talk, please consider me a listening ear."

What could she say to that? Thankfully, Adaleigh seemed to under-stand, because she stayed by Cora's side, though she turned to face the others.

"Have you decided where you'll live now that you're back?" Mindy looked across Cora to ask Adaleigh. "Obviously, you can't stay with Mrs. Martins since David is there, and he's courting you. It's sweet how much David has missed you all summer."

"Sweet?" Kyle grumbled. His strawberry-blond hair hid beneath his flat cap and around his neck hung a slender rope with something weigh-ing it down hidden under his collar. "I'm his First Mate and have to work with the man."

Samantha laughed, her bobbed black hair swinging as she shook her head. "You have to work with him, but I've had to live with him. Adaleigh, I love you, but you are never allowed to leave Crow's Nest ever again. Or if you do, take David with you!"

"I actually agree with her." Patrick muttered. Lankier than his brother, he slouched with his hands in his pockets, his mop of blondish hair uncovered, scruff lining his chin.

Adaleigh laughed, and David turned bright red.

"You should live with me above The Barn," Mindy continued. "I know it's the opposite end of the wharf, but David is halfway there when he moors his boat at the end of a day. Plus, winter is coming and the men won't go out on the boats."

"Then he's the one who should live elsewhere." Samantha crossed her arms. "Like with Uncle Mike. If we get snowed in, Adaleigh should be with us. And I want to get to know my future sister."

"Sam!" David turned even redder, if at all possible.

"She's right." Kyle shrugged. "You two should just get married. The way you mooned after her all summer."

"Kyle," David growled. Patrick rolled his eyes.

Mindy laughed. "They're right, David. You were a complete sap. If it wasn't for taking over for Captain Mann and helping Mrs. Whittlebush move her business, you would have been lost."

Adaleigh left Cora's side for David's, wrapping her arm around his. "I'm sorry you missed me. Unless Mr. Binitari drags me back for more paperwork or whatever else he supposedly can't handle, this is my home now. You know that. No matter what house I live in."

The smile David shared with Adaleigh cocooned them in a moment all their own. Mindy *aww*-ed, Samantha and Kyle nudged elbows, and Patrick pretended to gag. Cora glanced at Silas where he knelt several feet away, showing his nieces how to work their new yo-yos.

She stepped back, unnoticed. Her heart warmed at the interaction of these friends, people who cared for one another. At the joy of the children. But especially at the willingness of a man without children of his own to be the father his nieces could look up to. However, it made her all the more aware of how much she wasn't a part of this group. And seeing that no one noticed her slip away, it was time for her to go back to Tante's house. Alone.

Silas rolled his shoulders as he downed a glass of lemonade before again scanning the crowd for Cora. He'd lost sight of her while entertaining his nieces. Hopefully, she'd decided to eat, not leave. Though he'd wanted to join her for lunch to see if she was feeling better. Did it bother her that he put his nieces first? Of course he should have, right? Then why did the whole situation make him off-kilter?

He turned from the lemonade table and smacked into Greg Alistar of the *Crow's Nest Gazette.*

"Just the man I want to see." Greg's grin had a smarmy quality that matched his short brownish-blond hair, closely shaved scruff, and dopey expression.

"No comment." Silas sidestepped the man. He'd hounded David and Adaleigh this past spring, and Silas had no use for a reporter without scruples. How the man still held a job, he wasn't sure.

"I heard you're friends with the new lady in town."

Silas bit his cheek to keep from reacting. *That* was why the man still had a job. He had the ability to ferret out information, which he then used for his own gain. He baited people with it, and Silas would be hanged before he gave Alistar anything, especially when it came to Cora Davis.

"I take it you're in a romantic relationship with her." It wasn't a question.

Silas pinned his tongue to the roof of his mouth. He had to take care or this situation would deteriorate quickly. Even his silence could be misconstrued.

"I do hope she's not in the family way," Greg mumbled.

"How dare you!" Silas clenched his fists before he wrapped his fingers around the man's jacket. He'd let himself fall right into the man's trap.

Greg had the audacity to grin. "Ah, so the man does have feelings for the lady."

"Any decent man would defend a woman's honor."

"Come now, I'm a simple newspaperman looking for a story. And my gut is telling me that woman has a story. You're going to get it for me."

"No."

"Then I'll spread the rumor that she's carrying your child."

Silas took a step back, surprised at the strength of emotion Greg's words created in him. The desire to protect surged like an avalanche crashing through his body, fogging his head and blurring his eyes. A rumor like Greg's would destroy Cora's reputation, especially if her own illegitimate birth became known. She'd be ostracized in the very town she came to for refuge. If the Corinvetter Foundation heard, she would lose the job she loved so much. And her health … her health would likely serve to corroborate the falsities.

"Well, what will it be?" Greg pulled a notepad from the inside pocket of his jacket.

Wisdom said he should put distance between himself and Cora so no one would believe the rumors, but he couldn't do that. He wouldn't let her face Greg alone. He didn't care a fig for himself. His own reputation was so far down the line of concerns it was a minor inconvenience. One couldn't protect a person from a distance. It's why he left the ranch out West and came home. If he was to defend Cora against Greg's threat of rumors, he needed to keep close to her and toss Greg a bone that would send him scrambling in another direction.

Greg tipped his bowler with the back end of his pencil. "I will punish you for not getting me what I want."

"I won't be bullied for information. Cora Davis is a guest in our town, and I'll thank you to treat her as such. Not to mention, she is a lady and deserving of respect. If you print unsubstantiated rumors—"

"Who said anything about putting that information in the paper?" A calculating gleam lit Greg's eyes. "Insinuation is a wonderful tool. You saw how well it worked with your friend David and that girl of his."

"You almost got them killed!"

"Almost got who killed?" Buck Wilson appeared beside Silas, and for the first time, he was glad to see the head of the Crow's Nest Conglomerate. "What lies are you putting out now, Alistar? If I catch you spreading rumors, you know I can have you fired, and then Miss Sirland will see you don't get another job in journalism."

Really?

Greg had the good sense to look cowed before disappearing, but it was most likely an act. Silas made a mental note to tell Cora to stay away from the newspaperman and then have a chat with David and Adaleigh. Perhaps he needn't be alone in his fight to protect Cora's reputation.

He shoved thoughts of his plans aside and shook Buck's hand. He might not like the man, but he knew when to express gratitude. "Your timing was impeccable."

"I came to find you, so it wasn't happenstance." Buck slipped his hands into the pockets of his perfectly tailored trousers, the bottom edge of his gray-striped suit coat hanging over his wrists. "I hoped for a private conversation."

"Conducting business at church on Sunday? Not the most private place. Why not see me at home or the shop?"

"Follow me." Buck wandered toward the edge of the crowd. He kept his casual stance, but Silas could feel his tension, which raised his own. Something was wrong, or at least the information Buck was about to give him was unpleasant. No, worse than unpleasant. Silas might not care for Buck, might agree with David and his uncle that Buck worked on the edges of legality, but when trouble stirred, Buck could be counted on to help. He'd spearheaded the search for David's boat this past spring. He'd bought Mrs. Whittlebush's property after the storm so she could begin again. And he'd advocated for the businesses in town as they rebuilt the past summer. So if Buck was concerned about something, it wasn't for a minor reason.

"What's this about, Wilson?" Silas folded his arms when they came to a stop at the edge of Main Street, where the heart of the destruction—and restoration—had happened.

Buck met his gaze. "How is your mother?"

Silas jerked his chin back. "What does my mother have to do with anything?"

Buck toed the ground. The man was uncomfortable? "I came to the social today so people wouldn't think we were discussing business."

Silas's gut tightened. What came next wouldn't be good.

"Since your father passed away, the shop and its business have been in your mother's hands. I know your brother managed some aspects of it, as do you, but your mother entirely manages the accounting aspect."

Silas uncrossed his arms. "I've tried to lessen her load, but she likes to manage it, says she's done that ever since she sold eggs as a girl."

"I'm not surprised." Buck smiled. "She's a strong lady."

Silas yanked off his Stetson. "Get to the point, Wilson. It's not like you to not be direct."

"I hate these conversations, Silas. Especially when it involves one of the widows my conglomerate protects. Your mother is late on her dues." Buck held up both hands, stopping Silas's words. "I'm not trying to be difficult. I've carried her for two months already, but the bylaws won't let me carry her for a third month. She needs to pay by the end of September, or I can't protect her."

"Maybe she doesn't need the Conglomerate anymore." Not likely, but maybe Mom had changed her mind about them.

Buck's shoulders sagged. "That's the real reason I wanted to talk to you about this. She needs our protection, Silas, and I think the first step is for you to take over her business. All of it."

Silas paced away, Buck's words jumping around his head like a bronco, and he couldn't make sense of them.

"Have you noticed your funds reducing of late?"

Silas spun back to Buck. "I assumed it was the market trouble. People are struggling more and more."

"I'm sure that's part of it. Do you go with your mother on her finding sprees? The ones where she buys what you sell in your shop?"

"No, I thought Marian did, but she didn't this last time. The girls had something that required her attention, I think. Anyway, that part of the business is all theirs. You suspect someone is short-changing them? But that makes little sense. They're buying, not selling, on these trips."

"Therein lies the conundrum I've been attempting to unweave. Several of your mother's clients have claimed she hasn't paid for the items and so she pays a second time."

Odd. "Can you prove that?"

"I can't. But if she gains a reputation of not paying for her goods, then no one will sell to her, and your business will be over."

"She wouldn't *not* pay."

"I know that. That's why I'm sure there's something more going on. I've been investigating whether these claims are founded or whether the sellers are exploiting your mother. I think it's the latter, but, again, I have no proof. Does your mother keep records of sales? Where and from whom she buys her stock?"

"I think so. Or Marian does. Have you talked to her yet?"

Buck shook his head. "I came to you first because I know you want to protect your family. They need your oversight in this, or you won't have a business or an income before too long."

"Protect them from what?"

"That's what we have to find out. I suggest talking with your mother and Marian. I'll continue to investigate the sellers. The growing financial troubles are bringing out the more unscrupulous, but if your mother has paper proof, it will help. However, she's a woman and the people accusing her have little respect for her. They're the type to take advantage. It's why she needs you on these buying trips. If it's your word that the item is paid for, and you have a bill of sale, then I can advocate for you much more easily. So ... pay the Conglomerate dues and talk to your family. We'll get to the bottom of this."

Silas nodded, and Buck left him standing there, considering their conversation. He'd been home for a year and yet he'd missed this? He'd returned to protect his family, to be the man of the house, to take the place of his father and brother, and here he'd failed so utterly that their livelihood was at stake. And he thought he could protect Cora too?

He jabbed his free hand through his hair, then replaced his cowboy hat atop his head. He had to find Cora, needed to tell her about Greg. But what unnerved him most was the burning desire to lay the whole situation with his mother before Cora. She had this ability to see beneath a problem and he knew, just knew, she'd have the right words to say.

He scanned the church yard for her, only he spotted Mrs. Whittlebush just as she waved him down. Cora wasn't with her.

"Enjoying your food?" He sank to the grass beside her chair. Several of the town's oldest ladies were grouped around a table laden with a platter of desserts. He didn't want to upset them by showing any of the agitation he felt inside.

"Do you have plans this afternoon?" Mrs. Whittlebush lowered her voice to speak just to him. "Cora insisted on walking home and refused to let me take her. Refused to ask you for a ride, too."

"Why?" Of course he would have driven her home. Didn't she realize that about him?

"We all know you'd take her home, like the gentleman you are, which is why she specifically said not to interrupt you. She wanted to let you enjoy your nieces. A sentiment I understand coming from her."

So did Silas. "But if she isn't feeling well ..."

"She won't appreciate me leaving the social to mother her, but she might like a friend to check on her. If you don't already have plans, of course."

"You can get home all right?" Silas laid a hand on Mrs. Whittlebush's arm. His plans included talking to Cora, so no trouble there. And after everything that happened the last half an hour, he was itching to leave the social and find her. Marian and his mom always closed down a church social. Mrs. Whittlebush, too. The three women, plus his nieces, were among the most social chatterboxes he knew.

"I have my car, dear, and I'll see your mom and Marian home. Go on with you. And don't let Cora push you away, ya hear?"

Silas gave the expected nod, but he was anxious to put the conversation behind him and find Cora.

After alerting his mom and sister-in-law to his leaving, he got his family's truck on the road. It took all of five minutes, but each minute that ticked by increased his unease. If Cora felt as miserable as she did the first day he met her, how would she make it home okay? What if Greg found her in that state? The rumors he'd spread could destroy her. Then there was her tumble and her friend's death. What if she had been pushed and her friend killed? What if that person found her here in Crow's Nest and finished her off?

Silas pressed the accelerator. No. He'd get to her first.

CHAPTER SIX

Cora followed the road from the church toward Lake Michigan. Tante's house was easy to find since it overlooked the lake. Instead of taking the long way around, however, when she reached Tante's property, she ducked into the grove of apple trees that stood sentry on the north side. Tante had been out to check the apples every day since Cora arrived home. Any day now, they would be ready for harvest.

Cora plucked a particularly red one off the tree. She remembered the apple trees from Tante and Onkle's farm and found it comforting to know that when Tante moved to Crow's Nest, she transplanted a handful of the apple trees. Now, ten years later, those few transplanted trees numbered over two dozen. Tante explained the trees were a Minnesota variety that her father had particularly liked and chose to cultivate. Wealthy Apples. Cora smiled at the name. Wealthy in memory, for sure. There were also Gravenstein from Onkle's family, and probably a couple other varieties Tante had added over the years.

She snacked on the sweet fruit as she meandered toward the house. The air held the crispness of fall, and she adjusted her scarf so that it covered her shoulders. She moved slowly, taking in her surroundings and not jostling her head too much to avoid stirring up the dizziness. Although, now that she'd had a few bites of apple, her stomach wasn't quite so queasy as when she left the church.

More stable on her feet, Cora gathered her notes and settled on the front porch. The timing of Signora Pimonte's death did not sit well, but Cora couldn't investigate from half a world away. However, if that danger chased her to Crow's Nest, along with the statue, she wanted to be prepared. The wind rustled the trees as Cora situated herself. The hair on the back of her neck tingled. She knew that sensation from years of looking out for herself in foreign countries. It was a warning, *un presentimento*, or premonition, as Signora Pimonte would say.

Cora set aside the papers to scan the area. Memory of the earthquake returned. The moments before the ground trembled beneath her feet. She'd had the same warning feeling. She'd just unearthed a black *bucchero*, or jug, with Etruscan writing on it. Spearing pain shot through her head as she grasped the memory. Holding the find, the ceiling and walls collapsing around her, and then her memory went blank. She grasped her head.

Wait.

That was what was wrong. When she opened her eyes after the dust settled, she saw Harry Gordon not rescuing her. She didn't have the bucchero in her hands either. *He* did. She could remember it now. He'd taken her find from her unconscious hands instead of helping her. Had he left her to die? Was the bucchero that much more important than her life? What did it have to do with Signora Pimonte's questions?

She shuddered, and what began as a crisp lake breeze now felt sinister and cold.

Cora leaned her head against the porch railing, the chipped paint catching strands of her hair. She hated the lonely feeling that wrapped itself around her. The pain in her head from recalling the memory left her tired and achy. Her soul felt stretched thin, too. Did she think artifacts like the bucchero were more important than Tante? Was Cora no better than Mr. Gordon?

The sound of tires brought her head up, and she recognized the Wards' truck. Her insides bubbled with anticipation and yet her heart shrank back. Silas had scolded her that first day because he thought she was just like her colleague. That old pottery was more important than family. Ashamed that he would think that of her, she gathered her papers, considering a mad dash to hide inside the house. But her head wouldn't let her move quickly enough. She wasn't able to get her feet under her before Silas slammed the truck door and jogged toward her. Concern—no, worry—carved lines in his face.

"What are you doing here?" Cora smiled at him to lighten his intensity.

"Checking on you." He sat beside her, his eyes roving over her, assessing, and, she'd guess, cataloging the smallest detail. "Your Tante was worried, too."

Kind man. "I didn't want to take either of you away from the social. I'm fine, Silas. You don't need to stay."

"What if I want to stay?"

She blinked twice, hope swelling in her belly. "You do?"

"Absolutely." He rested his elbows on the step behind him and stretched out his legs, ankles crossed. "I don't enjoy socials all that much. I prefer to sit around a campfire, keep my cattle safe."

Tears smarted. "That sounds lovely right now."

Silas turned to watch her from under his Stetson. She studied the play of emotion on his shadowed face. The worry lines around his eyes had eased, but his tight jaw showed an underlying tension that caused her own nerves to tighten. The straight line of his shoulders, the muscles in his neck that appeared and disappeared only to appear again ... what did he hold onto so tightly? As if he were coiled inside, holding himself back. And from what? Then his chin dropped, those strong shoulders sagged.

"Is everything all right?" Cora spoke before she realized she'd put her hand on his arm. It broke her heart to see this good cowboy hurting in any way.

His eyes dipped to her hand, then up to her eyes. The space between them heated. Cora's heart pounded. Then Silas jerked back and jumped to his feet. He paced before her, rubbing his hand over his beard again and again.

Cora carefully maneuvered directly into his path so that he nearly stumbled over her. She put both hands on his chest to keep her balance, and he caught her arms. She looked up at him. "Silas, you're worrying me. Is something wrong? Why are you so agitated?"

His mouth opened, but nothing came out.

Cora frowned, then tugged him back toward the steps, making him sit beside her. Maybe she should try sharing something of her own. Perhaps if she explained more, she could chase the shame away. "Do you know why I enjoy my work? What makes me leave my aunt and travel the world over for those *things* you pointed out that first day we met?"

"Cora, I—"

"It's because of the stories." She wouldn't let him interrupt her now. "My friend who died, who left me the statue, Signora Pimonte, she was an older widow with no family, no one to remember her now that she's passed. Except me. At each dig, I travel into the surrounding communities looking for the storytellers, those people who keep the oral traditions alive. As my colleagues and I find various items, whether from a grotto or other type of dig, I ask the storytellers about those items. What were they used for, what do the markings mean? In that way, I can keep their history alive through the possessions their ancestors used during their lifetime. Whether or not those long dead have a name, living relatives or not, by bringing their story into the light, I give their memory fresh wings. Despite the actions of my mother and grandmother, I wouldn't want them forgotten, and I know how precious the memories of your brother are to you, your mom, Marian … his girls."

"That's …" Silas's throat bobbed. "That's why you do what you do?"

She threaded the end of her scarf through her fingers. "I don't want them to be forgotten."

"Forgotten?" He freed her fingers, then wrapped them around his own. "Has there been a time where you felt that way?"

"Do you know how scary the underbelly of Chicago is to a little girl?" The words tumbled out. "My mother insisted we leave our home in Colorado and travel to Chicago. Different names, different appearances. We'd been sleeping outside the first two nights when, the next night, she set me in a ramshackle cubby made of old boards under a fire escape and left me there with our meager belongings, promising to be back when the sun came up. I'm not sure how long I sat there as the world passed by the narrow alley opening, but I must have fallen asleep because when I opened my eyes, an older woman stood over me with a ticket to Tante's house. I never saw my mother—Jennie—again."

His cheek indented.

"Tante and Onkle took me in, and I won't do anything to harm her. I promise you that. She means the world to me. But my career fills a need, too. And not just for me. I can't stop thinking about Signora Pimonte. She was my friend. She took me to her church. She …"

"She left you her most prized possession."

Cora nodded, then pointed to his Stetson. "Things tell us stories about people. You are a cowboy, and if I'm not mistaken, the sadness you feel has something to do with leaving that life behind."

Silas's jaw slackened.

"You're not such a closed book, not for someone who unearths stories from the stone."

"Yeah, well, you're not a woman easily forgotten."

Tuesday, September 23

Silas scrubbed out his paintbrushes at the pump behind his shop. Pink water splashed the gravel at his feet—his dad's idea of a convenient wash area for the shop. Dad had lots of ideas to increase efficiency. Silas missed working side by side with him, watching Dad create something new from something old.

Overhead, fluffy white clouds dotted the late-morning sky. A warm breeze sanded the lake to a crystal glass. Too beautiful a day to mar with sorrow. Silas pushed memories of his father away, only to have them replaced with thoughts of a curly-haired woman. Irritation snagged through him.

On Sunday, he hadn't told her about Greg Alistar's threats, nor about his conversation with Buck Wilson. He hadn't wanted to add more weight to her shoulders. That's what he told himself, anyway. But for two days, he'd suffered her intruding into his mind, bringing up dreams of having a wife and family of his own one day. He thought he'd buried those when he returned from the ranch to care for Zee's family. How could he be so selfish as to nurture romantic thoughts when Cora's life and reputation were on the line, when his family could lose their business? He needed to stay clear-headed, not get muddled by thoughts of a certain archaeologist.

Silas jammed the handles of the brushes into his pants pocket and scrubbed his hands. The positive side of his mental turmoil was that during the same time frame he was going over the books—and finding nothing to answer Buck's concerns—he finished a dresser ordered for five-year-old Marylou Vashen. He'd drop it off later this afternoon. She'd be giddy, no doubt about it.

The furniture piece would pay for the Conglomerate dues. He'd see to that this afternoon as well. Thankfully, building furniture and repairing boats brought in a steady enough income for now. And contributing to his family's well-being made the loss of his ranch job a little easier, though he still missed spending his days outdoors. That was no longer an option, not with people out of work and banks failing.

The crunch of dirt alerted him to a new customer parking on the far side of the curiosities barn. Mom had been putting up vegetables non-stop today, getting the garden stored away for winter. Silas should be in the shop so Marian could help Mom, but she had banished him earlier with one look at his face. Between his grumpy attitude and the new lines he'd discovered bracketing his eyes and mouth this morning, she must've deemed him unfit to serve customers. He needed to talk with her about the business, but he'd wanted to find answers first.

Silas stored the brushes in the workshop and went to see if Marian needed him. As he wove through the rows of bric-à-brac, the front counter and the customer speaking to Marian came into view, and Silas's steps stumbled. Cora.

A barrette above each temple held her curly black hair away from her face. A brown dress wrapped around her frame, kept closed with a bow at her hip. And the same blue scarf she'd worn previously hung from her neck.

"There he is now." Marian flashed her trademark smile, the one that had snagged Zee's heart the first time he saw it—an encouraging sight indeed, especially with how rarely it appeared nowadays.

Then he heard Marian's words. Cora had come to see him? Nervous tension zipped down his arms. "What can I do for you, Miss Davis?" Silas looped his thumbs around his suspenders, hoping to affect a casual stance.

Her cheeks darkened. And her eyes matched her scarf, blue as the lake today. Goodness, she was pretty. "Wondering if you might show me that desk I helped you unload the other day."

Desk? The one with the secret compartment? He'd completely forgotten—

"Silas is the perfect person to show you around." Marian grinned at him, a message behind her unusually twinkly eyes. "Aren't you, brother?"

Uh ... He froze. Did Marian think something romantic was going on between them? Had Greg spread rumors already?

"My curiosity has gotten the best of me, and I hoped you hadn't sold it yet." Cora's gaze bounced between them, her shoulders rising to her ears and her fingers tangling in her scarf. "Could one of you point me to it?"

Sold it. Could it be one of the items Mom paid for twice? This was his opportunity to tell both women about his conversation with Buck, to ask Marian about Mom and the business.

"Silas would love to." Marian patted his shoulder and urged Cora forward with a hand to her back. When Cora's arm brushed his, Marian gave a wave and left them standing there, awkwardly alone together, while she disappeared outside.

He hadn't acted fast enough. In fact, he was acting like a schoolboy. If only he could think of words to say.

"The desk, Silas?" Cora smiled at him.

"Right. This way." He led her toward where he and David had left the heavy thing. "What do you hope to find by looking at it again?"

"Honestly? Nothing. Tante had a client fitting, and then Adaleigh is moving into Tante's other spare room, so I wanted to make myself scarce. Then I remembered the desk and figured this was as good a time as any to satisfy my curiosity."

"Right. Of course." Something in Cora's tone told him there was more going on. He glanced down at her and spotted the red stinging her cheeks. Could she have wanted an excuse to see *him*?

"I needed a fresh project. I've been poring over my notes from the dig, from interviewing Signora Pimonte, and not finding anything. The words are jumbling together in my head and making it ache."

Not him. Well, maybe not exactly, but she could have gone for a walk, investigated the wharf, watched the fishing boats. Instead, she'd come here. The thought warmed him.

"Signora Pimonte told me about living in Italy. About foods and customs. Her family ancestry, including the *Madre e Figlia* statue, the one time she made the pilgrimage to Rome. Nothing to indicate any secrets or dangers. Then there was the bucchero—a type of ceramic jug—I found during the earthquake. I have absolutely no notes about that, which is supremely strange. I couldn't recall anything about it until Sunday, and it makes me worried about what else I'm not remembering. Does it have anything to do with why I fell or was pushed off the cliff? Could I be putting Tante in danger by—"

"Cora." Silas grabbed her shoulders to stop the torrent of words. "Those are all insightful questions, but you came here for a fresh perspective. Set those worries aside for now and tell me about the desk."

Cora took a deep breath, the lines in her forehead easing. Still, Silas didn't remove his hands from her upper arms. Instead, he circled his thumbs and felt her sink into his hold.

Her eyes slid open. "Thank you, Silas."

He pressed his lips to her forehead and tugged her into his arms. "You can always find safety here, Cora. Whenever you're feeling lost or confused, please come see me."

Her head tucked perfectly under his chin. "I know. That's the real reason I came. You're always such a calming influence. Although ..." She tugged away, a sparkle in her eyes. "I do want to have another look at that desk."

"Here it is." He turned her toward it.

"The light in here isn't great, but I've made do with worse. This is a typical knee-hole design with the drawers on either side and one in the center, which was where we discovered the first secret compartment." Cora ran her fingers over the edging. "The mahogany and curves indicate it is a Chippendale, but I said all that when I first saw it. What I want to know today is whether there are other secret compartments."

"And how do you hope to find them?" Silas covered a smile with his hand. Her excitement was catching. He could see why she loved her work so much.

"By searching, of course." She was down on her knees now, crawling around beneath the desk like a child.

"There must be a better way. At least let me get you something to kneel on."

"Nonsense. This floor is much cleaner than most digs, and there are definitely less spiders. Now look at this." She tapped the gold keyhole in the center of the desk. "The carving around the keyhole is more than a simple pattern. I think that's a seal."

Silas leaned over her shoulder to see two horse heads carved on either side of the keyhole, along with intricate scrollwork. Her curls brushed his cheek. The smell of lavender swirled around him. A wave of longing washed over him as he closed his eyes. He shook off the feeling and shifted out of her light, only to spy a detail his carpenter's eye wouldn't miss. He pointed to the edge of the scrollwork. "See this? The scroll isn't carved from the front panel of the drawer. It was added afterward."

Cora pressed her fingers around the scroll work, then pushed her thumbs against the two horses. Something clicked, and the whole seal turned around the keyhole mechanism until the horses were upside down. The sides opened like double ballroom doors. Cora inhaled sharply, then reached two fingers into the small space and eased out a single piece of stationery. She looked up at him with eyes shining like a Christmas star. Color splashed her cheeks. Excitement radiated off her like a heat wave.

"What is it?" The question came out hoarse.

"I have a feeling this desk is going to have many secrets if we've found two so easily." Cora stood and unrolled the paper. She ran her finger over the lettering without touching the paper. "This looks like linen paper, and the handwriting is pre-1800s. See, the *s* looks like an *f*." She pointed to an example within the word *confess*. "This letter is likely from the Colonial era. I'd have to research whether the seal represents a certain family or a company. Is there a place we can look at it better?" She raised her head so that her eyes—and her mouth—were only inches away.

"Of course." His pulse hammered and he cleared his throat. "You're transforming into an archaeologist right before my eyes."

She ducked her chin. "It might be nothing. Probably is nothing. But I haven't had my fingers on anything like this in too long."

His heart stuttered as he took in the sight of her. "Of course you can look at it. I'm curious, too." About more than just the paper.

"You are?" Her eyes widened.

"Honest truth?" Truth he'd been wrestling with since he met her but only now could put into words, thanks to her. "You were right. I enjoy bringing discarded *things* back to life. So perhaps I was jealous of you and your adventures."

"Of me? Maybe the adventures." Her cheeks flushed with even deeper color. "How about we work on this together? If you ... I mean ... I ..."

Silas grinned. "I would like that very much."

Cora settled at Silas's work table, struggling to concentrate after the electricity that had arced between them. She'd never felt that way with another man before, but with Silas, he not only made her feel safe, he made her feel alive.

"Here we go." Silas laid out a pencil, unmarked paper, and a magnifying glass. "Talk me through what you do?"

Time to focus on the task at hand, not the handsome cowboy beside her. However, it would be fun having him there to join in on the camaraderie of discovery. She picked up the letter. "First, we look." She held open the paper, its ends curling from being in the desk. "This aged coloring is expected, but it's easy to duplicate with tea bags. The handwriting, too. As much as it looks old, anyone could write it that way to give the impression of it being written a century or more ago."

"How can you tell for certain, then?" Silas's voice rumbled beside her, and she ignored the shiver it sent down her spine.

"We research the provenance of the letter. By investigating the names on the document and the story it tells, we can potentially disprove its authenticity. If it still seems authentic, then we can do a handwriting comparison with a sample from the author of the letter. From there, we can look at the paper itself. Does it fit the timeline of when this person was alive? Paper, for example, has changed over the years." She ran her fingers over the bottom of the page. "This appears to be a sheet of stationery that has been torn. Perhaps something was written at the bottom that someone tore off to keep it from being found or read."

"Do you think this was originally a full-size eight-by-ten sheet of stationery?"

"Possibly. That's why it's helpful to determine the author first. Then we have parameters for whether the paper is authentic." She carefully held up the paper so that the light of the window shone behind it. "It wants to keep rolling up, so I suspect it's been in the desk for some time. But look at this, there's a watermark on the paper."

"What does that tell you?" He leaned over her shoulder. Mercy, she liked him sitting so close, more than was good for her, that was for sure.

"It can tell us a lot." She focused on the watermark. "Where the paper was made, who it was made for, maybe even when it was made. Or at least when the maker wants us to think it was made."

"Suspicious, are you?" The teasing lilt in the question brought out her smile.

"There's a reason art crime is a brisk business. Forgeries can bring a handsome amount for a worthless piece, and forgers are getting more skilled at covering their tracks."

"Is that why your work is dangerous?"

She lowered the paper and turned her full attention to Silas. Maybe answering this question would spark answers to the ones surrounding the death of Signora Pimonte and the missing bucchero. "Yes and no. Greedy people, not mindless thugs, often commit antiquities crime. However, where there is greed, more value is placed on money than human life. My company provides security for my colleagues and I while we are on a dig. However, digs are easy marks for someone—or some country—who wants uncatalogued items of value. With the provenance already authenticated, the only crime is having stolen it from a dig. Since these digs happen in out of the way places, it is difficult to prove. And as a woman, they believe I am a weak link and easily threatened."

"Then why put yourself in harm's way for another people's history?"

The question no longer seemed laced with judgment as when he asked it that first day. Rather, it felt weighted with personal concern. Cora's heart warmed. Perhaps more than just Tante would mourn if something happened to her.

She ran her hand over the paper. "Because I have the skills to offer information about their past. Female storytellers connect with me so that I am often tasked with gathering those histories." Something caught her eye on the paper itself. "Look. See how these lines are shaded darker on the outside? That says the mold used is likely older than—or a replica of one that is older than—the early 1800s."

"I don't see—"

"Watch." Cora angled the paper toward him with the window's light directly behind. "See the shading now?"

Silas shifted closer, his head inches from Cora's. "That's the same as the seal on the desk. Can you tell what it says?" He lifted the magnifying glass to the paper as she continued to hold it. The smell of sawdust wafted up from him.

"Winchaser Orchards. Seventeen ..." Cora squinted, and pain shot through her head as if someone speared her with a fiery blade. She laid the paper on the table.

"Hey, you okay?" Silas set down the magnifying glass and steadied her on the stool. "If this is too much, we should get you home."

"No." But Cora didn't move her head. That always made things worse. "I had forgotten about my symptoms for the first time since I got to Tante's house." Now they were back and full of vengeance.

"Do you know what's causing them?" Again, concern, not judgment, and it cracked open the part of her she'd buried like a forgotten urn.

"The doctor I saw upon returning to New York used words like *brain tumor* and *stroke*. Do you know how scary that is?" She sought his expression as she finally admitted the truth. The concern and compassion she found gave her the courage to go on. "I'm too scared to go back and face whatever tests they want to try. Don't tell Tante. I don't want her to worry."

Silas's eyes glimmered. "She is already worrying."

Cora smiled and dabbed her own eyes with the edge of her finger. "I hoped the doctor would wave away the symptoms and I could jump on the next ship back to Italy, but after my appointment, I felt so alone, and I was the closest to Tante's house I've been in years. So I got on the next train west. I hoped the rest would set me to rights. It hasn't yet, but this, the story behind this paper, the lives of the people who touched it, of the person who wrote it and the person he or she wrote it to, gives me something to cling to outside of myself and my own troubles."

He covered her hand with his strong one. "Cora, I—"

"What are you doing in here alone?" His mom's voice cut him off.

Silas jerked away from Cora and spun on his stool. "We found a—"

"You didn't answer my question, young man." Mrs. Ward stood with fists on her hips, a stance that Cora guessed Silas had seen many times growing up. But it sent a sense of unease down her spine.

"Cora and I—"

"You're not old enough to be canoodling a young woman. You know that."

Cora glanced at Silas to find his face a swirl of fear and worry.

Mrs. Ward didn't miss a beat. "I'll have Dad drive your young lady home. It's time for lunch."

"Mom ..." Silas's voice trembled. "Dad isn't here. He's ... dead."

CHAPTER SEVEN

The world tumbled around Silas as if he'd just been bucked from a horse. What was his mom talking about? Something was seriously wrong. He glanced at the phone box hanging on the wall of his workshop. Should he call for the doctor? He'd never seen someone forget their husband and son were ... dead.

The tap of her toe, the roll of her eyes, sent him back two decades, to when he was a boy playing on the wharf with his friends and forgot to do his chores. "Trying to get rid of me? I'm not blind, son, and when your father hears of you two being alone in here—"

Silas shoved back the embarrassment—and the memory of Greg Alistar's threats—and swallowed. First action in a medical emergency was to remain calm even though his mind raced. He'd get his mom to a safe place, then call Dr. Thompson. He cupped his mom's shoulder. "Dad isn't here, Mom. Remember?"

Confusion flashed through her eyes. "Did he and Zachariah go down to the wharf?"

"Mom. Zee and Dad—"

"Mrs. Ward?" Cora spoke quietly, demurely, and so unlike the spitfire he was accustomed to sparring with the last few days, that he stepped aside.

Their conversation smacked into him. *Brain tumor.* Beautiful, smart, amazing Cora could suffer from a brain tumor? Man, he'd been an idiot when he first met her. An insensitive, bumbling idiot. And now she was helping his mom.

His mom—did *she* have a brain tumor? Why else would she have forgotten a decade of time. Cora had forgotten weeks. But he hadn't seen his Mom act this way before. Could the customer issues be a symptom? How could he not have seen any of this?

Cora's cool hand on his arm snapped him out of his head. *Be calm.* He whipped his hand around to squeeze her fingers before he slowly approached his mother. Buck's question about his mother's health reverberated within. "Weren't you working in the kitchen, Mom? Preserving the garden?"

"I don't know you." Mom ignored him and glared at Cora. "Who are you?"

Cora took another step closer to Mom. "You know your friend Rose? Rose Whittlebush?"

Mom blinked uncertainly.

"I'm her niece. I'm visiting." She took Mom's arm and turned her out of his workshop, into the bright sunshine. "Your son was telling me all about the canning you were doing. What vegetable were you preserving today? Perhaps you could show me?"

"Well, I suppose," Mom muttered, but she let Cora lead her across the gravel between the workshop and the house.

Should Silas follow or call Dr. Thompson first? Indecision froze his feet and the warmth of the outdoors did nothing to ease the chill inside. Cora glanced over her shoulder with raised eyebrows. What did they do next? Silas sure didn't know.

"Mom?" Marian exited the kitchen, brushing loose strands of brown hair from her forehead. "The pot on the stove was boiling over. What's—" She met Silas's gaze and stopped.

"Pot of what?" Mom shook her head, then stared at her and Cora's linked arms. Suddenly, she yanked away from Cora. "Who are you? Why are you here?"

"Mom, it's Cora." Silas stepped between them. This wasn't his mother. She'd never yelled at them, even as trouble-making boys. Nor was this the woman who welcomed in strangers to buy the curiosities she found all over the area. Or who knit blankets for newborn babies. Or baked cookies for church functions.

"I don't know a Cora." Contempt laced Mom's tone. "I want her gone. She's trying to corrupt you."

Cora blanched beside him. This was a disaster.

"Mom, come rescue your carrots." Marian hurried forward, giving him a significant look that he felt helpless to interpret. "Silas is a gentleman, Mom, just like you raised him to be. He'll make sure Cora gets home safely. Come with me now. Zee's daughters will be home any minute, and you know how they love to help you in the kitchen."

"Yes. Zee's girls." Mom latched onto Marian's arm, the vitriol she'd spewed at Cora gone. "Nettie and Essie. I love those little girls." She remembered her grandchildren. That was good. *Right?*

"I know, Mom. They love their grandma." Marian looked over her shoulder at him, then nodded at Cora. "Walk the wharf."

"But—" The doctor. Unease added to the mash of emotions in his gut. Marian handled this situation smoothly, as though she'd done it before. But Silas had been home for over a year and had never witnessed anything like this.

He glanced at Cora. She kept a smile on her pale face, but she swayed as if a strong breeze would knock her over. Both Cora and his mother could use a doctor. He opened his mouth to say as much, but the glare Marian sent him shut his mouth. Why did he have such stubborn women in his life?

In his life? Cora wasn't in his life. He couldn't give her a future, especially if she planned to return to her work, which would take her to other countries.

"Are you okay?" Cora touched his arm again. Light fingers just barely grazing his wrist.

His gaze followed the line of her arm up to her shoulder, her neck, her eyes. Worry and concern mingled there, but one eye was slightly hooded, and her head dipped to that side. Had his mother's outburst caused her condition to worsen?

He cupped her cheek, the side that seemed to hurt her. Her eyes widened, but then she closed them and leaned into his palm. He ran his thumb over her cheekbone. "You're in pain." He was in pain for her.

She took a shuddering breath, and a tear slipped down her cheek. It gutted him, and the same protective streak that reared its head when she'd nearly fainted the first day he met her filled his chest once again. Marian had Mom in hand. He would take care of Cora until he could get her home to Mrs. Whittlebush. Then he'd insist on a call to Dr. Thompson.

"Come. We'll go slow." He wrapped her under his arm before turning them toward Lake Michigan and the wharf, as Marian suggested. Cora walked with him willingly. She seemed steady enough on her feet but let him keep her tucked next to him.

Beyond his workshop, the lake stretched out in all its crystal wonder. The wharf's weathered boards ended abruptly at the tall grasses behind the house. Three generations ago, this was a small farm, but his father wasn't a farmer—he was a shipbuilder and carpenter—and hadn't kept up the land. Zee had wanted to restart the farm, even cleared a patch of ground for potatoes. Then during one planting season, the horses spooked, and Zee got tangled in the plow lines. If Silas had been here, would he have been able to get him help in time? Surely, he would have been out in the field beside his brother.

But Silas knew better. He wouldn't have been farming. He hated farming. Being outside wasn't the problem—he craved the outdoors—it was the necessity of being tied to the land. Working as a ranch hand was different because the cattle had to be moved to different pastures or driven to market. If it wasn't for his ability to create new things, then deliver them all around the area, he might go a little crazy here in Crow's Nest. Is that what happened to his mother?

The clump of their feet on the wharf brought him back to the present. There would be time enough to talk to Marian and try to understand what happened with his mom—and to convince them both Mom needed to visit the doctor, if Marian hadn't taken her before, without his knowledge. He blew out a breath.

Cora ducked out from under his arm to stand at the edge of the wharf, her hands clasped atop a wooden post, her scarf fluttering in the breeze. At first, he wanted to reach for her, draw her away from being so close to the water. If she fainted as she nearly had the other day, she would fall right in. But her upright posture stopped him. Standing there, the wind ruffling her curls and her skirt, she resembled a seafarer, looking out to the horizon.

"How are you feeling?" he asked as a seagull cawed above them.

"Sometimes the pain in my head is like a crushing fist. Seeing the wide open space lets me breathe."

Could he feel any worse? "When did the symptoms start?"

"After I was trapped in an earthquake."

He cringed.

She peeked at him. "I told you my job has its dangers. The dig was in an ancient ruin of a town outside the village where Signora Pimonte lived. One minute, I was excavating the bucchero I mentioned to you earlier. The next, the building I was in crashed around me. I don't remember much else." Her eyebrows scrunched together. "Though, I recently remembered that I think my colleague was doing something with the bucchero before he pulled me free."

Silas crossed his arms. "He didn't immediately help you?"

Cora rubbed her forehead. "It hurts to remember, but, yeah. Harry Gordon doesn't approve of females on a dig. He was holding the bucchero. I can't make it make sense." She stepped away from the edge. "Has your mom ever ... forgot like that before?"

"No. Not that I know of. I intend to talk to Dr. Thompson." *As should you.* But he kept that to himself.

She pressed her palms to her cheeks. "I didn't mean to put you in an uncomfortable position with her. She didn't know what she was saying, I know that, but her thinking we—I'm so sorry."

"Cora." He needed to tell her about Alistar.

"And I wish I could have helped her more. I mean, I've forgotten weeks. Surely I could have helped her. If only—"

"Cora." He pulled her hands away from her face. "I was frozen, too."

"I know. That's why I wanted to help. I hate always being the needy one." She squared her shoulders and tugged free of him. He felt her absence keenly. "In fact, we should get back, then I'll drive myself home. And don't protest. I know you're just being polite to me when you really want to check on your mom. I'll be fine, I promise."

Stubborn woman. She was only half right. He wanted to check on his mom, and get some answers, but he also wasn't *just being polite* to Cora. He wanted to make sure she was okay. If he was being honest, he needed to know for his own peace of mind. "Let's walk this way for a minute first."

"I can't take you away from your mom. This has been too generous of you already."

"I need the walk." Silas shook his head as he told the half-truth. Or maybe it was mostly true. His insides were a crumbled mess and walking with Cora would definitely help. "It's quiet on this portion of the wharf because we dock all the fishing boats up toward the harbor, and of course the shops are centralized there, too. The closest shop to us is The Barn, where we found Nettie. The owner is a delightful older lady who makes the best sweetbreads."

Cora slipped her hand around his elbow, as if they were out for a date.

Instead of dwelling on the emotions that thought evoked, he continued. "Farther up is the Wharfside Cafe, which caters to the fishermen and serves breakfast, lunch, and supper. Mindy works as a waitress there. Next door to the Wharfside is David's fishing shanty." Which reminded him, he wanted to talk to Adaleigh about muzzling Greg. He'd wait to tell Cora until she felt better, or until he had better answers.

He glanced down at the curly head so close to his shoulder. He'd once warned David to free Adaleigh to return home to see to her responsibilities. Now that he had crossed paths with Cora, could he let *her* go?

That evening, Cora crept down the cellar steps below the kitchen, trying each wooden stair before putting her full weight on it to avoid any creaks. Tante dozed lightly on the first floor, and Cora didn't want to wake her—or Adaleigh, who now slept in a room on the second floor, across from Cora's. No need for all of them to spend the night awake worrying. Not that it was all that late yet, but the summer sun had set. Tante and Adaleigh had both retired early—Adaleigh explaining by reminding them of David's early fishing hours—leaving Cora alone with her thoughts.

Elaine Ward's episode had Cora struggling to wade through her emotions on the matter. Shame that she had thought Cora and Silas were being inappropriate. Guilt that Cora had taken Silas away from his mother, even if he insisted *he* needed a walk. And fear that she and Elaine somehow had the same diagnosis. That maybe one day Cora would forget a decade of her life. She couldn't remember a month, so of course that could happen, right?

The panic of that thought had her surging out of bed, grabbing a lantern, and descending into the dark space below the house in search of answers. Her lantern cast an eerie glow on the dirt wall closest to her, leaving the rest of the cellar in deep shadow. Shelves lined the walls, half filled with jars of preserved produce from the garden. A couple barrels rested on the floor, likely empty and ready to be filled with apples or root vegetables her aunt would harvest over the next couple months. Cora raised her lantern to peer inside one. Yes, three shriveled red apples lay at the bottom.

Tante had told her and Adaleigh at dinner how she planned an apple-picking social once the apples were ready. She'd invite the neighbors so they could bring in all the apples at once. Then she'd send a bushel home with every family.

When Adaleigh mentioned how Mrs. Martins, David's grandmother, was teaching her how to cook, Tante had promised to show her how to make a couple of apple recipes. Cora didn't like the possessive feelings that provoked in her. Of course, Tante had included Cora, too, but still … It was another reason Cora struggled to sleep tonight.

She shuffled deeper into the cellar, grateful it was cool and dry. Though she worked in environments like this all the time, her skin crawled with her anxiety. She hated it. Digging in holes, looking for someone's story was her life. But this time, she was searching for her own story.

Against the wall at the back of the cellar, she found the stack of boxes, crates, and trunks she hoped would hold answers to the questions today's events had sparked in her mind. She set the lantern on one stack, and it shone on a thick web that hung between two crates. She hated cobwebs. Too often, poisonous spiders dropped from them.

Lifting the first crate down from the tallest stack, she set it aside to reach a smaller trunk, which she set directly within the lantern's circle of light. The trunk was only three feet by one foot and only a foot deep. She popped the single buckle that held it closed and lifted the dusty lid to reveal the contents.

A thick, paperboard photo rested atop a stack of papers. She lifted it, a smile rising. Tante and Onkle in their youth. Their wedding day, based on the lacy white dress Tante wore. She looked so beautiful, so happy and young. Onkle, with his shoulders back and chin raised, appeared so proud and handsome. His German-ness—shocking blond hair and large frame—came through even in the colorless photograph. He came to America at eighteen and met Tante when he worked the farm next to her family's place. They married and tended her family's farm until Onkle passed away ten years ago and Tante moved to Crow's Nest.

Onkle was the one who encouraged Cora's desire to go into archae-ology. *Stories remind us of the people who lived them,* he would say. Cora always felt sad that he never got to have children of his own. If ever a man would have made a wonderful father, it was Onkle. Too bad blood did not relate her to him. Then maybe a happy marriage would be in her future, too.

But her mother was from Tante's side of the family, and Jennie Davis was the woman Cora came down here to find.

She picked up a small photograph of her mother that lay beneath the one of Tante and Onkle, uncomfortable emotions coursing through her. When Cora left for university, she'd packed up everything related to her mother and shoved it into this box, burying it in the cellar. Other than the photograph of Tante and Onkle, she didn't care if the rest got ruined. Still didn't. At least, that's what she tried to tell herself. Yet here she was, looking through documents she swore she would never read.

Tears burned her eyes as she came upon her mother's death notifica-tion. Cora had already been living with Tante and Onkle for two years when a lawman tracked them down to deliver the news. Jennie had died of some disease in a dilapidated old building in Chicago. She'd chosen her life on the street over her own daughter. Cora never understood. Tante and Onkle were more parental than Jennie had ever been.

Cora kept turning pages. Travel papers. Guardianship agreements. Another birth announcement, this one for Jennie's mother, Tante's much younger sister. She never met the woman, the unwed mother of her own unwed mother. She died a year before Cora was born, so not of old age. Her mother and grandmother were so different from Tante that it was difficult to see the relation. Tante was much older than—almost a mother to—her sister, Cora's grandmother.

She pushed those thoughts aside. There had to be medical information in here somewhere. A list of ailments, a letter, notes—something—that could bring understanding to her own situation. She didn't want to ask Tante—hated bringing up her mother or grandmother to her great aunt—but facing her own health problems, she needed to know if either of her maternal relatives had battled the same debilitating condition as she did. What if their wanton behavior or premature deaths were because of a brain tumor or whatever illness was affecting Cora now?

Her fingers trembled as she came to a letter from a young Jennie to Tante explaining that Cora's grandmother suffered heart trouble that had cost her a job as a saloon girl in Wyoming Territory and that they were moving to Denver. Cora grew increasingly aware of her own heart pumping hard and loud. Within five years, Cora's grandmother was dead, and Jennie was expecting Cora. Cora shuddered. She might be an archaeologist, but she didn't deal with bones or dead people. She preferred artifacts that showed how a person lived, not how they died.

Maybe this entire plan was a bad idea, especially to carry out alone, at night, in a dark cellar. Cora set the papers back inside the box, re-stacked it, and carried the lantern and photograph of Tante and Onkle upstairs. If only she could share the crate's contents with Silas.

Silas? Why would she want to share this information with him? Then again, they both had lived in the shadow of the Rocky Mountains at some point in their lives. Is that why she felt a kinship with him? He certainly was different from the cowboys that filled the faded stories her mother had once told her.

"There you are." Tante's voice nearly had Cora dropping the lantern.

"I hoped you'd sleep through my escapade." She clutched the photograph to her chest.

"Don't sleep so well these days." Tante slid a cup of peppermint tea across the table toward an empty chair. "Come sit."

The smell wrapped itself around Cora even from several feet away. She set the photograph on the table and tucked her legs up onto the chair, then cradled the cup in her hands. "Is Adaleigh still asleep?"

"I think so. She wanted to see David before he took his boat out fishing in the morning." Tante chuckled. "That's love for you. They'll be hitched before long."

Silence stretched between them until Cora blurted, "Do you wish I would've stayed nearby instead of working an ocean away?"

"No." Tante cocked her head, lantern light flickering on the many wrinkles she'd sprouted since last Cora saw her. "I miss you, make no bones about it. But do I want to see you living a full life? Yes, of course. And I fully believe you are at your best when you're bringing other people's stories to life."

The words were a comfort, just like the peppermint tea as it slipped down her throat.

"You have a gift, Cora." Tante set her cup aside to lean forward, the gray hair that escaped her braid loose about her face. "You can bring back to life what the rock has hardened into stone."

Cora smiled. She couldn't help it. "Does that notion not excite you, Tante? I miss it. I've never been away from my work this long, and not knowing when I can return is torture."

Tante adjusted her dressing gown. "What of the letter you found at the curiosity shop this morning?"

She'd told Tante everything about her day. Well, almost everything. Not the connection she'd felt to Silas. That was disconcerting and not relevant.

"It has the potential to be interesting." Cora hid a smile behind her cup. She could guess at Tante's real reason for asking that question. She'd used the same tone with Cora throughout her coming-of-age years, whenever she suspected Cora had her eye on one boy or another.

"Oh dearie, someday love is going to sweep you right off your feet."

Cora felt her cheeks warm, and not because of the tea. Then, like a cold wind, thoughts of Silas's mother snuffed out the heat. "Has Mrs. Ward shown memory problems before?"

Tante rubbed at an invisible spot on the tablecloth. "Shortly after her son died, she had an episode like the one you told me about today. She saw Dr. Thompson, who declared it was simply stress from Zachariah's death. I doubt she ever told her family and I haven't noticed anything like it since."

"What would have brought it on now?" Would Silas have told her if another family member recently passed away?

"I don't know." Tante glanced at the telephone box hanging on the wall. "I know for a fact that Elaine refuses to have a telephone in the house, so her late husband installed one in the workshop. And a certain handsome cowboy often works late. I, for one, would like to know how Elaine is faring after her episode today."

Embarrassment washed over Cora. How could Tante play matchmaker at a time like this?

Tante laid her hand on Cora's shoulder. Squeezed with a strength that belied her age. "Call him, sweet child. It will do you both good. Then come tell me how Elaine is doing when you wish me good night."

Cora stared at her cup long after Tante's steps faded down the hall. Mrs. Ward's confusion had rattled her. She waffled between wanting to know how she fared and fearing the news she'd worsened. What if that happened to Cora?

After she washed the two cups and put them away, she stood before the telephone box, chewing her lip. Memory came of Silas's hand to her back, on her arm, strength and comfort transferring from him as she battled her own weakness.

Weakness ... the word triggered a memory. A verse Tante had her memorize when she was a girl. How did it go? Something about grace being sufficient. And God's... that was it! *Strength is made perfect in weakness.*

Truth was, she did want to know how Mrs. Ward fared. She also wanted to know how Silas was doing. Today had shaken him, too. She lifted the receiver—*Lord, be my strength when I am weak*—and asked the night operator to put her through to the Ward's extension.

Silas closed the back door behind him, assured the house and store were both locked up tight. The night air held a crisp chill, warning of the coming autumn. If he wanted to paint Mrs. Whittlebush's front porch, he needed to do it soon. And it would give him an excuse to see Cora, away from potentially upsetting his mother and igniting Greg Alistar's rumors.

Mom had refused to discuss going to the doctor. Silas had spent supper trying to convince her a simple check-up wouldn't cause harm. Marian had added her insistence. But Mom waved off the worry. A slip of the tongue is what she called her forgetful moment. Silas didn't agree, especially after hearing of Buck's concern.

As Silas wove through his workroom toward the interior door to the storage area, he assessed as many encounters with his mom over the last year he could bring to mind. Had he missed other forgetful episodes? His mom seemed too young to be forgetting things, and nothing stood out.

Silas trudged up to his loft, discarded his shirt, and splashed lukewarm water from his washstand over his face. He was grateful for this place of his own. Not only did it give him a chance to escape his mother and Marian's mothering, but it reminded him of the bunkhouses he'd lived in on the ranch. The semblance of independence eased his wanderlust, especially after getting a taste of it in Montana. What he wouldn't give for a glimpse of that vast blue sky. The wind in the grasses. The mountains against the horizon.

He tugged an old cotton shirt over his head and left his suspenders hanging by his hips. The garment had long ago lost the smell of hay and manure. All his belongings had. Strangely, he missed that smell. The sweat of a horse as it helped him drive cattle to a better pasture. Sun shining down whether it be summer or winter. That sure wasn't the case here. Once winter set in, cloud cover came to stay.

His gaze snagged on a letter from his old foreman, Carl Anchorman, at the Crooked Tooth. They were hiring on for the next season, and he wanted—no, begged—Silas to come back. Even just for the spring cattle drive. He scrubbed a hand over his stubble. Could he leave Mom and Marian for months? Especially after today?

Cora's image flashed through his mind.

He tossed the letter aside. He couldn't answer it. Not now. Not in this frame of mind. He might as well take out his frustration on a piece of furniture that needed sanding. He had just the piece, too. An old elm candle box worn down by age and use. Once he sanded its faded sides, he could stain the wood so that it looked like new.

Back in his workshop, he carried the foot-and-a-half-tall box from the storage room to the table. Only five inches square, it fit easily in his hand. He wiped sawdust from his workbench and gently laid the candle box on top, then took up his sandpaper.

As a youth, he'd spent countless hours here, side by side with Dad. The smile that thought brought lifted his spirits despite the man having been gone for over a decade now.

Working with even pressure, he methodically sanded down the top with slight movements. The minute work the sanding forced his muscles to perform felt good.

A breath to blow away the sawdust. Then he ran his hand over the candle box top, testing the evenness of his sanding. Almost perfect. He adjusted his position on the stool, eyes darting over to the one beside him. The one Cora had sat on earlier today. He'd put the letter she found in a safe place after his mom's episode.

The jangle of the telephone shattered the peace of his workshop. Who would call this late? He set aside the sandpaper and answered the phone hanging in the corner. Praying nothing serious had happened.

"It's Cora. Tante and I wanted to ask after your mother." Her voice came over the line, and the warmth of it wrapped itself around his shoulders, easing a burden he hadn't realized weighed him down so heavily.

He smiled and leaned a shoulder against the wall beside the telephone box. "She says she's fine. Hopefully, rest will set things right again." Especially since she wouldn't see Dr. Thompson.

"I hope that, too."

Silas tucked the inside of his cheek between his teeth, torn over the next words he should say, the ones his heart wanted him to say versus the ones his head insisted he mutter. Honestly, he wanted her company. Not tonight, of course. Tomorrow.

"It's late ..." she said. "I should ..."

Maybe it wouldn't hurt to test the waters. "The old letter is waiting for your expert eyes. Come by tomorrow after lunch to have another look at it?"

His heartbeat doubled as he awaited her answer.

"I'll be there."

CHAPTER EIGHT

Wednesday, September 24

The next day, Cora set up at Silas's workroom table, a magnifying lens in her hand. She'd left Tante sewing in the shop room Silas helped her design, preparing for a client fitting later. Where Silas had disappeared to, she didn't know.

The gentle lap of waves followed the sunlight through the open door. She could use a little more breeze, as the thick air made for stuffy conditions. Not that she wasn't used to that from working around the Mediterranean region. But something about being in the building alone unsettled her.

An ache worked its way up her neck, warning of another headache. She rolled her shoulders, concentrating on relaxing her muscles. She'd focused on the paper found in the secret compartment while she could. It appeared to be a simple love letter from one Claude to one Martha, the words taking up only a quarter of the page, which was unusual for that time since paper was expensive and people generally tried to fill it as full as possible to make the most of the cost.

Cora gently unrolled the paper and read the letter again.

Dearest Martha,

All goes well but for missing you. I confess, it will not be long before I join you. Do not fret, for I will make arrangements for our treasure to stay between us. My love will never dim.

Yours until the end,

Claude

Simple. Short. Stilted. Something bothered her about that, but she couldn't pin down what it was. She'd let it ruminate and come back to the writing later. With no last name, how could she find more information about either Claude or Martha? So she turned to the paper itself.

Lighting a short candle she carried in her gear, she set it up to backlight the document, allowing her to study the watermark. She held the magnifying lens to the paper as she bent over it, careful to keep the letter from getting too close to the flame.

"How's it going?" Silas materialized behind her, making her jump.

She clutched the paper to her chest as she turned. He smiled and removed his hat. Her heart gave a little *pitter-patter.*

"It's interesting." Cora set aside the magnifier and letter, then blew out the candle, strongly aware of Silas's presence with each movement. "It appears to be authentically made paper."

"How can you tell?" He pulled out the stool next to her, tossing his cowboy hat to the side.

Her work—she could talk about that no matter how she felt. "Paper prior to the 1800s was made in molds with chains across the bottom to allow the water to drain. Rags would be mashed and shredded into pulp, then pressed into the mold until it created a thin paper parchment. The chain design made the watermark. Hence the name."

"And the watermark tells you what?"

"It's the same as the seal from the desk—two horses. Obviously, the letter and desk are tied together, but I'm not sure how."

"The letter itself seems unusual." Silas reached for the paper. "I'm not poetic, but even I could write a better love letter than this."

Oh? Did Silas have a lot of experience writing love letters? Someone as handsome as he probably did. What would he write in such letters?

"I need to talk to my mom about her latest purchases, so I'll also ask her where she got the desk." Silas spoke as if Cora's thoughts hadn't become a runaway train. He scratched his chin. "Perhaps that will tell us who this Claude or Martha is. A last name to start with, at least."

"Good idea." Then his words registered. "What do you mean, you need to talk to your mom about her latest purchases? Has she experienced other lapses like she did yesterday?" Should she mention what Tante said about an episode after his brother died?

"Not that I'm aware, but it appears there may be more going on." Silas hooked his heels on the rungs of his stool and rested his elbows on his bent knees. "Has your aunt mentioned the Crow's Nest Conglomerate?"

Confused at his change of topic, she set aside her work and turned to fully face him. "Tante mentioned it. It's like a union, isn't it?"

"Less formal, but yes. It's a way to protect the businesses of Crow's Nest. Or it should be."

"Meaning?"

Silas straightened. "There's a question over Buck Wilson's integrity."

"Money. It's always about money." Every danger she faced on a dig came because of greed.

"But nothing has been proven, and he has helped people, like your aunt." Was he trying to convince her or himself? "He made sure she was well taken care of this summer after the storm."

She remained skeptical. "If the Conglomerate is like a union, then that means Tante pays for their services, so it's not out of the goodness of Mr. Wilson's heart to help, unlike you and your friend Mr. Martins, who I know have cared for my aunt while I've been gone."

"Astute." Silas rubbed his chin as though he was hiding a smile.

"I work alongside men like Mr. Wilson. Men who put money before anything else." Which made her wonder about Harry Gordon, the bucchero, and whomever she was talking with before her fall. Was it Mr. Gordon? Why would they be having an emotional argument that ended with her being dizzy and perhaps him pushing her off a cliff? Was it about the bucchero or even Signora's statue? She reached into her memory, but the space was a blank hole.

"Hey, where'd you go?" Silas was at her side, a hand to her back, his deep voice in her ear.

A shiver of fear snaked through her, and she leaned into him. "I can't remember."

"Can't remember what?" Silas's hand made small circles on her back.

"What happened after the earthquake. I'd dug up the bucchero, the quake collapsed the walls, and I woke to see Harry Gordon holding the bucchero. Then blank until an emotional argument with someone. I can't see their face in my mind. Then I was hitting the water. The next day, I was on the boat home." She sought Silas's eyes. "Why can't I remember anything more?"

Silas pressed her head against his chest and stroked her hair. "Do you have an emotional memory of those days? Do you remember feeling excited, fearful?"

Another shiver. Cora swallowed. "Fear, definitely fear. What if my decision to leave Italy was because I was afraid for my life? And here I am trying to get back? I thought Corinvetter Foundation didn't want me to return. What if I'm wrong?"

"Hey, now." Silas moved around so that he cupped her face in his hands and looked right in her eyes. "Just because there may be something sinister going on doesn't mean your health problems don't exist. I've caught you twice now when you looked like you might faint away. The dizziness and nausea are real, and a real reason not to put yourself in more danger."

Cora attempted a nod, but Silas didn't let go.

"There's nothing simple about your situation. I see that now and I want you to see it, too." He ran his thumbs over her cheekbones, then put space between them. "Do you have someone at your company that you trust, who you could talk to about what happened after the earthquake, especially in light of Signora Pimonte's death?"

"I can send a letter to Dorothy Burnett. She's at the New York office and the one who knew to send my letters to Tante." Cora massaged her temple. "I'm sorry, Silas. I didn't mean to take over the conversation. You were telling me about your mom and the Conglomerate. Do you think they are taking money from you?"

"It's not important." Silas returned to his stool with a wave of his hand.

"It is important. What does Mr. Wilson have to do with your mother's health?"

"Are you sure you want to talk about it?"

"Silas."

He hooked his thumbs around his suspenders. "Buck warned me about trouble facing our business. I'm not proud of it, but I missed the signs entirely."

"Are you sure there is trouble, or did he create it?"

"I've been noticing our profits have been getting smaller, but with so many people out of work, I attributed it to not having as many sales. However, Buck believes my mom has been double-paying for the items she purchases."

Cora picked up the candle to have something in her hands—she'd taken off her scarf to work—while her mind studied the problem. "Does your mom have proof of sale? Working in antiquities, that is a vital part of the business."

"She does, or I thought she did. I'm only finding proof of one sale, so I don't know who has charged her twice. Buck says there is rumor spreading that she isn't paying her bills. And if that gets around, we'll lose credibility and customers. It doesn't help that—never mind."

"Uh-huh." Cora wagged the candle at him. "Doesn't help that what?"

"It gets more complicated because our town newspaper has an unscrupulous newspaperman who would like nothing better than to get his hands on this rumor." Silas met her gaze with an intensity that had her sitting up. "Unfortunately, you need to watch out for him, too. He'll use anything to get a story, including lies and blackmail. I haven't wanted to add to your troubles, but simply knowing each other could ruin your reputation. If he knew we were working on Claude's letter together ..."

Panic wrapped a band around her lungs, not because of the newspaperman, but at the thought of losing Silas's friendship. "Has he made a threat?"

Silas nodded. "I'm sorry, Cora. I should have told you right away. He threatened to insinuate that we are ... involved."

Embarrassment filled Cora, and she dug out the matches to light the candle, again to have something to do with her hands. It bought her the moment she needed to make her voice calm. "If I let rumors dictate my life, I would hide in a hole. I'm the illegitimate daughter of an illegitimate daughter. I'm an unmarried woman who travels to dig after dig. If I let one newspaperman's threats change what I do, then where would I be?"

"Are you sure? He made Adaleigh and David's life difficult and he wants information on you."

She faced him. "He threatened you to get information on me?"

Silas's jaw ticked. "Yes."

Cora tapped the matchbook against her chin. "We could give him something innocuous to get him to leave you alone."

"No." Silas left no question in his tone. "I am not playing his games, especially not with your life."

That warm, fuzzy feeling was back. "All right, then. What about your mom? Have you asked her about the money?"

"Not yet." Silas rubbed his leg, the confidence from a moment ago seeping away before her eyes. "I keep trying to find the proof so I can present it to her."

"What about Marian? Does she know?"

"She hasn't noticed anything out of the ordinary, and I haven't wanted to worry her about the specifics yet."

"Silas, you can't protect them if you don't find out the answers, which means telling them what's wrong. It might be a simple solution."

He lowered his chin. "I guess I've been hesitant to discover the truth."

"Because it might mean there is something worse happening? Like maybe your mom is really sick?" The words hit her chest like a mallet. "I know those feelings, Silas. I live with them. There is definitely something that appears safe about not facing the truth, burying one's head, but it is not really safe, is it? Avoiding the tests that could discover what is really going on with me is putting off answers that could fix me."

Silas reached across the space between them but didn't touch her. "Would you consider seeing a doctor again? I'd go with you."

"Maybe." The truth swarmed around her head, and instead of facing it, she relit the candle. "Let's look at the watermark again. Maybe you'll recognize it."

"Cora, avoiding isn't the answer for either of us."

She held the paper over the candle. "I know, I just—Look!" Black markings had formed below Claude's letter.

Silas leaned closer. "What—"

Cora shushed him, as if speaking would stop the markings from revealing themselves. Lines grew longer. Rectangles appeared, then squiggles that looked like bushes or trees. "A map?" Wonder saturated her words.

"I think I know where this is." Silas pointed at it. "It looks like Crow's Nest Cemetery."

Cora whirled to face him, but her words died when she realized how close that brought her to him. Inches separated them. Yet neither moved. Perhaps they didn't even breathe. Cora didn't know. She couldn't think. Not after the emotional conversation they just had. Nor with the way this cowboy looked at her with those warm brown eyes, as if she were a beautiful treasure, like one of the rare discoveries she made it her life purpose to bring back to life.

"Should we follow the map?" Silas asked, his voice lower than usual.

Cora nodded, all ability to speak gone.

"I just need one promise from you first." Silas cupped her cheek. "Promise me you'll be honest about how you're feeling. If you get dizzy or need to rest. Anything. Tell me. Deal?"

Cora's heart pounded. Rushing filled her ears.

"Cora?" He ran his thumb along her cheekbone. "Do we have a deal?"

"Yes, yes, of course." She pulled away from him, needing to find her equilibrium. "Following this lead will be better medicine than sitting at home."

"Not at the expense of your health."

"The walk and fresh air are good for me, too."

Silas grumbled under his breath but left her at the worktable to rummage through his collection of tools. He returned with a paper and pencil, and together they carefully heated the letter to reveal the map again, then copied it down. Silas stored the letter and told Marian they'd be back later.

Excitement battled the growing dizziness as Cora settled into the passenger seat of Silas's truck. The mystery of the map, combined with her love of visiting cemeteries, meant she wouldn't let her health derail her. Not this time. No matter what Silas made her promise. Cemeteries, like grottos, were monuments to the memories of people who lived, loved, hated, and fought. Names of people who may be lost to the annals of time or remembered in stories told to children. They fascinated her.

"We'll park near the entrance and walk in from there," Silas explained as he drove toward the north end of Crow's Nest, west of Tante's house. The road followed the curve of Crow's Nest Creek, which was more of a river that isolated Crow's Nest from the rest of the state. "It's a small place, so we should be able to get our bearings without walking far."

"I'm not worried about that." Even if she was, she wasn't sure she'd admit it. She needed this outing. The adventure of following the map fed her soul as much as finding a treasure. The company was kind of nice, too.

Silas chuckled. The sound soothed her raw nerves, and she leaned against the seatback. It eased the ache in her bones and the ringing in her ears. Even her heart rate slowed so that she could take a deep breath for the first time in ... a while. Silas's presence did that for her.

"The cemetery is as old as the town." Silas rested an elbow on the window frame, his other wrist hanging over the steering wheel. "The founders of Crow's Nest built the original chapel on top of Crow's Nest Hill, after which the town is named, and now the headstones surround it like rings in a pond. My brother worked as the groundskeeper, in addition to farming. He saw beauty in the most uncommon places."

"Is your brother buried here?" Cora asked as Silas drove the car under the archway that indicated the entrance to the cemetery.

"Yes. On the east side."

"The morning sun would be beautiful as it appears over Lake Michigan," she offered, knowing her words were inadequate, but needing to say something.

Silas gave a silent nod and parked just off the road that ended at the quiet grounds. They walked down a dirt footpath, Silas setting a wandering pace as he wrapped her hand around his arm.

When they reached the first crossroads, he pulled out the copy they'd drawn of the map. "I could tell this was a map of this cemetery because of how it's laid out. See the circular pattern? But from there, I'm at a loss to know what we're looking for."

"Let me see." Cora wiggled her fingers for the paper. "First question is whether there is an indication of directionality. Is there a sense of Lake Michigan, the river, or the chapel?"

Silas looked over her shoulder, bringing him within Cora's personal space with the scent of pine. "Would the top of the page not point north?"

"Not necessarily. Claude used invisible ink, so he didn't want the map or the location readily found. The fact that Crow's Nest has a uniquely laid out cemetery would be known only to locals, so that allowed Claude to avoid using a name to indicate a location."

"Can we back up to 'invisible ink'? Wouldn't that discredit the supposed date of the letter?"

"Just the opposite, actually." Cora turned to look at him with a smile, but once again, the man stood so close, emanating such a sense of security she never expected from a cowboy. The realization sent needle pricks down her back, but she was powerless to look away from him. If she were even willing to do so.

"Tell me about this invisible ink." Silas's gaze roamed her face with a teasing glint. Did he know the effect he had on her? She needed to brush it off. Shift. Move. Something!

"The Revolution." The words croaked from her throat, and she cleared it. "They used a solution of tannic acid Washington called the *sympathetic stain*."

"You are a fount of knowledge." He tucked her hand around his arm again and led them toward the chapel and the heart of the cemetery. "Instead of looking for the lake, let's see if the chapel has record of a Claude or ... what was her name?"

"Martha."

"A common name, but maybe we'll get lucky and they'll have the same last name."

Cora held in a sigh. Everything in her wanted to sink into Silas's strength, but she was getting entirely too comfortable. She couldn't come to rely on him—not that he wasn't reliable. That was becoming an indisputable fact despite him being a cowboy like the men who were her father and grandfather. He was just so responsible and loyal to his family and this community. He left his job, the life he'd built for himself out West, in order to be here for them. And that was the crux of her problem. She didn't want to be here. Her heart was thousands of miles away, buried in the dirt and rock that surrounded the Mediterranean Sea.

"Here we are." Silas pulled open an oak door and removed his cowboy hat. Reverence settled over them as their footsteps echoed in the hallowed place.

"Wow," Cora breathed as they entered the interior chapel.

The ceiling rose in a cathedral arch. Above the stained-glass windows on either side were painted frescos of cherubs and saints, angels, and the Stations of the Cross. On the front platform, a table stood prominently, a plain lectern off to the side and a more ornate pulpit tucked into a far corner, waiting to be brought forward. She'd been in enough sacred buildings to recognize the attempt at an ecumenical place, able to cater to the variety of Catholic and Protestant beliefs, at least.

"Through here is the registry." Silas reached for her hand. She hadn't realized she'd let go of his arm and welcomed the connection. He took her into an anteroom lined with dark paneling and darkened windows.

"What is this place used for?"

"The preparation or gathering area for a family before the funeral." His throat bobbed with obvious emotion.

"Silas, you don't have to be here." Why hadn't she thought of it before? "Go back into the sunlight. I'll look for their names. Better yet, take me home, and we'll sit on Tante's front porch together. This is too much to ask of you so soon after your brother passed away."

"And let you uncover this mystery all by yourself?" His teasing tone sounded strained. He patted his thigh with his hat, the sound oddly loud in the quiet place. "Unless you aren't feeling well enough to continue?"

She wove her fingers between his. "I'm fine. I'm only thinking of you."

He tossed his hat onto a chair and took both of her hands so that they faced one another. He kept his head down as he rubbed his thumbs over her wrists. Could he feel her pulse picking up speed?

"Silas?"

"I'll be honest, I didn't anticipate how it'd feel to be back here, but I wanted …" He raised his eyes to hers. "I want to follow this mystery with you."

Tears pricked. Oh how wonderful it felt to be treasured.

Saints alive, never had the cold wind blowing off Lake Michigan felt so good. Silas squared his Stetson as he waited for Cora to check the map again. They'd found a Claude Herman in the registry, his tombstone located in the oldest quarter, but Silas had lost his mind if not his heart in the anteroom.

He'd almost kissed Cora—kissed her! Not on the forehead or the cheek, but had he not stopped himself, he would have kissed her fully on the lips. Instead, he'd directed her attention to the registry, which captured her attention, leaving him time to regain his self-control.

"Why would the map, written by Claude, lead to his grave plot?" Cora squinted at the paper. She rubbed her left temple. "I can't make sense of it."

"Your head?" He nodded his chin toward her left eye, which drooped more than the other.

"It'll be fine." She marched past him, headed for the first line of gravestones on the south side of the chapel where the first burial sites were located. "When did you say the cemetery was founded? These stones have been worn smooth."

Stubborn woman. He hooked his thumbs around his suspenders as he followed her. "The town was founded in the mid-1800s."

She stared down at the tombstones. "Something doesn't add up, but I can't get my mind around it. The letter indicates it was written in the late 1700s, so he would have been a young man when he wrote the letter if he was buried here around 1850."

"Let's find Claude's marker, then take a break." He needed to get her home so she could rest.

They walked down three rows to a line of tilted, mismatched stones. The one with Claude's name was a simple gray marker in between two tall family markers—Adenauer and Siegel. Cora dropped to the ground, putting herself level with Claude's stone. Silas joined her, the coolness of the grass seeping into the backside of his trousers.

She ran her fingers over the stone. "Claude lived from 1763 to 1849. So he feasibly could have written the letter, but how would he know he would be buried here? The wording of the letter has an odd quality to it, too. What makes no sense is, how would anyone know Claude Herman would be buried in this spot, and why put it in invisible ink?"

"Do you see Martha's stone anywhere?" Silas wandered down the row. None of the tombstones held the name *Martha*, or even a first name that began with the letter *M*.

"No. So when Claude assures Martha he'll plan for the *treasure to stay between us*, what else could he mean?" Cora rubbed her temple.

"I think you've had enough thinking for today." Silas captured her hand. "Come on, let's rest before I take you home. I'll show you my favorite spot."

She followed willingly, which had to mean she'd reached the end of her strength. The bench was just around the hill and would give her time to recoup before the walk to the truck. Silas hadn't been to the cemetery since they buried Zee, but before he left Wisconsin, he'd come to this spot whenever he needed some place other than the workshop to think. The old bench was still under the gnarly oak on the northeast edge of the hill.

"The lake is gorgeous. It's like you can see the end of the world." Cora sank onto the bench, shoulders sagged and weary lines etched into her face. "It reminds me of working in Crete. The scenery is all wrong, but the water is the same sparkling crystal."

"Crete?" What other places had she traveled to?

"That was my assignment before Italy. They'd discovered a house carved out of the rock that had been overgrown for centuries. I was there to identify the household items destined for a local museum. Because I work for an independent company, we often work for more local governments. Not all the time, of course. But in Crete, that was the case."

He watched her profile. She sat perfectly straight, leaving space between her back and the bench, atop which he'd laid his arm. Just as he was about to move, in case she felt uncomfortable, she sighed and rested the back of her head against his arm. He froze.

"I miss my adventures. I miss discovering new people and places. I miss the stories. But what if my seeking those stories was the reason for the argument before I fell, or the reason for Signora Pimonte's death? I always thought uncovering artifacts would show me how people lived, but I wonder now whether I've put inanimate objects ahead of people."

Silas slid closer so he could wrap his arm fully around her shoulders. "Perhaps it's because you were afraid you'd be lost to time, as they seem to be. But now, you have people here who—" What? Care about her? Support her? *Love* her?

"If I don't tell other people's stories, who am I?"

Silas hung his Stetson from his knee. "Who am I without my hat, without cattle to herd and a ranch to help run?"

Cora looked up at him. "You're a kind man who cares about his family, who protects those around him, who has managed to turn my world upside down and yet right side up all at the same time."

Silas pulled her even closer. "And you're a treasure worth more than the rarest artifact." Then he leaned forward and gave into a kiss.

Chapter Nine

Cora sank into Silas's arms, his kiss enveloping her in wonder. He thought her a treasure. In that moment, the world could crumble around them and she had no doubt he would keep her perfectly safe.

Her shoulders relaxed, and then she felt the breeze, heard the crash of waves, and suddenly, she was back in Italy on the edge of the cliff.

She hadn't just been arguing with someone. He'd physically ripped the bucchero from her arms before sending her over the edge.

The memory sliced through her head, causing her to gasp and yank away.

"Cora." Silas caught her shoulders. "I'm sorry, I—"

Cora shook her head, the violent motion churning her stomach. She would not throw up. She would not!

"Cora, darling, please." The concern in his voice broke her heart.

"Hold me?" she whispered.

Without hesitation, Silas pulled her to his chest. They sat in silence, with only nature for background, for many long minutes. Gradually, the nausea subsided as he held her.

Her mind drifted back to the last time she saw her mother and how she'd wished for comforting arms to hold her. She thought over her years abroad and how she'd clung to her independence like a shield. Yet it was here, allowing someone to protect her, that she felt the most at ease, that her lost memories were returning.

Not just someone. Silas. She straightened so she could look him in the eye. Such compassion she found there that she pressed her hand to his beard. Uncertainty flashed across his face, undoing her and emboldening her. She reached up and laid her lips against his.

He answered for a moment, then pulled back. "Cora."

"It wasn't your kiss." Cora lifted her scarf to cover her head and wrap around her neck, needing some barrier between them if they were about to talk about what just happened. "It was, but ... some of my memories returned. They were unexpected and intruded, and I wish they hadn't interrupted." Now her cheeks heated and she jumped to her feet.

"You wished they didn't interrupt?" The hopeful tease in Silas's voice had her spinning around. Sparring with Silas was safer than the emotions filling her chest.

"Don't get a big head about it. That was my first ki—" She clapped her hand to her mouth, her embarrassment complete.

Silas was before her in an instant. Then he leaned down and whispered in her ear, "And was it as you dreamed it would be?"

She was going to explode like a stick of dynamite. "Not that it's any of your concern, sir. You're missing the important part. I remembered. I remember almost everything from those missing days between the earthquake and taking the ship home."

"Maybe I should have kissed you sooner."

She stuck her tongue out at him. "Stop your nonsense and listen."

He chuckled, and she turned away before he saw her smile.

"The area I was excavating revealed quite a few household items, like bowls and tools. Those tend to be my area of expertise. I'm not as interested in the art side of artifacts. I want to know how people lived. The practical items. Since my colleagues don't favor those types of finds, I was tasked with the excavation. Which is what made finding the bucchero so interesting."

"Come sit down while you tell me more." Silas directed her back to the bench.

"I hadn't dated the excavation yet, but we were primarily focused on finding Etruscan artifacts in the area. Because of that, I suppose I shouldn't have been surprised to find the bucchero, but I was. The black ceramic was unlike any of the other artifacts I found in the shelter. It had writing on it that—wait." Pain sliced through Cora's temple. "Did I ask Signora Pimonte about it? She wasn't a scholar, so why would she know about Etruscan artifacts?"

Silas placed a warm hand on her shoulder. "Stay to the story."

"I had just freed the bucchero from the ground when the earth began to shake. It happened so fast, I didn't react as quickly as I should have. The walls crumbled around me. I must have hit my head because I was definitely unconscious for a period of time."

"Did you tell your doctor about that? Could that be why you have the headaches?"

"I could only tell them what my colleagues told me, and they said I didn't have any of these symptoms right after the earthquake. Now that I'm remembering, my colleagues were right. The dizziness developed days later and got steadily worse until my fall off the cliff. However, if these symptoms are related to being hit on the head during the earthquake, maybe whatever is wrong is not as severe as what I was thinking it could be. Maybe it won't end my career. Maybe I'll get better."

Silas smiled, but there was a sadness in his eyes.

"And then I'll leave Crow's Nest." Cora turned toward the lake, unsure how she felt about that. She never dreamed of giving up her archaeology, and Tante wouldn't keep her from leaving. But that was before she got to know Silas. Before that kiss. Suddenly, the path ahead didn't feel so clear.

"Go back to your story. What happened after you woke up from the earthquake?"

"Right. Harry Gordon was holding the bucchero. Things are still fuzzy, but now I remember spending time with Signora Pimonte afterwards, and we talked about the bucchero." Had Cora gotten her killed because of it?

Silas took her hand. "It wasn't your fault."

"I can't help feeling that maybe it was. Though I don't know why she would be targeted or by whom."

He rubbed his thumb against her wrist. "Tell me more about this bucchero."

Cora leaned against the bench, the sun warm on her back. "As I told you before, a bucchero is an Etruscan jug. The Etruscans lived in eight hundred to nine hundred B. C. in what is now central Italy, until they were wiped out by the Romans. Not much is known about them other than what we find in archaeological digs, which makes the bucchero a valuable find. There was an inscription on it, I remember, and I think I had interpreted a few of the runes, but that is still fuzzy to me. As is why Harry Gordon would have taken it from me while I was still buried in the earthquake rubble."

"Perhaps that's what you asked your friend about." Silas stretched out his legs, crossing them at the ankles. Their shadows stretched long before them. "It seems you still have missing chunks of memory over the course of a one-month time period. We know what happened began with the earthquake. Between then and your fall from the cliff, you studied the bucchero."

"It should have been cataloged into our records. Why would I fight someone about it?"

"Unless that someone aimed to steal it. In that case, you may have been protecting it."

"I wish I could remember." Cora pressed the heel of her free hand to her forehead. "Though I don't know what I can do about it here in Crow's Nest. I can't ask the *polizia* about Signora Pimonte's death. I can't look at the records to see what's become of the bucchero. Maybe I need to set the questions aside and concentrate on getting well."

"Will you be able to rest without answers?"

"No. Especially since the missing memories are tied to my health. I remember the dizziness, have all along. It's this feeling deep inside that makes the world tilt, and even when the rest of my memories were gone, that sensation has stayed with me the whole time. That's why I was sure I fell off the cliff, as my colleagues said. But now I remember arguing with someone. I can't picture who. It's fuzzy. But it was a man."

"This Harry Gordon?"

"Could be. Could have been our leader, Signore Camposano. There were two other male archeologists on the team, Mr. Marcus and Mr. Flatt. Of course there were plenty of other men around, but why I would be arguing with them about the bucchero? I can't remember what we were arguing about either. But I do remember the emotion, the nausea and dizziness. Then the person yanked the bucchero from my arms and I went over the cliff."

Silas shifted in on the bench. "I don't like that you could still be in danger. They might not trust that your memories won't return and follow you here to finish what they started. You left Italy quickly after that fall. I think that's reason enough to find out what happened. We can tell this to David's uncle, Detective O'Connor."

Cora stared at the horizon, where the water of Lake Michigan met the sky, and considered what Silas said. "But we don't know for sure that they will follow me here. No one but my friend in the home office knows my address."

"Can you live with the uncertainty?"

"My health is uncertain. What's one more thing? However, if I want to go back to work, then I need to put this behind me, which means finding the solution."

"And you want to go back." The sadness in his voice stabbed Cora in the heart.

"I'm sorry, Silas."

"Don't be sorry." Silas wrapped his arm around her shoulders. "I told David to let Adaleigh return to her life. He didn't listen, but I need to take my own advice. I can't hold you back from pursuing your dreams. My choice to give mine up for my family is mine alone. I was wrong to judge you for your choices when we first met. Going forward, I will do everything I can to make sure you can get back to your digs, safe and healthy."

Tears smarted. Was going back really what she wanted? She could stay in Crow's Nest without the pressure to heal. She would no longer need to hide her familial connection to Tante to keep her safe. Perhaps she could even forget about the danger that potentially awaited her return, and maybe whoever pushed her would forget about her, too.

"Let's get you home. Evening is nearing, and I have a delivery yet to make this afternoon."

Cora nodded, but as they left the cemetery, it felt as if she'd buried a new set of dreams there. Ones that included a future with a cowboy named Silas Ward.

Thursday September 25

The next day, Silas was determined to get to the bottom of Buck Wilson's concerns. After Nettie and Essie left for school, he asked his mom and Marian to meet him in the shop. He'd prefer to speak with them in the house, but he didn't want to upset his mom before the conversation even started by closing the shop. She hadn't had another forgetful episode as far as he'd noticed, but she'd been pricklier than he ever remembered.

"What's this about?" Mom bustled in, wiping her hands on her apron. "Can't this wait until I finish canning the beans?"

"Yes, why'd you call a family meeting?" Marian sat on a stool behind the front counter. Her expression and tone were ones of curiosity, not edging on hostility like Mom's.

"We need to talk about the shop." Silas set his Stetson on the counter, braced for the expected argument.

"What about it?" Mom crossed her arms. "It's doing fine."

Marian's gaze bounced between them.

"It appears we are not making as much profit as I expected." Silas spoke carefully. "The money in the bank is not covering our expenses, and we have been receiving complaints that we haven't been paying for our purchases."

"That's utter rot." Mom untied her apron with a jerk and slapped it onto the front counter. "I pay each one and make a note of it in my ledger before giving you the money to deposit in the bank. Do you think I'm keeping money back?"

The thought hadn't crossed his mind. Could that be where the missing money went? Were Mom or Marian needing it for the girls or the business?

"I can see your wheels turning, young man." Mom wagged her finger in his face. She might be a head shorter, but he still bowed his head beneath her scolding. "I am not stealing from my own business. I use the money to purchase items to sell in the shop, and the rest I give you to put in the bank. You pay our expenses. Are *you* mishandling the money?"

"Mom," Marian hissed.

"He accused me of stealing, and I know I'm not doing anything wrong."

"I'm sorry." Silas rubbed his chest. "I didn't mean to imply that you're not trustworthy." Just forgetful. Or ... something.

"You didn't imply it, young man. You flat out told me I was." Mom's voice rose. "You think I would purposefully destroy the very business my husband and I worked to build from nothing? I would not do that to him. Don't think I won't tell him about this meeting. Calling a family meeting without him. He'll have words for you when he gets home."

A knife to the stomach would hurt less. "Mom, Dad isn't—"

"Don't make excuses." Mom snatched up her apron, angry sparks flying from her eyes. "You can finish this conversation with your father."

"But ..." Silas let his protest fade when Marian shook her head. Instead, he watched his mother storm from the shop. What he wouldn't give to have Cora here at this moment. Her understanding would soothe his aching heart.

"She was going on about Zachariah the other day." Marian straightened the knickknacks on the counter, though they didn't appear to be in disorder. "I didn't put it together until she scolded you about Cora. She thought Zachariah was still alive."

"We need to convince her to see Dr. Thompson." Silas pressed his palms to the top of the counter. "Three memory lapses in so many weeks isn't good." To put it mildly.

"I'll set up an appointment and figure out a way to get her there. But Silas, I don't know how to answer your question about the money either. As far as I know, besides the money we set aside for acquisition, the rest goes to you to put in the bank." She pulled a ledger from the shelf. "We just filled this one. It has every purchase we've made in the last three months, the seller's name and address, the date purchased, and the amount we paid."

Silas paged through the ledger. "Do you think Mom could be paying twice? If she paid for an item but forgot to mark it down immediately in her ledger, forgot the transaction, then paid for it again?"

"I suppose it's possible. I'll go through our receipts and match what I have with the ledger."

"Thank you. I can't find the discrepancy any place else. If she's forgetting Dad and Zee are no longer with us, then why not forget that she paid for something?" Silas set his hat on his head, but as he tugged the brim, he remembered the other question he wanted to ask. "What about the desk you purchased last week? You bought it from a family who was about to lose their house. Cora found a note inside, so I'd like to contact the family. Are those records in this ledger as well?"

"Yes." Marian turned to the last page and pointed to the last entry. "This is their information. It shows we paid for the desk, but like I said, I'll match the entry to the receipt. The receipts have both Mom's signature and the seller's, so it's proof of sale."

"Thanks, Marian." He placed a hand on the ledger. "May I keep this for the rest of the morning?"

"Of course. I'll work on gathering the receipts for when you're finished."

Silas tucked the ledger under his arm, took three steps, then turned back. "I'm glad you and the girls stayed after Zee. You're good for my mom."

Marian gave him a sad smile. "My parents are lumber camp nomads, and it's no place for the girls. But I'm glad I'm here, too."

Back in his workshop, he set the ledger and his Stetson on his worktable and turned to the last entry, where he found the record he was looking for, then asked the operator to patch him through.

"Robert Cox." The desk's prior owner answered, his voice placing him in later middle age.

"Hello, sir, my name is Silas Ward, and my mother purchased a desk of yours."

"Ah, the woman who stole my desk."

Stole? "We have a record of the sale, sir. Why do you believe she stole it?"

"Because she did! Until I chased her to the car and demanded she pay me. Now what do you want?"

Was this proof his theory was correct? Or proof of a seller taking advantage of his mother? Even if they found the receipts, they wouldn't be able to prove it either way. Best smooth things over in hopes negative impressions wouldn't spread. "I'm sorry for the confusion, sir. It's a beautiful piece of furniture."

"Sure is. I had to sell it to keep my house. You planning to rub that in my face?"

"No, sir." Why would Mr. Cox think he'd do something so ungracious as that? "I was actually hoping for more information on the history of the desk."

"Why would you want that? It's nothing special."

"On the contrary, sir, it's a Chippendale."

"It is? I mean, of course it is." The man spluttered. "I think our conversation is over."

Before Silas could say a word, the man hung up. Silas stared at the ear cone for a moment before setting it on the hook. If the previous owner didn't know its value, he likely didn't know about the letter inside or have any connection to Claude Herman. Either Robert Cox got the desk from someone else and that someone must be the connection to Claude, or Robert Cox knew much more about the desk and didn't want Silas digging into anything.

With Mr. Cox's hostility, they'd probably not get more information from him regarding the desk. So that direction of investigation into the letter was likely at an end. However, he didn't like how confident Mr. Cox was about his mother taking the desk without paying. Could the man be behind the rumors? No matter, the fact he didn't seem to know the desk was a Chippendale desk made Silas uneasy.

He'd return to the desk dilemma in a minute. First, he placed calls to the next five names in the ledger to ask about Mom paying them. Three of the five admitted Mom hadn't paid them at first. Two of those three were nearly as hostile as Mr. Cox. The other expressed concern for Mom, that she seemed disoriented, and thought the mistake was merely an oversight.

The theory growing in Silas's mind prompted him to set up a meeting with Buck Wilson, then he invited Detective O'Connor to join them as well. He had an hour before the meeting, so after returning the ledger to

Marian, he set to work on the rocking chair Mindy had requested for her parents. They lived on a farm outside of town, and Mindy sent home as much of her paycheck as she could. He quoted her the lowest price she would accept for the gift, a thank you for sitting with Nettie the other day.

As he sanded a back slat, he let his mind drift to Cora. He'd been able to keep her out of his head most of the day. Now, however, she flooded his thoughts. Hopefully, it was a good day for her. She'd had so many bad ones. Would she consider seeing Dr. Thompson? The man was a small-town doctor in his eighties, and she'd mentioned seeing a doctor in New York, so she might not think it worth her time.

He also hoped the trouble she faced in Italy would not visit her here in Crow's Nest. If he was honest with himself, he didn't know why it wouldn't follow her here. She'd been in America for at least two weeks, if his calculations were correct. If the person who pushed her left Italy directly after her, they would already be here, wouldn't they?

What about her friend in Italy? Was Signora Pimonte's death at all related to Cora's troubles? If only there was a way to get answers about what happened on the other side of the world. The specter of danger might hang over Cora forever.

Such dark thoughts dogged him all the way to the Wharfside Cafe. An chill wind blew in from the lake, and clouds hovered low over the blue and green water, matching his mood. The harbored boats clanged as they bounced against their moorings. He turned into the cafe's outdoor seating in time to see Detective O'Connor securing his massive dog, Samson, to a post.

Silas patted the dog's head, receiving a slobbery dog smile in return. "Thanks for meeting me, Detective."

"Let's hear what all this is about." Detective O'Connor led the way into the Wharfside. Close to seventy, the man hid stark blue eyes and gray hair behind a wide-brimmed hat, similar to Silas's Stetson.

"Hello, gentlemen." Buck Wilson waved them to a table in the back corner. About Silas's age, the man stood tall in his expertly tailored blue-striped suit. It hung open, revealing a matching shirtwaist, starched white shirt, and blue tie. It made Silas feel exceedingly beneath him. "Miss Zahn has already delivered us coffee."

Mindy lifted the carafe in her hand and smiled. "Good to see you both. Has Nettie been staying closer to home?"

"Yes." Silas removed his Stetson. "She's excited about attending the Harvest Festival now and talks about it every chance she gets."

Mindy grinned. "I don't blame her. It's a highlight! Adaleigh told me today that Mrs. Whittlebush's apples will be ready this weekend, and she's planning her Picking Party for Saturday. Will you be there?"

Silas schooled his expression, but anticipation rose at the thought of picking apples alongside Cora. Though a large group would also be there, so would she.

"Would you gentleman like any food with your coffee?" Mindy asked.

Silas shook his head and the others declined as well. Did Adaleigh know Cora was Mrs. Whittlebush's niece? It didn't appear as if Mindy knew. Silas tucked away the question to ask Cora later. Perhaps it was time for the town to know the truth. They would welcome her and protect her, especially with how much they loved Mrs. Whittlebush.

"So why are we here, Ward?" Buck pulled his attention to the here and now. "Must be something big if you got O'Connor and me together."

"I have a theory." Silas rested his forearms on the table. "The problem is, it's just a theory, and I can't prove anything yet. However, I think I know where the missing profits have gone from my family's business. I'm hoping the law and the Conglomerate can help me."

Detective O'Connor's bushy gray mustache bobbed. "I'm assuming it's something on the shady side of the law, or you wouldn't have asked me here. But why do you need Buck and the Conglomerate?" Considering the detective was actively investigating the organization, the man would probably love nothing more than an inroad to something he could finally pin on Buck.

"The shop is part of the Conglomerate, O'Connor." Buck glared at the detective. "Whatever you think of me, I do protect my members, especially widows. And despite Silas being involved, Crow's Nest Curiosities is operated by two widows. I won't stand by and let them be taken advantage of."

The table fell silent, so Silas cleared his throat. "Buck first brought the problem to me because sellers are complaining that my mom isn't paying them for the items she collects to sell in our shop. I called the last couple and discovered it seems to be the case, at least some of the time."

"Seems? Some of?" Buck crossed his arms. "Is there any proof she hasn't been paying, or is it their word against hers?"

"Proof is in short supply. Marian is going through the sales receipts, which hold both Mom's and the seller's signatures. I do have a ledger which records each transaction. But it's not definitive proof because it only shows the final transaction. Not her forgetting to record information or paying twice." Both men opened their mouths as if to speak, but Silas held up his hand to forestall them. "I called the last several sellers, and one of the conversations planted an idea in my head, which is the reason I asked you to meet with me. Frankly, the more I consider it, the more weight it has. My mother appears to be having a health crisis of some kind. She won't see a doctor, but she's shown confusion and forgetfulness. She forgot my dad and Zee were gone."

Detective O'Connor smoothed his mustache. "And she won't see Dr. Thompson?"

"Utterly refuses, though Marian is going to try again." Silas rotated his coffee cup clockwise. "The sellers who claim she forgot to pay them were very hostile to me, except the one. He explained he had to walk Mom through the payment process, the receipt, recording it in the ledger. It makes me wonder just how easily an unscrupulous person could take advantage of her and whether those hostile sellers could hide behind their bluster."

"It's a sound theory, but, like you said, there's no proof." Detective O'Connor took a sip of his coffee. "I doubt I can do much at this point. However, give me the names of the hostile sellers. I'll look into them, then we'll talk again."

"And once Marian has gathered all the receipts, bring them to me." Buck tapped his fingers against his biceps. "I'll keep them as evidence while I do some digging on my own. I want to know who is spreading the rumor about the situation. Hearsay is damaging, and even if there's a thread of truth to it thanks to your mother's health, it certainly shouldn't be broadcast throughout the county."

Silas nodded. As grateful as he was, more immediate answers would have been most helpful.

Buck glanced at Detective O'Connor. "Would you like me to keep you abreast of what I find?"

Detective O'Conner's eyebrows bobbed. "Of course."

Buck grinned. Did Buck like antagonizing Detective O'Connor? If Silas didn't have more pressing matters taking up his attention, he'd find the matter curious.

"What do you know about the woman staying with Rose Whittle-bush?" The detective's question startled him. Where had it come from?

Buck chuckled, a glint in his eye. "I think he's getting to know her quite well."

Silas ignored the barb. "She's an archaeologist and—" Silas stopped. Should he tell the men about the letter and map they found in the desk? Was it relevant? He should tell Detective O'Connor about the possible danger following her from Italy, but was it something he wanted Buck to learn as well? He'd come prepared to discuss his mother and his family's failings, not Cora.

"I see." Detective O'Connor grinned beneath his mustache. "Then perhaps you can provide an introduction at Rose's Apple Picking Party on Saturday, and I'll ask her my questions myself."

Mindy saved him having to respond when she arrived with the bill. Buck insisted on paying and Detective O'Connor refused to let him, so Silas handed Mindy enough for all three of them. Not that he had the money to spare, but it had been his idea to meet here.

"Good plan. Those two would argue the afternoon away." Mindy winked. "Tell Nettie I say hello."

"I'll do that." He glanced at the timepiece in his coat pocket. "I'll leave you to manage them. I want to catch David before he leaves the shanty."

Mindy smiled, casting sunshine on his day. Silas tossed a goodbye to the still-bickering men and hurried next door. Short of telling David about Cora's familial connection to Mrs. Whittlebush—and that he'd kissed Cora—Silas needed a friend's advice. His attraction to Cora couldn't go anywhere if she insisted on returning to her work, and the advice Silas had given David reverberated in his head. He could only hope David had better wisdom than Silas had offered him, because not having Cora part of his life wasn't an answer he was prepared to accept.

So distracted was he that he rammed into Greg Alistar coming out of David's fishing shanty.

"Have you considered my offer?" Greg Alistar held the door closed, not permitting Silas to enter.

Frankly, he'd forgotten about it in the aftermath of Cora's kiss. He should have told Detective O'Connor about the threat right away. As Buck said, hearsay was dangerous and Greg was proving why. Silas attempted to shoulder past him. "Leave me alone."

Greg blocked his way. "I need a story, Ward. Since the storm this spring, it's been dead quiet, and my deadline is tonight."

"Then talk about the upcoming Harvest Festival and leave me—and Cora—alone."

Wrong thing to say, considering the spark in the newspaperman's eye. "Will you escort Miss Davis to the dance?"

Anger simmered, but he kept tight control over it. Any reaction would give Greg the fodder he needed to spin a yarn.

"Not interrupting, am I?" A voice behind Silas made him turn. David adjusted his flat cap as his gaze studied Silas and Greg. He owed the man dinner for his perfect timing.

"I was just leaving." Greg scrambled past them, but he muttered a single word under his breath as he passed Silas that turned his anger to ice.

Tonight.

CHAPTER TEN

Saturday, September 27

Morning dawned warm and breezy. Cora, Tante, and Adaleigh sat on the side porch that overlooked Lake Michigan, drinking their coffee, eating scones Tante helped Adaleigh bake yesterday, and watching the sunrise before preparing for the Apple Picking Party. Anticipation had Cora's heel bouncing.

Her dizziness had to stay away so she could enjoy her aunt's special day, especially since Tante planned a dance after the potluck dinner. Would Silas ask her to dance? Girlish of her. Perhaps foolish since she planned to be half a world away as soon as her health cooperated. Yet, memories made were ones she could take with her.

"I never tire of watching the sun rise over the lake." Adaleigh set her chair rocking. "In the attic room at David's grandmother's house, I had a perfect view of it. David gets to see it every day, since the boats go out before dawn. One day, I'll convince him to let me work a catch."

"He hasn't let you yet?" Tante set her sewing in her lap, sounding offended on Adaleigh's behalf.

Adaleigh chuckled. "No. His boats only have a crew of three each, and since he lost the *Tuna Mann*, he combined crews. Kyle is David's first mate. Once he can add a third boat back to the fleet, he wants to make Kyle captain."

"Is that what's keeping Kyle from formally courting Samantha?" Tante asked. Cora recalled the black-haired young woman and red-headed young man from church the other day.

"I suspect so. Kyle's dad lost his job at the factory this summer, so Kyle is supporting his parents and three siblings. With winter coming and the fishing season ending, I suspect he might head up to the lumber camps." Adaleigh traced the top of her cup with her finger. "David might go with them."

Tante's jaw dropped. "Why?"

Adaleigh chuckled. "Just because I have an inheritance doesn't mean David has no pride. He wants to provide for us, and fishing didn't bring in as much as he hoped this year after losing the *Tuna Mann*."

Cora rested her elbow on the arm of the chair and cupped her chin. She'd guessed Adaleigh came from money, seeing that she spent time in Europe, but she couldn't deny a fascination with her relationship to David.

"Is that why I haven't heard wedding bells yet?" Tante huffed, jamming her needle into the flowered fabric. "He needs to provide for you even though you have means?"

Adaleigh's cheeks reddened, but she spoke evenly. "It's partially my fault. I was gone all summer, and I just ... well, I'm still healing from everything that happened this spring, and David has the patience of a saint. Anyway, we plan on using my inheritance to fund philanthropic opportunities, not a wedding."

"As long as that boy isn't dragging his feet." Tante patted Adaleigh's hand. "Just because you weren't in town doesn't mean I didn't see what you were doing from afar. I appreciate how you worked with the Conglomerate to rebuild Main Street after the storm."

Adaleigh helped Tante also? Cora couldn't help feeling a bit left out. So many people had helped her aunt while she was half a world away. She should have been here, too, as Silas told her that first day.

"Grandma Martins told you, didn't she?" Adaleigh shook her head. "I didn't mean for everyone to know."

"She can't help doting on you." Tante wiggled in her chair like a bird nesting an egg full of wholesome gossip.

Adaleigh blushed. "It was the least I could do for the town that harbored me when I needed it most."

Her words wrapped around Cora like a shawl. She could understand Adaleigh's sentiment because she felt as though she'd found refuge here and hoped to find healing as well. What if ... what if she didn't hurry back to her work?

"However, I want to do something else," Adaleigh continued. "A bigger project that would benefit everyone. David and I have a list we've been brainstorming, but so far we haven't felt the Lord leading in one direction or another."

Where before Adaleigh's words comforted and inspired, now they convicted. How much time had Cora spent asking God for direction in her life? Was she afraid of God's answer? Yes, because what if God told her she couldn't return to her work? It wasn't an answer she'd wanted to hear. Even now, her heart pounded at the thought.

"Hey, are you all right?" Adaleigh touched her shoulder. "You look a little pale."

She felt a little dizzy, too. *Not today, please, God.* "I'm fine." She forced a smile. Neither Adaleigh nor Tante looked convinced.

"Was it something I said?" Adaleigh pressed.

Cora hesitated. Could she share her struggle? Would Adaleigh understand how torn she felt inside?

"It was, wasn't it?" Adaleigh set her cup on the porch and turned her chair to face Cora. "I'm terribly sorry. Please forgive me."

"No need to apologize." Cora gently shook her head so as not to exacerbate the dizziness. "I needed to hear what you said."

Adaleigh glanced over her shoulder at Tante, who stood. "I'll let you two dears have a nice little chat. I need to begin preparations for the party."

"You don't—" Cora's protest fell short as Tante walked around the corner of the house. "She didn't have to leave."

"No, but whatever you say to me will stay between us." Adaleigh set her chair rocking again. "I'm here to listen if you'd like to talk."

The offer eliminated her hesitation, and she blurted out the first question on her tongue. "What made you stay in Crow's Nest? Was it David?"

"No. Well, yes, partially. I would have stayed even if David hadn't wanted to call on me. I found family here. Not blood family, but David's grandmother is like my own grandmother. His sister, Samantha, is like the little sister I always wanted. Mindy has become a dear friend. I love Mrs. Whittlebush, too, so I'm honored to have a chance to get to know her better by living here. Of course there's David's uncle, Detective O'Connor. And Buck Wilson has become a surprising acquaintance. I know he has a shady reputation, but we understand each other." Adaleigh cocked her head. "I wonder if perhaps you and I have more in common than we think."

Cora agreed, but asked, "And you aren't sad to leave your old home behind?"

"I had nothing to leave behind but an empty house and a business I didn't care to run."

The hope that had been sprouting withered. "If I stay, I would have to give up my dreams."

Adaleigh narrowed her eyes. "Then I ask, why would you choose to stay? What's drawing you here? And don't say Silas Ward. I don't believe the rumors that you two are ... involved. Friends maybe, but I know him well enough to know he's an honorable man who wouldn't sully a woman's reputation."

Cora's cheeks heated. Involved? Surely, a kiss didn't spawn those kinds of rumors. "No, I wouldn't give up my dreams just for a man. It's ... Mrs. Whittlebush is my aunt."

If Adaleigh was surprised, she didn't show it. "Is she your only family?"

Cora nodded.

"I see." Adaleigh brushed her skirt. "And you think she wants you to sacrifice your dreams to live with her?"

"No." She was confident of that answer. "Quite the opposite."

"Then why do you think you must stay?"

"If I ask God whether I should stay, isn't that what He would say?"

Adaleigh rocked for several moments, her gaze turned out to sea, before she turned back to Cora. "Do you believe God wants your happiness?"

No. She caught her answer before it slipped out.

"Look at the beauty of Lake Michigan, the pink clouds, the rising sun ..." Adaleigh waved toward the horizon. "God loves beauty."

"It might be true, but not every story has a happy ending." She'd heard too many tales of heartache to believe otherwise. Her own story aside.

"I know. We all experience hardship and challenge, but that doesn't mean we can't see beauty and goodness around us."

Signora Pimonte had told her a similar thing. Even though she'd lost her husband and had no family left, she told story after story of God's blessings. And yet, her life had ended prematurely. Would she still say God was good? *Yes.* The assurance of that answer settled in Cora's soul. Signora Pimonte believed in heaven and often spoke of how she couldn't wait to meet Jesus.

Tears pressed behind Cora's eyes. No longer did Signora Pimonte have to suffer with rheumatic joints or scrape out a living as an aging widow. No, she was with her husband in heaven. So ... could Cora believe in God's goodness, like Signora did?

Adaleigh squeezed Cora's hand. "I'll let you think and go help your aunt in the house."

"Thank you," Cora said before Adaleigh could disappear. Adaleigh simply nodded, then left Cora alone with her thoughts.

Silas shouldered an overflowing bushel of apples, careful not to lose the fruit someone had precariously mounded on top, and headed for the barn where Mrs. Whittlebush, his mom, and Mrs. Martins sorted the apples. Some to the apple press, some to baskets for people to take home, and some to Mrs. Whittlebush's cellar. Each trip to the barn, he kept an eye out for Cora, but he had yet to see her. Her aunt said she'd run into town, but she didn't know why. Silas couldn't help but be concerned.

"I think there are more apples this year than last." Buck Wilson met him coming from the barn. Buck wiped his brow with a handkerchief, but for once, the man wore only trousers and a simple cotton shirt, the sleeves rolled up to his elbows, making him look like any of the other fishermen helping Mrs. Whittlebush.

"I missed last year's harvest season." Silas adjusted the bushel on his shoulder. Zee had died in the spring, but Silas had been on the trail and hadn't heard the news till summer. It took until mid-October for him to make it home. Six months after Zee's death.

Buck shifted, unusually uncomfortable.

Silas braced for what it could mean. "More bad news?"

"I received another complaint about your family's business practices today. Another payment request. Has Marian finished gathering the receipts? We need to prove whether or not you owe them money."

Silas's shoulders slumped. Last night, he'd been working on a bed frame, a wedding present commissioned by a groom's parents in Hawk's River. It'd been an unexpected job, one that was needed quickly—something about the other carpenter skipping town when his debts were called in—and so Silas had worked from the moment the commission came in until the wee hours of the morning, only to rise early and work until bringing his family here, leaving no time to follow up on the receipts. "I'll ask her tonight."

"Good. And bring them to church tomorrow. I don't like to do business on a Sunday, but, in this case, I feel the Lord wouldn't mind us working to protect one of His widows."

Silas didn't hide his surprise. Buck rarely graced the doors of the church, so he hadn't expected to hear him speak so freely about God.

"I need to fetch another basket before one of the ladies in there comes after me with a cane." Buck laughed, but perhaps he was covering for his previous words.

Silas delivered his own basket of apples and had no time to ask after Cora—again—before Mrs. Whittlebush sent him back out to the orchard for another bushel.

"No rest for the weary, huh?" Patrick Martins met him in the doorway. The kid—well, man now, but Silas had a hard time seeing him as anything but the sullen ten-year-old who had lost his mother—had filled out in the years Silas was away.

"Before you know it, we'll be dancing the night away." And Silas had plans to ask Cora for one.

"It's good honest work, brother." David appeared with a shoulder ladened with a bushel of apples.

Patrick rolled his eyes. "Gotta work before play. Yeah. I know. At least Adaleigh reminds you not to work so hard."

David frowned and Patrick laughed. Silas quickly slipped away. The brothers were as opposite as day and night. Silas had heard plenty from David about how irresponsible he thought his brother, and how much David prayed that Patrick would grow up to be a good man. Seemed Patrick had indeed grown up, but what type of man he'd become, Silas didn't know.

He shrugged off thoughts of the Martins brothers. They couldn't have asked for a better day for the party. Though it was warm for hard work, it would make the evening perfect. They didn't have many days like this left before winter settled over Crow's Nest. He wanted to spend it with Cora. So where was she?

As Silas passed a group of pickers, Mindy fell in step with him. "I have something to ask you."

Her seriousness took him aback and yanked his thoughts away from Cora. "All right."

"This is mighty uncomfortable." She huffed. "Maybe I should tell David, and he can ask you. Or maybe I should ask Cora, but she isn't here. Are you why she isn't here?"

His concern grew. He sure hoped he wasn't the reason. Or namely, that their kiss the other day wasn't the reason. "I haven't spoken with Cora today."

"Hmm." Mindy folded her arms, her sunny disposition clouded like a thunderstorm.

Silas pulled Mindy out of earshot of any of the other pickers and set the empty bushel at his feet. "What's going on? I can't recall a time when you were this, well, not yourself."

Her face flamed apple red. Mindy was never nervous or embarrassed, and she often had cause, since many of the fishermen who frequented the Wharfside Cafe didn't keep their hands to themselves. What if one of them had pushed too far?

"Mindy, are you in trouble? Do you need my help?"

"No, not me. You and Cora." She covered her face but peeked at him through her fingers. "I overheard a rumor and don't believe it, but when I didn't see Cora here, I wondered. I'm sorry! I don't want to think the worst of you. You've always treated me with respect, and I have to think you'd do the same to Cora. Why wouldn't you? So the rumors can't be true. No, why would—"

"Mindy." He grasped her wrists to stop her torrent of words. "Take a breath and tell me the rumor." Though he already suspected.

She lowered her hands. "That you and Cora ..."

"You don't need to say more." He was going to have words with Greg Alistar.

"It's not true, is it? No one knows Cora, so they think she seduced you."

"That's not true. None of it." If anyone found out Cora's background, that she was the daughter and granddaughter of saloon girls, no one would believe him.

Mindy planted her hands on her hips. "Why aren't you at least calling on her, then? I can see, plain as a prairie, that you care about her."

He couldn't now. "And feed the rumor?"

"Hogwash. The rumor will feed itself. I can help counteract it if I know the truth. You aren't sweet on her?"

Now heat climbed his neck.

"You are! Has someone caught you kissing her?"

"Mindy!" Silas turned away from her and yanked his Stetson from his head. His heart pounded because, even if no one saw them, he was still the reason for the rumor. If he'd given Alistar something, anything, Cora's reputation wouldn't be dragged through the mud.

"Silas Ward, you have kissed her—don't you lie to me by denying it—so why aren't you calling her official-like? Does she not like you back?"

Silas slapped his hat against his thigh. "She's not staying in Crow's Nest, Mindy, so drop it."

Her eyes widened, and he scraped a hand through his hair.

"I'm sorry, Mindy. I'm not mad at you. The rumor is my fault. Cora is completely innocent and shouldn't be caught in the middle of a war of words."

"You know who started the rumor, don't ya?"

Silas nodded.

"Who?"

Should he say?

"As God is my witness." She stopped her foot. "I'm going to whup ya upside the head if you don't tell me. I can help. Don't you believe that?"

"How can you help? A rumor is like yeast. Once it starts, it keeps on growing."

"By spreading the truth. You know how many people come through the Wharfside every day. A carefully dropped phrase will plant the truth in people's minds. No one will think twice about me saying it, and if they hear it enough times, they might start believin' it. It's worth a try, ain't it?"

"I'm not sure how much of the truth I can share." Would Cora want Mindy—or the whole town—to know she's Mrs. Whittlebush's niece? That she was here to get well from something in her brain? That they were looking for a treasure because of a secret map they found in a desk? He scrubbed his face. He couldn't say any of that.

Mindy tugged his hat from his hands. "Tell me what you think of Cora."

"She's strong, brave, smart." The words tumbled right out of him.

"And you like her." Mindy stretched on her tiptoes to put his hat back on his head. "I've made my share of mistakes, but I'm trying to do better. Adaleigh is a good influence for me. But holding back is not something I'm good at, and I don't aim to improve that area, not when it means helping a friend. What do you have to risk when the whole town thinks you two are ... you know? Tell her how you feel about her. If nothing comes of it, at least you tried, right?"

He could be honest with Cora about his judgment of her, but could he be honest about his heart too?

"At least ask her to dance tonight." Mindy's laugh rang like a wind chime. "Might as well give those gossips something to talk about."

Cora sat on the exam table in Dr. Thomson's office. The place was poorly lit, albeit clean enough. The older man shuffled in, eyeing her over a hawkish nose.

"What brings you in today, little lady?" he asked with a raspy voice.

Was this a wise idea? She'd decided to pay him a visit after talking with Adaleigh, even if it meant missing part of the Apple Picking Party, and she'd needed to act on the impulse before her bravery fled.

Now where to begin? "I'm having headaches and dizziness."

"Hmm." The doctor looked at his paperwork. "You're staying with Rose Whittlebush, I see."

"Yes, sir." Did she tell him Tante was her aunt?

The doctor raised an eyebrow. "Wait, I know now why I recognize your name. You and Silas Ward need to see a preacher about getting married."

What? "Why? Mr. Ward and I are not a couple."

Both brows lifted now. "Is that so?"

"I'm helping him with a project that falls within my area of expertise. I'm an archeologist."

"*Pftt*. A woman who is not at home is no lady." He removed his spectacles to glare at her. "I will treat you because I am a doctor, but I strongly suggest you talk to a preacher about how you have chosen to live your life."

Her jaw dropped. She'd heard plenty of criticism for her chosen profession over the years, but this caught her off guard.

"Now what was ailing you?"

Cora gripped her fingers. "I told you, I have headaches and—"

"I'll give you some powders. Anything else?"

Cora's shoulders fell. Dr. Thompson wouldn't help her. This was a waste of time. "No, nothing else."

She took the powders and left, more disheartened than she had felt since arriving in Crow's Nest. The heat of the day did nothing to push out the coldness that wrapped around her heart. What did the doctor think she and Silas—Oh no. Could his mother have had another forgetful spell and shared her misconception from the first time? How could she return to Tante's and face him?

Walking up Main Street, she passed the newly restored buildings and empty spaces—like where Tante's shop used to be—and thought again about Adaleigh's words. Cora saw herself in these buildings. The future would not remain the same, but she could either become empty or rebuild her life. Not here, not if rumors were spreading about her and Silas. She couldn't do that to him.

Anyway, Crow's Nest didn't feel like home. At least, it didn't have the feel of family that Adaleigh had said caused her to stay. Cora loved her aunt, but she'd grow restless if she had to stay here. She suspected Silas felt similar. He'd returned for his family, but if Marian remarried, would Silas stay? If his mom's health continued to decline, he probably would. However, if she got better, then what would he do?

If Cora found answers to her health, she wouldn't have to remain in Crow's Nest either. Rumors aside, did that mean she and Silas had or didn't have a future together? Could they explore the sparks between them while they were together in Crow's Nest? Dare they wait until they were both free to leave? On the other hand, did she want to return to the Corinvetter Foundation? Or was she open to exploring another path—a path with Silas—even if it meant staying in Crow's Nest for an indefinite time?

The question surprised her. She always thought she had two options—Crow's Nest or archeology. But perhaps she had a third option, one that could involve Silas. She wouldn't know unless she got her headaches and dizziness under control, because otherwise, she was stuck in Crow's Nest whether or not she chose to be. And that was no foundation on which to build a future. Now, since Dr. Thompson was no help to her, she needed to travel back to New York to see the doctor she first saw after her return.

She backtracked to the post office, which also held the telegraph office, and sent a request to her friend Dorothy to arrange an appointment for her to see a specialist in the hopes she could be cleared to return to work. Then she'd decide what steps came next.

Twilight fell as the remains of the potluck were put away and the barn lit for dancing. As Silas predicted, the absence of sunlight allowed for a night breeze to cool the warm air. A couple of the old fishermen brought out their fiddles and other instruments, striking up a lively tune so that he couldn't help but tap his boot. Mindy pulled Detective O'Connor onto the dance floor, and several other pairings quickly followed. He spotted his nieces hovering around the sweets—apple pies and penny candies—along with a few other children.

For the hundredth time, Silas's gaze darted to where Cora and Adaleigh talked in the corner of the barn. Cora had arrived sometime after his conversation with Mindy, but with Greg Alistar's rumor circulating, he'd kept his distance until he could speak with her privately. He needed to know how she felt about the rumor before fanning it by working near her all day. Not that they had time to chat. Mrs. Whittlebush and Mrs. Martins had kept them on task, dangling supper and dancing to keep everyone motivated.

"You going to ask her to dance?" David held a glass of lemonade as he appeared beside Silas.

He knew exactly to whom David referred, but said, "Do you think Adaleigh would dance with me?"

David slapped his shoulder. "Cora. Are you going to dance with Cora?"

"I don't know."

"Wrong answer."

"The rumors."

"I heard." David sighed. "Have you thought about going with her? Back to Italy?"

"What?" The concept had never entered his mind. Could he? No. He needed to provide for his family.

"Granted, you'd have to marry her first." David's eyes twinkled. "The way you've been watching her this afternoon, I don't think you'd mind."

"My family—"

"There's a town of people who would be happy to help take care of them. Anyway, getting married means putting your wife first. Providing for her becomes the most important task, even before your current family."

Then nothing could come of his feelings for Cora. The realization hit him like a hoof to the stomach. He would never wish an unhappy marriage on her, and if he couldn't put her first, then he wasn't ready to be the husband she deserved. Instead of voicing any of that, however, he latched onto an undertone in David's words. "Thinking about marriage, are you? I see the way you watch Adaleigh. I don't think you'd mind."

David blushed as Silas parroted his words back at him. "Fine. I'm planning to join Kyle up at the lumber camp this winter because I want to pay for a ring myself. My dad gambled away my mom's ring years ago, and Grandma still wears hers, so there's no family ring. Is it so wrong that I want something special on her finger that's just between me and Adaleigh?"

"No, of course not." If anything, jealousy rose in his chest. He wanted something special with a special someone. Not just anyone. Cora. But he'd been right to tell David to let Adaleigh go this past summer. Of course, she chose to stay. Cora would not make the same choice. Her soul was made to wander. He understood that because he had the same spirit. If only he was free to wander with her.

"Ask her to dance." David squeezed his shoulder. "If you part ways, at least you'll have that memory with her. Rumors be hanged."

Before Silas could respond, Nettie dragged him onto the dance floor in time for a polka. Then Essie demanded a dance. Of course he danced with his mom and Marian. Mindy and Adaleigh both claimed dances, and both used the opportunity to scold him for having not danced with Cora yet. David had been one of the first men to ask Cora to dance. She even said yes to Buck Wilson. Silas had noted each partner. He'd also overheard the rumors, but they'd died down as she danced with others and not with him. Would dancing with her bring the questions to the forefront again?

"Are you waiting for permission?" Mrs. Whittlebush slipped beside him, tucking her arm around his. "Because if you are, then you have my blessing."

His shoulders sagged. "The rumors."

"When isn't there gossip about a new couple? Sure, some enjoy spreading base rumors, but as you stand before God, you know the truth about how you've treated my niece, and I have no doubt it is honorable."

"Then I should keep my distance, Mrs. Whittlebush. I can't offer her my heart when I need to provide for my family."

"Dear Silas. How do you know Cora will leave? I wouldn't bank on that. Her health is not improving."

"And when it does, even if it's ten years from now, she'll resent being forced to stay."

"How do you know you will still be in Crow's Nest ten years from now? Come, come. If you two care about one another, you'll find a way through those answers together. One step at a time. Life does not stay the same. It's a river, and you never know what twists and turns will come your way."

Cora laughed at something Buck said, and Silas's feet were in motion before he said goodbye to Mrs. Whittlebush.

"And there he is now." Buck held out a hand to shake his. "Cora was telling me about the furniture you designed for Mrs. Whittlebush. I've heard you do fine work, but now I must see for myself."

His jealousy evaporated beneath the unexpected compliment. "Thank you."

"I'm assuming you've come to ask the pretty lady for a dance, so I shall take my leave." Buck bowed to Cora. "Fine speaking with you, Miss Davis. I hope we shall converse again soon."

Cora smiled. "Likewise."

Buck left, and Silas cleared his throat, drawing her attention. "Might I have this dance?"

She paused, ear to the music. "It's another polka. They move too quickly for me."

"Then may I claim the next acceptable one?" Why did he sound so stiff?

Cora nodded.

"Are you feeling all right tonight?" He tried to make his tone casual but wasn't sure he succeeded. "I was worried when I didn't see you earlier today."

"Better than I expected." Cora reached for her throat, then lowered her hands. She wasn't wearing the scarf she'd been wearing most of the days he'd seen her. Instead, she wore a simple, straight dress, the color of autumn leaves. "I went to see Dr. Thompson."

"You did!" He would have gone with her. "And?"

Her beautiful face crumpled.

Rumors be hanged, indeed. He grabbed her hand and pulled her into the shadow of the barn wall. "What happened, Cora? What did he say? Does he have answers for you?"

Those blue eyes were as watery as the lake. "He dismissed me."

"Is it because of the rumors of us?" *Please, God, let it not be so.*

Her cheeks pinked. "Only partially—" She stopped him from interrupting her. "It's nothing I haven't heard before as an unmarried woman who works in archaeology, but I hate that you are implicated, Silas. It's not fair."

"It's not right either, and you don't deserve it." He'd give Greg Alistar a piece of his mind next time he laid eyes on the snake.

"It's why I telegraphed my friend Dorothy. She is setting up an appointment for me in New York. I'm going back to see the specialist as soon as possible."

New York? Silas pushed back disappointment at her leaving. He needed to support her, and if this was the only way he could, then ... "I'm glad you decided to find answers."

"I'm still scared." Her voice a whisper.

The song tempo changed. A waltz. He tugged Cora onto the dance floor and used the song as an excuse to hold her in front of their friends and families. Having her so close to his heart, words slipped out before his head could stop him. "I wish I could go with you."

"Do you?" She leaned back and surveyed his face, hope shining on full display.

God only knew how it could ever happen, but he told her the truth. "I do. I'd go to the—"

"Pardon me." A man tapped Silas on the shoulder. "I apologize, but it is most urgent I speak with Miss Davis."

Silas glared at the stranger. No way was he releasing Cora until the end of the dance. The man was dressed in a simple gray suit, rumpled and travel-dirty. He had black hair, lanky limbs, and a satchel thrown over his shoulder. He looked more accustomed to a desk than manual labor, especially with spectacles. Was he one of Cora's colleagues?

Cora stopped, and another couple nearly ran into them. The action allowed Cora to slip from Silas's arms, and the stranger escorted Cora from the dance floor, leaving Silas to trail after them out the barn door and into the chilly, starless night. He wasn't about to let her out of his sight but wasn't close enough to stop the stranger from cornering her against the side of the barn.

"I understand you are Cora Davis?" The man's tone wasn't harsh, exactly, but it wasn't kind either. Silas threw back his shoulders, preparing to meet the man as he would a bull.

"What is it you want, sir?" Cora raised her chin.

The stranger's gaze darted toward Silas. "Tell me the name of your friend."

"Silas Ward?" She gestured toward him. "You have nothing to fear from him unless you mean me harm."

She was correct about that.

"No." The hint of an accent slipped through, and Silas recognized it as similar to, but not exactly like, that of a ranch hand he'd met once from New York. "I mean your friend in Italy."

"Signora Pimonte?" Cora whispered and backed against the barn wall.

Silas stepped to her side.

The man relaxed a smidgeon. "And tell me, did she consider you a friend or something else? Something with more meaning, perhaps?"

What was with the third degree? Cora glanced at Silas before facing the stranger. "She thought of me as a daughter. But who are you?"

"*Grazie Dio* I found you in time." The man grabbed her shoulders. "Your life is in danger, and I'm here to save it."

CHAPTER ELEVEN

Cora stared at the man as Italian rolled off his tongue, sounding just like Signora Pimonte. "How do you know my friend?"

Silas rested his hand at the small of her back. "No, what do you mean, her life is in danger?"

Oh, right. She'd heard that, but she wanted to know about her friend. "Did you know Signora Pimonte? Do you know what happened to her?"

The man looked over at the barn doors, then at Silas, before pointing toward the house. "Let's speak away from the crowds."

"No." Silas pulled Cora to his side. "You need to tell me who you are before we leave the safety of this group of people. Or do I need to call my *friend*, Detective O'Connor, to come out here?"

Cora wiggled out from Silas's embrace but squeezed his wrist before putting space between them. She appreciated his protective actions, but they weren't necessary at this moment. She knew how to learn whether this stranger was friend or foe. "Tell me how you know Signora Pimonte."

The man adjusted his spectacles. "My family lived next door before immigrating to America when I was a boy. My sister stayed behind with my grandmother, but after Nonna died in the earthquake this summer, Isabella made plans to join our family in New York."

Isabella. She could remember an Isabella about her same age.

"After your unusually quick departure, Signora Pimonte sent a package with my sister, along with a detailed letter to me."

This was the man Signora Pimonte trusted? Him and his sister?

"Miss Davis." The man shot a glance at Silas before concern tightened his angular features. "I understand you were injured during the earthquake and have been experiencing headaches, dizziness, nausea. I am a medical doctor in New York, and Signora Pimonte specifically asked me to look into your wellbeing. However, your friend, Mr. Ward, and I likely agree your health takes second to your safety. My sister arrived in New York with news of what happened to Signora Pimonte, which is why I left her with our parents and came here straight away. Someone wants to silence you over an Etruscan bucchero."

Cora could only stare at the man as she attempted to absorb all that he said. The bucchero was at the root of all of this?

Silas wrapped her arm around his and tugged her toward the house. "There are chairs on the porch where we can talk. Follow me."

Cora let him lead her, which allowed her mind to sort through this new information. First of all, Signora Pimonte had told this man about her health, and he wanted to help. Did that mean she wouldn't need to travel to New York to see a doctor who would listen to her condition? Would he have answers for her? A way for her to get better so she could return to her work? However, as he said, that took second to her safety.

Again, Signora Pimonte must have trusted him—and his sister—if he was the one to whom she sent the statue. Cora risked a stabbing pain in her head to call up a memory of who the sister could be. The Isabella she remembered was taller than other Italian women, with a long black braid and inquisitive brown eyes.

Did she and her brother have the statue Signora Pimonte desired to give Cora? Other than a bittersweet memory of a woman who thought of Cora as a daughter, what good would the statue do her when it was her work with the bucchero that got Signora Pimonte killed? If only she had never found it. What did it matter when it cost people their lives?

Silas handed her to the same rocking chair she'd sat in that morning when she'd talked with Adaleigh. He took the one in the middle, leaving Isabella's brother the one on his far side, where Tante preferred to sit.

The lake was noisy tonight, crashing against the cliff face. No moon or stars shone, either, which likely meant that a change of weather was on the way. Silas lit the lantern Tante kept on the porch for just such evenings. The light cast long shadows, the lawn beyond cloaked in blackness.

Cora adjusted her chair to see the two men better. "First, let me offer my condolences on the loss of your grandmother. I recall your sister. *Matrone* was her last name."

"Isabella Matrone, yes." His smile softened. "You said it correctly, too, with the *ay* at the end instead of a hard *n* sound. Not many outside of our New York neighborhood get it right. And I'm Nick. My sister probably calls me *Niccolo*."

The name sparked a memory. "She and I went to market together a couple of times, and I do remember her telling me of a doctor brother whom she missed. I can't recall if I saw her after the earthquake."

Nick frowned. "Has your memory returned at all?"

"In bits and pieces. Silas has helped me a great deal." She smiled at her cowboy. *Her cowboy*? If only. He sat with his hat hanging on his knee, his broad shoulders relaxed, though he was no doubt attentive to their conversation and everything around them. He exuded such a protection that she could question Dr. Nick Matrone without fear. Was she willing to give that up just to return to playing in the dirt?

"Good. I am glad for that." Nick turned to Silas. "Can I count on you to help protect Cora?"

"I already have been." Silas folded his arms. "Based on what Cora can remember, I am not surprised to hear the bucchero is the reason for your concern. Is Harry Gordon who you suspect means her harm?"

"Yes." Nick kept eye contact with Silas—perhaps it should bother her that these two men were planning her protection, but just now, knowing they would keep her safe eased the ache in her head. "From what my sister explained, he wanted credit for the bucchero find and set about discrediting you over several weeks. It came to a head one day when you argued, and he hit you with the bucchero, knocking you off a rise into the river. Signora Pimonte learned you were sent back to America immediately after that, and she began to ask questions."

Grief knifed Cora's heart. "She shouldn't have. It's what got her killed, isn't it?"

"I'm sorry. It's very likely. However, she did send Isabella away with a package for you. I don't know what it is, and I'm not sure Isabella knows either. But Isabella told me this Henry Gordon visited Signora Pimonte, and when he left, Isabella went to check on her only to discover her dead."

Cora pressed a hand to her chest. The news hurt so much.

"Is there any indication that Henry Gordon left Italy?" Silas asked, and again she was grateful for him. She couldn't have spoken if she tried.

"When Isabella arrived with the news and Signora Pimonte's letters, I went immediately to the Corinvetter Foundation's main offices and spoke with a Dorothy Burnett. Unfortunately, I was the second person that day to request Cora's address. Miss Burnett didn't see harm in giving it to Mr. Gordon because he'd told her they sent him to escort you back to Italy, that he'd convinced Signore Camposano to allow you to return.

When I told her what actually happened, she gave me your aunt's address right away. I could only hope I would arrive in time. Have you seen him?"

Cora shook her head. Harry Gordon had caused all of this? Had killed Signora Pimonte and then planned to travel here to ... do what? Kill Cora too? Was there any hope that Nick had it wrong, that Mr. Gordon actually meant to escort her back?

"Then I think we need to make sure as many people know as possible so they can keep an eye out for him." Nick spoke with the authority of one used to being listened to. "We must be alerted if he chooses to confront you."

"Detective O'Connor is here." Silas stood. "I'll get him so we can fill him in. We can trust him."

"Excellent," Nick said.

Silas looked at Cora. "Would you like to inform him together?"

What he was really asking was, did she feel comfortable enough with Nick to stay alone with him while Silas was gone? "I'd like to talk to Nick more about my headaches."

"As you wish." He settled his cowboy hat on his head.

"But Silas ... hurry back?"

He touched the brim, and her heart fluttered.

As Silas's steps departed, an awkward silence settled between her and Nick until he cleared his throat. "Is he ... are you ..."

"We're friends." Cora wrapped her arms around her middle.

"You're cold." Nick slipped out of his coat and rested it over her shoulders. "Are you *only friends* because of your health or because of your work?"

She startled at his bold question.

"I'll not deny Signora Pimonte wrote glowingly about you as well as mentioning that you have no husband or beau, her intent obvious. I would not say I had hope for a match, but my concern for you as a doctor and as someone who meant something to Signora Pimonte hastened my travels here. However, I see that your heart belongs to another, and neither of you have anything to fear from me."

Again Cora stared at Nick as, one by one, his words sank in. First, that Signora had suggested her as a possible wife for Nick, then that he cared about her although he didn't know her, and lastly, that he thought she'd given her heart to Silas. But she hadn't, had she? There were decisions to make before her heart ran to find refuge with a cowboy.

"I'm sorry if that has upset you. I felt honesty was best in this situation." Nick took Silas's chair. "While we wait for your man's return, tell me about these headaches."

Her man? Silas? *Focus, Cora.* "The month between the earthquake and my fall is still a blur. I struggle to know the difference between what my colleagues told me I felt and what I actually felt. How much did Signora say? I'm sure I told her everything."

"Based on her letter and Isabella's account, my initial thought is that you are experiencing some type of amnesia. You were unconscious after the earthquake and then hit in the head with the bucchero. Both events could have caused your lack of memory during that time. You said you have begun to remember?"

"Slowly, but I can't recall who hit me with the bucchero."

"And your headaches, when do you think they began?"

Cora rubbed her temple. "When I have an emotional reaction or try to think too hard, they get worse. I also have dizziness. A couple of times, I have almost fainted. Or maybe the ground was moving like a ship and I simply lost my balance. It's hard to know sometimes."

His head bobbed as if her story was as he expected. "I'll admit, I'm not a seasoned doctor, but I do believe you suffered two brain injuries. One during the earthquake and again when you were struck. That combination, along with the emotional turmoil of someone attacking you, has produced this combined effect."

"Does that mean I can get better?"

He sighed. "I'm afraid that's all up to your brain. Neither you nor I can predict how it will heal. However, rest and quiet will give it the chance it needs."

Hope sprouted. "You mean I won't need brain surgery for a tumor or anything like that?"

"I would require a further exam before I could say for certain, but in my professional opinion, I believe all your symptoms are related to those two events. I also believe you appear to be having migrainous headaches." He steepled his fingers. "My mother experiences them, and that was my first thought after reading Signora Pimonte's letter. My mother retreats to the darkest, quietest room until they pass, which is difficult to do in New York City. There is talk of researching headaches within laboratories. But for now, I cannot offer you much relief other than typical headache powders, which never work for Mamma."

"I can't believe a diagnosis could be as simple as all that. I'm at risk of losing my career, and other doctors are ready to operate on my head or simply dismiss me."

Nick adjusted his spectacles. "I have the benefit of youth, in this case. Unlike many of those who have been in medicine for decades, I am still open to the latest advancements."

Cora's relief at a non-life-threatening diagnosis quickly gave way before Nick's previous words about his inability to offer relief. "What did you mean about there not being treatments? There is hope I'll get better, isn't there?"

Nick gripped her hand. "Signora Pimonte, my mamma, even my sister, would tell you there is always hope. But I feel I should be honest with you. I don't know. Those three women are praying women, but after the disease, poverty, and darkness I have seen in my work among the poorest in New York, I admit to not knowing whether I believe in God anymore. Medically speaking, only time will show whether you can heal. But your headaches may stay forever."

Cora's stomach dropped. Forever?

Nick squeezed, providing her some sense of stability. "I have made plans to stay until Christmas, if necessary. I want to make sure you're safe and on the road to recovery. However, this is the first Christmas my family will spend all together in fifteen years, so I must be home."

"Of course. Family is important." Cora couldn't help glancing toward the barn where Tante was likely enjoying the Apple Picking Party. When was the last holiday she'd spent with Tante? All those Christmases she'd missed, leaving Tante to celebrate alone. Of course she knew families like the Wards and Martins had included Tante, but it wasn't the same as spending it with a blood relative. What pain had she cost her aunt in order to pursue her own dream? Realizing that now, even if she could return to her archaeological work, could she do so with a clear conscience?

"Would you like to see the package Signora Pimonte sent you?" Nick released her hand and lifted his satchel onto his lap. "I kept it as safely inconspicuous as I could."

Cora's heart beat hard. Now that she knew she'd never hear another story about it from Signora Pimonte herself, did she want to see it?

Nick lifted a bundle wrapped in cloth from the bag and handed it to her. She took it gently, feeling its weight, and set it on her knees. Layer by layer, she divested it of the cloths until the pink marble shone in the lantern light.

The carving was of a mother, with wrinkled face and stooped shoulder, wrapping her arms around a young woman. Signora Pimonte had explained one of her ancestors—a great-great-great-grandfather—worked in marble, and on the daughter's wedding day had gifted her this statue. The daughter then gave it to her eldest daughter on her wedding day, and on down the generations until Signora Pimonte, who had no daughter, no child, to give it to.

Except Cora.

Grief overwhelmed her at the loss of her friend. That her discovery of the bucchero had played a role in Signora Pimonte's death. The sorrow pressed tears to her eyes and a sob to her throat. Her ears rushed as she pressed her forehead to the statue, drowning out worried voices around her. What she wouldn't give to be back in Signora's kitchen, to hear another of her stories while they cooked together. Or to be a girl again on Tante and Onkle's farm, gathering apples to make pies for every neighbor within five miles.

Strong arms came around her and awkwardly held her, the chair's arm between them. Silas. She recognized his comfort immediately. And somehow, it unlocked an even deeper vault of grief she'd hidden away since she was a little girl. What if her mother hadn't left her that day in Chicago? What if she could have seen her one last time?

Grief overwhelmed her like a tidal wave and her sobs shook her whole being. She leaned her head against Silas's shoulder as sorrow rolled through her.

Then Silas hooked his arms under her legs and lifted her from the chair. His heart beat beneath her ear as he held her against his chest. This cowboy wouldn't desert her like the ones who left her mother and grandmother. No, Silas was stalwart to the point of sacrificing his own happiness for those he cared about. Was she one of those? Could she be one of those?

Silas's steps climbed the stairs, the movement lulling her. Safe and secure, she allowed the grief and sorrow to drift away.

When she opened her eyes, she immediately felt the loss of Silas's arms, as if they had been but a dream. Now she found herself in bed. Tante knitting in the dark beside her, humming a German lullaby she'd sung the first night Cora came to live with her. Peace settled on her bruised heart, and she fell asleep.

"So this is the desk that brought you two together?"

Silas looked up from where he searched by lamplight behind Marian's counter for the receipts. Nick appeared in the shop, hair damp and trousers clean. The man couldn't stay at Mrs. Whittlebush's house with Cora and Adaleigh there, so Silas had invited him to bunk above the workshop with him. He gave a nod of acknowledgment before returning to his searching. He couldn't find where Marian had put them.

"Are you going to let her get away?"

"What?" *Her*? Silas blinked. *Cora.* His mind still whirled from the evening, from hearing her sobs and running up the porch to find her nearly bent in two. He'd blamed Nick at first, but Nick had looked shocked by Cora's emotional state. Then Silas had seen the statue in her lap, and he hadn't thought of rumors or anything other than comforting her. So he'd held her. Until Detective O'Connor returned with

Mrs. Whittlebush and she escorted them up to Cora's room where Silas reluctantly left Cora in her aunt's care.

"You haven't even changed your clothes." Nick's presence loomed beside him. "Are you planning to sleep tonight?"

Silas shook his head. He couldn't rest while worry reigned. He wanted to know Cora was okay and he wanted to keep watch to make sure she was safe. But Mrs. Whittlebush promised she wouldn't leave Cora's side, so he might as well find the receipts Buck had asked him to bring to church tomorrow morning.

"Time and distance are no match for love." Nick folded his arms and leaned a hip against the desk. "My father traveled across an ocean without my mother, in hopes of giving her a better life. It took two years for him to have enough money to send for her."

Anger spiked through him. What did this stranger know of it? "I'm already struggling to provide for my family." And he wouldn't subject Cora to waiting for him. He touched each ledger's spine as he scanned the shelves again.

"I couldn't help but notice the letter you left on the washstand in your room."

Silas still hadn't replied to Anchorman and now had a second letter waiting for a response. They would let ranch hands go over the winter, but without a doubt, his foreman would cut a handful more if he could get Silas back. The man had understood Silas's need to return home after his brother's death. However, after a reasonable grieving period, he'd been relentless about hiring him on again. If Silas waited much longer, his old boss would have to move on. There were too many workers and not enough jobs.

"Why don't you take your family west with you?" Nick pressed.

Silas turned from the shelves. "I can't take Mom and Marian away from Crow's Nest. It's where their husbands are buried. And Marian's folks work the lumber camps up north, so she and the girls see them in the summer on occasion."

"And Cora?" He said it quietly, but there was steel in his tone.

Silas squared his shoulders. "You keep prodding me about her. Why?"

Nick met his gaze. "Because Signora Pimonte charged me with her protection. Not just physically. She wanted me to marry her."

"What!"

"There's the emotion I was looking for."

Silas balled his fists. "Are you telling me the truth or trying to get a rise out of me?"

"Both." Nick rounded the counter until he stood directly in front of him. "You care about Cora Davis, and if you're not careful, you're going to break her heart. I won't stand for that."

Confusion tempered Silas's anger. "Then you don't want to marry her?"

The man muttered something in another language. "I don't know her, but if that's what it took to keep her safe, I'd do it for Signora Pimonte. However, I won't have to because Cora has you. I see how highly you think of her. How protective you are of her." He stabbed a finger into Silas's chest. "Are you going to go the distance? Or is your sense of responsibility going to get in the way?"

"My sense of responsibility is necessary. I'm the only man in my household. They need me."

"And Cora doesn't need you? Why not make her part of your household too?"

Silas returned to searching the shelves. "Trust me, if there was a way we could work it out, do you think I'd let her go? I don't think I have a choice. If I can't prove Mom paid for her purchases, I'm going to have to leave my family in order to provide for them."

"What do you mean?" Marian's voice had both men spinning to face her. She tugged her robe tighter with one hand and held a lantern higher with the other. "You're leaving?"

Silas pushed past Nick. "Buck Wilson told me of another seller claiming Mom didn't pay. Did you find the receipts?"

"I left them tucked next to the ledger you returned to me." Marian hurried over to the shelf—Nick scrambling out of her way—and set the lantern on the counter, pulling a ledger off the shelf. Then another and another. "They were both right here before we left for the apple picking."

Silas exchanged a glance with Nick. "Is there anywhere else they could be? Could Mom have misplaced them?" He hated to ask.

Marian was already shaking her head. "Either you or I were with Mom and the girls from the moment I put them away until we got into the truck."

"Did you find anything in them?" Silas asked.

Marian met his gaze. "I did. There was proof of purchase. Mom isn't forgetting."

"Forgetting?" Nick placed a hand on the counter, bringing himself into the conversation. "What do you mean?"

Silas quickly explained that Mom had thought both Dad and Zee had still been alive, as well as the confusion she exhibited during her acquisition trips, which seemed to leave an opportunity to pay twice for items. "Now the proof of her purchases is missing."

"And someone else is claiming she hasn't paid?" Marian asked.

Nick rubbed his now clean-shaven face. "Has your mom seen a doctor?"

"She refuses." An idea struck. "Wait. You're a doctor. Would you consider speaking with Mom?"

"You're a doctor?" Marian elbowed Silas. "Why didn't you introduce him as one before you crammed us all into the truck?" It hadn't seemed relevant at the time. Now, however …

Nick gave a self-deprecating chuckle. Before he could answer, Marian turned back to Silas. "First, go back to what you said about leaving."

"If we have to pay for the wardrobe Mom purchased from that family in Hawk's River again, we will have to make a sale in order to buy flour or pay the milkman."

"What about the bedframe you're making?"

"The electric bill is due at the end of next week."

Marian sank to the stool that stayed behind the counter. "Where else can you find work?"

Nick tapped the counter. "I should—"

Silas waved him to silence. "My old foreman offered me a job. If we can't find the receipts and Buck can't help us, then I have no choice but to go back West."

Marian glanced at Nick, then back at Silas. "What about Cora? I know you have feelings for her."

Nick raised his eyebrows.

"I …" Silas blew out a breath. He didn't know what to do.

CHAPTER TWELVE

Monday September 29

"I'm going to do you a favor today," Nick announced Monday morning as he blew into Silas's workshop with a gust of wind.

Silas looked up from the bedpost on which he was etching a swirl design.

Nick smoothed his gray suit. "You're going to drop me off at this Dr. Thompson's clinic so I can speak to him about our shared profession, then you'll pick up Cora and bring her here."

Silas's heart jumped at the idea, but he tamped down his excitement. He hadn't seen Cora since carrying her to her room Saturday night. Neither she nor her aunt were at church yesterday, Adaleigh delivering the news that Cora was abed. No wonder. After the emotional evening she had, of course her headache and dizziness would be too much for her. Nick had immediately left to pay a medical call, telling Silas later there wasn't much he could do except let her rest. Silas wished he could have seen her, helped ease her pain, but it wasn't his place.

It could be.

"Then you can spend the day working on that letter together," Nick was saying, "and make sure you tell her everything that's going on with your family and your finances. Ask her opinion whether you should go to the lumber camp your friend David mentioned at church yesterday or return out West. See what she says. She might surprise you if you ask whether she'd go with you."

Silas chewed on Nick's words as he drove him into town thirty minutes later. Neither he nor Marian had been able to find the receipts, which he told to both Buck and Detective O'Connor after the church service. They had come to the shop to poke around yesterday afternoon. Buck spotted scratch marks on the lock securing the large barn doors, which they all agreed could mean someone stole the receipts. It could also have been from one of them struggling to get the key into the lock. Marian planned to turn the house inside out today to see if Mom took the receipts and ledger. If they still couldn't find them, Silas would have to pay—again—for the wardrobe from Hawk's River.

So Silas planned to spend his day working on the bedframe while Detective O'Connor and Buck investigated the connections between all the others who claimed they hadn't been paid. If they couldn't get to the bottom of the trouble within the next few days, and unless an unexpected windfall came in, Silas would have no choice but to seek other employment.

What if Cora was willing to go with him out West? Hope tried to spring up, but Silas shot it down. First, the cost of an extra train ticket alone forbade it. And the rails were no place for Cora. Second, there were no wives on the ranch, let alone unmarried women. She'd have to live in town. Alone. The risk to her reputation was unacceptable. He'd already caused rumors here in Crow's Nest.

Then again, was he willing to offer marriage as Nick had been ready to do? Even if it meant leaving her here in Crow's Nest until he could return? As David had implied, marrying Cora sure wasn't a hardship to think on. Silas could see a future with her. He could see Cora as his wife, having children together, growing old side by side.

The timing, it was all wrong. He couldn't provide for her, and he didn't want her to make a decision until she was in a position to make it without her health making it for her.

He pulled to a stop outside Dr. Thompson's clinic. Nick opened the truck door, but Silas stalled him with a hand to his bicep. "Tell me the truth. Do you think Cora's headaches will improve? Will her memory return? And the dizziness, will it keep her from returning to her work?"

Nick closed the door and turned to him. "Honestly? I don't know. Her brain has to heal, and the medical field doesn't know yet how that works. There's talk of experiments to attempt to learn more, but that could be years away. Imaging the brain is still difficult and requires improvement of the equipment. If that even holds an answer. The best recommendation I can make is for her to rest. The emotional turmoil she's been under, the loss of Signora Pimonte, the fear that her colleague could be after her ... none of that has helped. However, I saw how she relaxed when you held her the other night on that porch."

He'd felt it, too, and had a difficult time releasing her care to Mrs. Whittlebush once he laid her in her bed.

"If you must leave sooner, I can stay in town until mid-December to watch over her." Nick reopened his door. "But I'm not the person she needs, Silas. Talk to her."

Could he do that? Be completely honest with her about ... everything, including his feelings for her?

Silas drove slowly toward Mrs. Whittlebush's house as he recalled the first day they met. Honesty was one of the first things they'd agreed on, even if the harshness of it caused friction between them. Yes, honesty was required now. If only he had more time before needing to make a decision on the best way to provide for his family this winter. He wanted time to court Cora properly, not rush into a marriage because he might need to leave.

Oh, the irony—him leaving Crow's Nest, not Cora—it wasn't lost on him.

He parked in front of Mrs. Whittlebush's house, surprised to see the older lady's car gone. She and Adaleigh had promised that one of them would always be with Cora until Detective O'Connor had information on Henry Gordon. Had Cora run an errand with her aunt, or was Adaleigh home? One glance toward the water's horizon suggested Adaleigh wasn't here. David wouldn't be fishing with how angry the lake looked today, and Adaleigh would be with him.

Worry chased him up the walk. He pounded on the front door, memory of that first day stronger now.

Answer, Cora, please. Answer the door.

No sound came, not even a crash.

He pounded once more, then tried the knob. Locked. Again.

Still, no one came to the door. He jogged down the porch steps and circled the house, only to discover the back door stood ajar.

He broke into a run, bursting into the house. "Cora!"

Silence greeted him.

Cora struggled against Henry Gordon as he dragged her into the grove of apples. She tried to scream, make noise, something to alert the person who'd knocked at the front door—Nick, most likely—that she was behind the house.

Fifteen minutes. That was how long it took for Mr. Gordon to strike.

The waves hadn't allowed for fishing this morning, so David had surprised Adaleigh with an outing. Tante already had a ladies' meeting, but she'd offered to stay until Nick arrived as promised. Cora had been sure fifteen minutes alone wouldn't make a difference. If only she hadn't assumed it was Nick who knocked at the door. She'd been careful to crack it open just enough to see the visitor, but the split second it took to realize her mistake was enough for Henry to barge in and aim a gun at her.

That gun he now used to force her toward the place where the orchard ended at the cliff face. She knew what was at the bottom this time. Water, yes, but rocks. Many, many rocks.

Why couldn't Nick have arrived three minutes earlier? Even two would have caught Henry pushing through the front door. Nick was right. Her life was in danger, and it had taken her too long to remember the truth of it.

"Scream and I'll shoot you. Understand?" Henry pushed her against one of the outlying apple trees. Picked clean just the other day, there wasn't a round weapon at hand. Cora leaned against the low-hanging branches.

"What do you want, Henry?" She fought through the pain in her head. "I can't remember."

"Likely story." He paced, the lake roaring behind him. The wind jostled his bowler hat and whipped his unbuttoned coat. He slashed his gun through the air. "You were so determined to keep your name as the finder of the bucchero, I had to smack the pride out of you, and your hard head broke it."

What? The memory fought for purchase in her mind. "I found it. Of course I should get credit."

"You're a woman!" he shouted at her, causing her to jump. "So no, you shouldn't get credit. It was my find, and you had to take that from me."

Like the flash of a camera bulb, a silent film of their argument came back to her. They'd had a similar argument before he struck her with the bucchero, sending her over the cliff. What all was said, Cora could not yet bring into focus, but feelings of anger, shame, and surprise welled from the memory. Gordon wanted the bucchero, wanted the honor and praise, and lost it all by hitting her with the artifact.

Would he do the same here, only with the butt of a gun? Could she dodge it this time since she knew to expect it? A wave of dizziness and nausea washed over her, the same as it had that fateful day in Italy.

Gordon leaned close to her face, his hot breath on her cheek. "You made me break the bucchero, and I thought all was lost. Then I learned about the statue the old lady sent you. I'll take that as payment for costing me the bucchero. Now where is it?"

His words might as well have been a fist to her stomach. "You killed Signora Pimonte?"

He pressed the gun under her ribs. "Tell me where it is, and I'll consider not tossing you into the lake."

False promise, that. She tightened her hold on the apple tree branch, knowing if she didn't, she'd crumble. Showing Mr. Gordon the full extent of her weakness was a risk she couldn't take, seeing that she doubted Gordon would ever let her go. At best, she'd tell the Corinvetter Foundation, and they'd fire him. At worst, she'd tell the police what he'd done to her. Though it was her word against his. Would he be willing to bank his career that no one would believe the word of an unmarried woman born out of wedlock? *She* couldn't take that chance. She had to stall, had to find a way for Nick—or whoever had been at the front door—to find her. If the statue saved her life, Signora Pimonte would be fine with her giving it up.

She cleared the bile from her throat. "It—it's in the house. We have to go back."

Mr. Gordon laughed. "I don't trust you to send the cowboy away."

The cowboy? Silas! He'd come for her, not Nick. Oh, Silas. The Italian doctor might be nice and all, but knowing Silas was here flooded her with both hope and fear. She trusted him so much more than Signora Pimonte's friend, yet Silas could be injured just as Signora Pimonte had been. Silas would protect her with his life if he must.

Henry cocked the weapon. A pistol, maybe? Her thoughts swirled. She truly knew nothing about modern guns. Ancient bows and siege weapons, even swords she could discuss. But guns didn't appear in history until the ninth or tenth century, beginning in China. It was a couple hundred years after that they made it to the Mediterranean region, her region. Her more recent digs showed civilizations that lived that many years BC, so—

"Miss Davis." Mr. Gordon yanked her back to the present, pulling her away from the tree. "Will you get rid of the cowboy, or must I?"

"I will." She'd never let him hurt Silas.

Mr. Gordon hid the weapon behind her back and Cora had no choice but to lean on his arm as he escorted her back to the house. The ground shifted under feet as if she stood on the deck of a boat. Tears pricked her eyes. How was she supposed to get out of the situation when her body failed her so?

And Silas ... how was she to send him away as Gordon demanded? She drank in the sight of him as he stood on the side porch, looking out toward the lake. Looking for her? His profile exuded strength, his hat low over his eyes. Cora clenched her jaw. This situation might cost her life, but she would do everything to make sure he survived.

They must have made enough noise as they neared the house because a moment later his head whipped around. In an instant, he'd bounded over the railing, landing lightly on his feet. He dashed toward them. "Cora! Are you all right?"

Mr. Gordon dug the gun into her side.

"I'm all right, Silas." She held out a hand to stop him, praying he couldn't see through her lie for his sake.

"Who is your friend?" Silas drew himself up, large and intimidating. She remembered that first day when he'd defended Tante. He had a protective streak as wide as the Rhône River. How was she going to call him off?

"Cora." Mr. Gordon hissed in her ear. If she weren't suffering these symptoms, how easy it would be to throw her head back and smash his nose, then whip around to snatch away the gun. She could do those things ... before.

Silas stepped forward.

"Stop Silas, please." Too much desperation, but she didn't trust what Gordon would do if she didn't follow his direction. "Do you trust me?"

His gaze mined into hers. Questions aplenty shone in his eyes. How much could he read in hers? Surely the pain was evident. He always seemed to see that. But did he guess how hard this next part would be? She had to get him to leave without causing an argument. If Mr. Gordon harmed her, she couldn't bear for the last conversation she had with Silas to be one of hurtful words.

Gordon tightened his grip on her arm, and she fought off a whimper. Silas wouldn't leave if he heard one. "Silas, please. I need a few minutes to speak with my colleague here. I'll be over later to work on our project. You go on ahead." She held her breath, praying Silas would concede.

"Cora ..."

She shook her head, the action causing her to stumble. Silas stepped forward and Gordan clicked the hammer of his gun.

But that one step was all Silas took. "Okay Cora. If that is what you wish. I'll see you at the house later." His tone was even, but there was something there that hinted at a double meaning. Did he have a plan to rescue her? Hope warred with fear.

"Later, then?" She forced herself to smile.

Silas tipped his cowboy hat and backtracked toward the house. Cora's heart pounded, the same beat banging inside her head. Mr. Gordon waited until Silas drove away before instructing her to enter the back door.

"Now where is the statue?" He pushed her through the kitchen.

"Upstairs." She dragged her feet as she led him to her room, her brain mush when she needed it sharp. What was she supposed to do now? If she gave him the statue, Signora Pimonte would understand, but he still wouldn't let her go.

Gordon shoved her toward the bed where the *Madre e Figlia* lay. He snatched it before Cora could recover.

"She's a beauty." Mr. Gordon caressed the pink marble, then turned an ugly grin on her. "And you are not."

He aimed the gun at her heart. Cora tried to stand, but dizziness made the room spin around her. She stumbled forward and Gordon pulled the trigger.

Silas dove at the gunman as the gun blast pounded his ears. Was he in time?

They landed on the floor with a thunk and he sank a fist into the man's cheek, rendering him unconscious. Then he scrambled for Cora, who lay a few feet away in a crumpled heap. He lightly ran his hands over her arms, then cupped her cheek. "Are you all right? Tell me you're okay."

"Silas?" She looked up at him with the bluest of eyes, then pain scrunched her face and she touched her hand to her side. Blood. "I think …"

"Shh." Silas examined the wound through the tear in her dress. A crease. Deep, but it didn't go through her gut. "You're going to be fine, my darling."

She gave a ghost of a smile and closed her eyes. "Gordon wanted … the statue. I think … he killed Signora Pimonte."

He glanced over at the unconscious man. Good thing he'd punched him while given the chance. Silas shuddered. He hadn't seen the gun when he first spotted Cora and Gordon on the back lawn, but Cora's ashen face, the pain and fear in her eyes, and the gentleness of her request for him to leave … he'd known something was wrong.

To give the impression of leaving, he'd jogged to his truck, driven around the corner, and ran back to the house. He'd seen the gun, heard the pain in Cora's voice as she attempted to send him away. He hoped she knew he would never leave her, even if he had to make it look like he had.

"Thank you," Cora whispered, reaching for him with her unbloodied hand. "I—"

"Shh." He kissed her forehead. He needed to get Nick to see to her wound and her health in general. "Do you have rope anywhere?"

"In the barn."

"I'll call Detective O'Connor and Nick. You stay put." He pressed his handkerchief into her hand. "Keep this here on your side. I'll be back. I'll always come back for you. Now stay here."

He hadn't meant to say that aloud, but also didn't take the time to examine why he did, considering his own uncertain future. Instead, he hauled Gordon over his shoulder like a sack of grain and clomped down the stairs. He not-so-graciously dumped him in a kitchen chair while he used Mrs. Whittlebush's extension to place a call to Detective O'Connor. To find Nick, he tried Dr. Thompson's. He was still there, and Thompson agreed to drive him over.

Gordon was just beginning to wake when Silas finished his calls. Silas grabbed Gordon's upper arm and forced him to his feet. He'd take the man to the barn with him for that rope.

"Unhand me, sir." Gordon twisted, but Silas had no trouble keeping hold.

"Why did you shoot Cora Davis?" Silas directed him out the back door.

Gordon spat blood into the grass between the house and the barn. "She can't remember anything so you can't trust a thing she says. She should be in an asylum."

The man was a snake. "Just because Cora is a woman doesn't mean you can make up tales about her." Silas pushed him into the barn. "Now don't move or I'll punch you again."

By the time Silas located the rope, tied Gordon's hands, and led him back to the house, Detective O'Connor had arrived with his boss, a Chief Sebastian, as well as an Officer Caleb Palmson. Palmson escorted Gordon to the station with Dr. Thompson attending his bruises, while Detective O'Connor and Chief Sebastian stayed to question Silas and Cora.

Silas gave his statement as Nick treated Cora. Silas wanted to see her as soon as possible but had to wait until the lawmen were finished. He paced the kitchen, stopping only to note Nick's arrival before starting up again.

"Coffee?" Nick stoked the woodstove. "She'll be fine. We'll watch the wound so it doesn't get infected, but I have every belief it will heal perfectly."

It was a relief, but ... "What if Gordon lies about what happened? He already tried to plant ideas in my head about her being mentally unstable."

"That's not good." Nick glanced over his shoulder. "From what my sister told me, he used a similar tactic in Italy. That's why Signora Pimonte was concerned when Cora left for home so suddenly."

Silas crossed his arms. "Do you think Gordon killed Signora Pimonte?"

Nick closed the door to the firebox and shifted the kettle to a front burner before turning to face Silas, his expression dour. "I don't know. And, to be quite frank with you, all Cora said to me upstairs was to ask whether you were all right."

Warmth spread through Silas, and he hid a smile behind his hand.

The twinkle in Nick's eye said he saw it, anyway. "Now, what do I have to say to get it through your thick head that she cares about you?"

"I know it, I just—"

"Excuses." Nick rummaged through the cabinet for two cups. "I won't let this go."

"Give Cora time to heal." And Silas time to figure out whether providing for his family meant returning to the ranch. "I'll talk to her."

Nick gave a noncommittal agreement, and fortunately, Detective O'Connor and Chief Sebastian entered the kitchen, ending the conversation.

"We have all we need." Chief Sebastian spoke first.

The man had been a lowly policeman before Silas first left for his western adventure. Since then, Detective O'Connor had been awarded the special investigations position over Sebastian, and then Sebastian became chief. Didn't matter what position the man held. After the hard time he gave David and Adaleigh this summer, Silas didn't trust him.

"At this time"—Sebastian cleared his throat—"I don't think we'll level any charges against Miss Davis."

"What?" Silas stared at the arrogant man. Not choosing to charge Gordon would be bad enough, but charges against Cora? "She was held against her will and shot!"

"Silas." Detective O'Connor subtly shook his head.

"*Harumph.*" Sebastian's smile was sickeningly condescending. "Women notoriously exaggerate these types of claims, Mr. Ward, and Mr. Gordon was sure about what happened. He did not take her anywhere she did not lead him."

"That's a lie," Nick muttered.

"You weren't here, Mr. Ma-tron." The chief mispronounced the man's name badly, and Silas winced.

"It's *Doctor* Ma-trone-*ay*," Nick growled.

Sebastian adjusted his pants. "It doesn't change the fact that you weren't here."

"But I was." Silas crossed his arms. "And I know what I saw."

"She previously told you to leave, Mr. Ward, which means she was okay being alone with Mr. Gordon. I shouldn't wonder, since she's obviously free with her affection."

"Of all the—" Silas's anger was cut short by Nick's grip on his shoulder.

"I need to see to my patient's rest." Nick spoke with cold formality. "If you gentlemen would kindly allow me to see you to the door, since you have all you need for the case …"

Nick showed Chief Sebastian out of the kitchen. O'Connor stayed, rescuing the whistling kettle from the stove. Silas's whole body trembled with the emotion coursing through him.

Anger, frustration, concern. All churned like the lake outside, dredging up silt that darkened his mood. He pressed his palms onto the wooden table, trying to ground himself using the medium with which he spent the most time.

Detective O'Connor set a cup of coffee between Silas's hands. "You know how he treated David and Adaleigh, so this shouldn't surprise you."

"How did that man get into office?" Silas gritted his teeth.

"He's a politician who knows what to say and when to say it. He's also friends with the county sheriff. Don't worry, I'm learning to let Sebastian have his bluster, then make sure the paperwork is right." Detective O'Connor sipped his coffee. "To tell you that is not the whole reason I stayed. I have news about your other situation. I hesitate to tell you now since it is not good news, but you need to know."

Silas pulled out a chair, needing to sit. He wrapped his hands around his cup.

Detective O'Connor rested his hip against the table. "I've spoken with a county officer who connected me with several sellers who have sold items to your mother. Almost all of them have admitted to having to remind your mother to pay them. None, of course, admitted to her paying twice. But I've been a policeman long enough to know that half of them were lying about that, especially since those ones were down on their luck and needed the money."

"What about Cox?" His connection to the desk and secret letter singled him out in Silas's mind.

"His wife has already left him to live with his grown son in Milwaukee, so I expect him to rabbit soon. However, without proof, there's nothing you can do to get that money back."

Silas bowed his head. "I should have gone with Mom. Been the brawn and protection she needed."

"Your brother and father never went with her—does Marian?—so why should you? This is your mother's business." Detective O'Connor stroked his mustache. "But I suspect your mother's memory troubles have been going on longer than you realize."

"I concur." Reentering the kitchen, Nick made a beeline for the coffee carafé. "The reason I went to see Dr. Thompson today was to introduce myself as a doctor. It never pays to overstep as a young physician without having an older doctor's blessing. He welcomed me to help him out while I'm here, including speaking with your mother regarding her memory."

"Very smart, young man." Detective O'Connor gave Nick a nod of approval that colored Nick's neck.

"In the meantime, we're out the money my mom double paid." Silas pulled his watch from his pocket. "I need to get back to my work. If Marian can't find the receipts today, Buck offered to loan me the money to pay this latest seller. I'll ask him to join me as a witness to the paperwork."

"Wise." Detective O'Connor nodded. "Though asking that man for a loan is not."

Silas grimaced. He hadn't told anyone about his last visit to the bank. "Buck said the bank hasn't given a new loan in months. They're calling in loans instead, which is why so many around us are selling their furniture.

Adaleigh told us yesterday that with the number of people selling their belongings and losing their jobs, there's a chance the economy won't turn around like President Hoover insists it will. If that happens, our business won't make it to Thanksgiving. Not after the financial losses of the last few months."

"You'll lose your shop?" Cora stood in the doorway.

He hadn't meant for Cora to learn about the direness of their financial woes this way, but his heart warmed at the sight of her. He jumped to his feet, words caught in his throat. She wore a loose house dress, her hair in a braid over her shoulder and a twinge of color in her cheeks. Beautiful.

"Sit, Miss Davis." Detective O'Connor offered her his chair, and she sank into it with a whimper. "Dr. Matrone, can you pour her a cup?"

Nick watched her with an expert eye before he nodded.

If only Nick and Detective O'Connor would vanish so Silas could pour out his heart to Cora. He was ready, having begun the conversation with the two men. But where would it lead? He didn't want to lose Cora, not after she could have died. Yet that's what could happen if he laid the options before her. She might not wish to risk her heart on someone who could be gone from Crow's Nest for a year ... or two.

He bowed his head, tried to pray, but he didn't trust God to answer in the way he wanted Him to—that money would somehow descend from on high, that Cora would instantly be healed and still wish to stay here, with him. Of course, it *could* happen just that way, but Silas didn't have the faith that it would.

Nick patted his shoulder and invited Detective O'Connor into the hall.

As soon as the two left, Silas reached across the table for Cora's hand. "I don't think I'll make enough with my carpentry to support my family.

Several of the men are already planning to go up to the lumber camps this winter. I'm considering going west."

Her eyes lit up—not what he expected. "You can ranch again? I'm happy for you."

"I don't want to leave."

"But you can provide for your family by doing something you love. How many men get that choice? Especially right now."

Silas stared at her.

"I know your family will miss you. You won't have to leave before the Harvest Festival, will you? Nettie will still get her dance?"

"I'll be there. I won't let Nettie miss her dance." He'd ask Cora to dance, too, but why was she being so agreeable about him leaving? His heart stuttered. Did she plan to leave, too?

"Many men are in the same position, Silas. Adaleigh was saying David is considering going up to the camps this winter." Cora's hand rested on his. "You're showing your care for your family, even if you aren't present."

Silas wove their fingers together. "And you? Will you stay in Crow's Nest this winter?" Did he have a hope of returning one day to find her here? Or did going west sacrifice ... everything.

"I don't know. Now that Mr. Gordon is in jail and the trouble past, I can pursue getting well. Perhaps I can convince Signore Camposano to allow me to return despite my headaches and dizziness. I didn't fall because of them, after all. I'll write to him to determine my next steps."

Where did that leave them? "I only want your happiness."

"And I yours, Silas Ward."

There was a finality to their words. Nothing could come of their attraction to one another. Not now, with both of them aiming for opposite sides of the world. Silas would never forget Cora Davis or these days with her that could never turn into a future together.

"Do you know when you must leave?" Cora asked.

He should have released her hand, but he couldn't make himself.

"Not yet." Of course, there was always a chance he wouldn't need to go, but it would take a miracle. Anyway, if he didn't take the job now, the opportunity to work at the ranch would slip away.

"Then there's still time to solve the mystery of the secret letter. Tante will be anxious once she hears what happened with Mr. Gordon, so I should be here when she returns. But may I visit another day this week to work on the letter?"

"What about tomorrow?" He couldn't go a day without seeing her, not when each might be their last.

CHAPTER THIRTEEN

Tuesday, September 30

Cora situated herself on the wooden stool in Silas's workshop, Claude's letter before her. In the far corner, Silas assembled the bedframe he'd created. An uneasy silence settled between them and had her attempting to think of a way to bring up their conversation from yesterday. It took until midnight last night for her to realize why she felt so melancholy over it when she should be happy for him. He would get to return to his favorite place, and with Henry Gordon in jail, perhaps she could return to her archaeology. Only now, she wished Silas had suggested she go west with him instead.

How brazen a thought was that?

There was no way for her to go alone with him unless they were married. Was she truly thinking of hitching herself to a cowboy for the rest of her life? Going from avoiding all cowboys to contemplating marrying one was quite a turn around. Too big to take lightly. Was she so drawn to his protection that she conveniently forgot all the other reasons for not wanting anything to do with cowboys? Exhibits A and B being her father and grandfather, the two cowboys who left her mother and grandmother to face their futures alone.

Cora lit her low candle and held the letter over it in order to better study the watermark. She had a feeling the two horses of the seal told more than how to open the desk's secret drawer. She looked through her magnifying glass.

Silas wasn't like her father and grandfather. He'd returned to take care of his family.

But he was leaving her.

Ugh! Cora rubbed her forehead. A headache had bloomed overnight.

"Are you okay?" Silas's low rumble beside her caused her to open her eyes. "The sawdust can't be good for you, and the letter can wait."

Oh, her heart was a goner. Before she could think of words to say, the crunch of footsteps approaching had Silas putting distance between them.

"Ward?" A man's voice called from outside.

"In here, Buck."

Buck nodded at Cora as he removed his fedora, then turned to Silas. "Did you find the receipts?"

Receipts?

Silas shook his head. "They aren't here. Marian and I looked everywhere."

"I'm sorry." Buck hung his hat on the coat rack by the door. "I can loan you enough to pay this most recent seller. We have to put an end to this happening, or you'll be over your head in debt."

"How can I?" Silas demanded. "We can't prove anything. At this rate, every one of the sellers from the past three months could demand a repayment. Those receipts are the only hope of saving our business."

Buck placed his hands on the band of his trousers, holding his coat open. "There may be another way, but it means getting Cox to admit to what I'm pretty sure he's done. Doing."

Silas's countenance darkened. "What are you talking about?"

Buck shot a glance at Cora. "I've had one of my men following him, and he met with Greg Alistar this morning. I believe he means to leverage you."

Cora's ears burned at the words Silas let loose under his breath. While not uncouth words, as she heard from many of the men with whom she worked, they hissed like a branding iron.

Buck appeared unfazed. "Only time will tell what additional rumors those two are cooking up."

Additional ... Goodness! They'd already dragged her reputation through the mud trying to hurt Silas. What else would they do to blackmail him? What could she do to shield him?

The thought stunned her. She wanted to protect Silas just as he desired to protect her.

"When we deliver the payment to this most recent seller," Buck was saying, "I want to press him about whether he knows Robert Cox or any of the other sellers who have demanded more money. Too many sellers have the same idea to scam your mother because she's forgetful. She's become an easy target."

Silas rested his palms on the stool beside him, as if he needed to anchor himself. "You'll go with me to deliver the payment?"

"Absolutely." Buck gave a firm nod. "It might be wise to pay Alistar a visit afterward." Cora flinched at the newspaperman's name.

Silas bowed his head. "I'm not sure I can be civil toward the man after he attacked Cora's character."

Yes, she had to figure out a way to help him.

"I heard." Buck's gaze snapped to hers. "Considering the source, I doubt there is any substance to the rumors. Have they negatively affected you, Miss Davis?"

She felt Silas's attention, too, and she shook her head, though her cheeks reddened. The people she'd met thus far had the same reaction as Buck, save for the town doctor. And, since she'd battled such rumors in her career, she tried not to let them bother her. What did anger her, however, was how they affected Silas ... that the newspaperman was using her to get to him. It was unconscionable.

"And your aunt?" Buck asked. "Has she treated you well despite the negativity circulating about you?"

Cora startled. "How did you know she—"

Buck chuckled. "I'm good at recognizing facial similarities. You and Mrs. Whittlebush share the same chin."

They did, but few people thought them related, seeing as how different they looked. She focused on his implied slight of Tante. "Of course she has treated me as she always has, and to think otherwise is a gross misjudgment of her."

"I'm glad for it." Buck smiled. "I like her very much and expected no less."

Her ruffled feelings calmed. Maybe Buck wasn't as bad as everyone claimed. Smooth, and she didn't quite trust him. But perhaps he did not seek to do ill.

"It's a regular gathering." Detective O'Connor ducked into the workshop. He ignored Buck as he acknowledged both her and Silas. "Mrs. Whittlebush explained where to find you. I have bad news to share."

More bad news? The muscles in her neck tightened.

Silas leaned against the worktable beside her and stuffed his hands into the pockets of his denim trousers. "Gordon was released, wasn't he?"

"What's this?" Buck stepped forward, keeping himself in the circle of conversation despite Detective O'Connor's cold shoulder.

Cora couldn't leave Buck in the dark, not after the help he offered and kindness he'd shown. "A colleague thought to steal a gift from a friend. One worth quite a bit of money." What if she sold the statue in order to help Silas's family? Surely, Signora Pimonte would approve.

"Uh-uh." Silas whirled, bending to glare into her eyes. "I see those wheels turning. You are not using your gift to appease anyone. Neither the man who attacked you nor people who would take advantage of an old, forgetful lady. Is that clear?"

She jerked her chin up. "It's my statue. I'll do just as I—" Her bluster faded. He'd read her mind. "How ..." He cocked his head and tears smarted. He cared about her. It was good Detective O'Connor and Buck were here, or she'd throw herself into Silas's arms. A safer place she couldn't imagine.

Detective O'Connor cleared his throat. "Gordon's word carried more weight than either of yours with the chief."

Of course it did. "What does that mean?"

"It means you're still in danger." After addressing her, Silas whirled to face the detective. "The man shot her and tried to kidnap her. How am I supposed to keep her safe if I can't stay in Crow's Nest?"

Buck stepped between Silas and the detective, a hand to Silas's chest.

Detective O'Connor's eye twitched. "I plan to find Mr. Gordon and make sure he understands he's to leave Miss Davis alone. Beyond that, we have to hope to catch him before he strikes again."

If she didn't give away the statue, Cora had to hide it as soon as possible. She wouldn't let anyone steal it.

"I won't accept that." Silas swiped Buck's hand away. "Cora came here to heal, to get better. Not be in a position to be attacked again."

Cora's pulse picked up speed, and the pain in her head exploded against her skull. The floor tilted beneath her feet, and her stomach rolled like waves crashing into a cliff. Without a word to any of the men, she dashed outside and didn't stop until she reached the lake. The fresh air and open sky.

Before the earthquake, life had been normal. Not easy or simple, but good. She loved her life, her job, the people she met along the way. Even Mr. Gordon had seemed like an okay chap. Now everything had been upended, and she couldn't make the world right itself.

Lord, what am I supposed to do?

Though he itched to run after her, Silas finished his conversation with Buck and Detective O'Connor, set up a day later in the week to pay the seller, then followed Cora out to the wharf. She stood silhouetted against the gray-blue of the sky and turquoise of the water. A solitary figure. There was no doubt in his mind after talking with Buck that he needed to contact Anchorman to accept the position out West. His family wouldn't have enough to make it through the winter with the way these sellers were draining them dry.

Then there was Cora. She was in danger as long as Gordon was loose. He couldn't let her face that danger alone, so he'd deliver the bedframe tonight, and tomorrow, he'd paint Mrs. Whittlebush's porch so he could keep an eye on them. Hopefully, Detective O'Connor would catch up to Gordon before Silas finished the project or left for the ranch. The porch wasn't a paying project—he'd never accept money from either

Mrs. Whittlebush or Cora—but there had to be a way to both provide for his family and protect Cora, at least until he left Crow's Nest.

He rested his forearms on one of the posts that held the wharf's planks in place and stared out at the water. Choppy waves splashed his boots. Not large, but not smooth sailing either. Fog hovered over the middle of the lake, and clouds dodged the sun.

"If I don't have Signora Pimonte's statue, then Mr. Gordon would leave me alone," Cora said without looking at him.

"I don't think so. He smashed the bucchero over your head and tried to kill you. He can't let you tell anyone about that."

"Except no one believes me." She huffed. "They'd rather believe that newspaperman's rumor that you and I ..."

"Alistar likes his power." Silas folded his arms and turned so that he leaned his back against the post. "So does Sebastian. Likely, Gordon and Cox, too. However, don't let them take something that means a lot to you just to appease them. That statue may or may not have financial value, but it does have memory. It's not just a *thing*. You taught me that. There is a story behind it. It is infused with the memory and love of a woman who considered you her daughter."

Tears filled Cora's eyes. Her lips trembled.

He cupped her cheek, bringing her to face him. "We're going to find a way through this." *I could take you with me*. The knife in his heart twisted.

She nodded, winced.

"Your head." Silas ran his thumb over her brow, then drew her to his side, where he wished she could stay. "Let's get you home."

After he left Cora in Mrs. Whittlebush's capable hands, he returned to his workshop to finish the bedframe. He took all his emotion out on the wood so that by mid-afternoon, he loaded it into the truck with Nick's help, and they left together to deliver it.

They'd barely crossed the river out of Crow's Nest when Nick brought up Silas's mother. "I helped her in the kitchen today and used it as an opportunity to get an understanding of her current condition."

Silas's pulse hammered. With everything else going on, he'd accepted her forgetfulness as just that. What if it was more? Something serious?

"Have you noticed your mother losing consciousness? Fainting? Anything like that?"

Silas tightened his grip on the steering wheel. "Sounds more like something Cora would experience."

Nick gave a slow nod. "One of the conditions I considered for Cora was a type of apoplexy. I don't believe she has it. However, it may be true for your mom. An attack may not have happened when you could see it, but it would explain the intense episodes of confusion followed by normalcy. Dementia tends toward a continual decline, which, from what you and Marian have told me, doesn't appear to be the case."

Apoplexy? Dementia? "What does that mean?"

"I'll mention it to Dr. Thompson, of course. But there isn't a way to predict an attack. As I told Cora regarding her condition, imaging of the brain is still being developed. Scans just aren't clear enough for us to see anything other than bone."

"So there's nothing to be done. One day she could just ..." Silas couldn't say the word *die*.

"Unfortunately, yes." Nick sighed in that particular way of doctors delivering bad news. "However, that's the case for any of us, Silas. I've seen seemingly healthy young men die in an accident and frail old ladies outlive all their friends. It's why you shouldn't hide your feelings for Cora."

Silas glared at him.

Nick chuckled but let the topic go.

They delivered the bedframe, and Silas immediately went to the electric company to pay the bill with the money from the sale. It left him with enough to feel comfortable giving tomorrow to Mrs. Whittlebush's porch. It would take more than a day, but perhaps he'd get another job before the bedframe money ran out. In fact, he might as well start on the porch while there was still light to be had.

He left Nick with his mom, grabbed his tools, and pointed the truck toward Mrs. Whittlebush's house.

When he arrived, Mrs. Whittlebush explained Cora was not receiving visitors though confided that she couldn't get Cora to tell her what was wrong. Silas wouldn't tell her about the morning if Cora wished to keep silent. So Silas worked, once again taking his convoluted emotions out on the boards. Mrs. Whittlebush tried to feed him, but Silas refused. His stomach wouldn't tolerate anything until his brain sorted things out. He'd sanded most of the porch floor by the time the sun began to set in earnest and he still had no answers.

"Losing daylight, Ward," David called as he and Adaleigh approached.

Silas glanced up. He hadn't heard a car.

"Such a beautiful evening, I walked her home." The smile in David's voice showed his love for Adaleigh but churned Silas's gut.

"Where's Cora?" Adaleigh asked. "I'm surprised she is not sitting out here with you."

"You and me both." Did he say that out loud? He tossed his sandpaper aside. Only five more planks of the porch floor left to work. He wanted nothing more than to spend what time he had left in Crow's Nest with Cora. He scrubbed his hands over his face and through his hair. He needed to deflect before either David or Adaleigh figured out his train of thought. "I also might have gone off on your uncle, Martins."

David chuckled. "I might have done the same thing when Adaleigh's life was in danger."

Silas's fist closed of its own accord.

"You two talk. I'm going to find Cora." Adaleigh reached up and kissed David's cheek. "Good night."

David turned quickly, catching her lips in a kiss that made Silas wish for Cora. He folded his arms and turned toward the lake. Saturday evening, he hadn't been able to stop himself from holding her when it appeared her pain would tear her apart. He shouldn't have, though, not if he couldn't follow through and marry her. He wouldn't even ask her for a promise or a long engagement. Who knew how long he'd have to be out West?

The screen door opened and closed, then David stood beside him. "Got any sandpaper for me?"

Silas dug in his tool bag and handed a rectangle to him. "With the grain." Then they knelt side by side and sanded the worn wood in the corner of the porch. Minutes stretched and Silas waited for the proverbial shoe. David aimed to say something, so why didn't he just get it out of the way?

David leaned back on his heels. "I met Nick—what was his last name?—at the Wharfside today. He was having supper with Dr. Thompson. What do you think of him?"

"About as annoying as you are." Silas glared at his friend. "I know what you're doing."

"Escorting my girl?" David raised his eyebrows.

Silas scowled. "She's inside already."

"Fine, then. I'm helping my friend." David slid the sandpaper along the plank. The scratch of the paper on wood usually soothed, but Silas had to hold back his irritation.

"You never help me with my woodworking."

David laughed. "That's not what I'm talking about, and you know it."

Silas grunted.

"Adaleigh told me you're probably leaving. Taking your old job out West to provide for your mom, sister-in-law, and nieces."

That was the other task he'd accomplished today. After leaving Nick at home, he'd sent a telegram to accept the ranch job. "Just waiting for my old foreman to tell me when to be there."

"What about Cora?"

Silas finished sanding his plank and started on the last one. What could he say when he didn't even know the answer?

"You're an idiot, Ward."

"Don't I know it?"

"You're going to let her get away."

Silas sat back and tipped up his Stetson. "I suppose you think I should convince her to stay in Crow's Nest."

David grinned. "It worked for me. Granted, Adaleigh had to go away for a couple months first, but it made the reuniting all the sweeter."

Silas rolled his eyes, but it was all for show. He was happy for David. Honest. But for himself? Then he remembered how Nick had talked about his own parents and said something similar about their two-year separation. His irritation morphed into sorrow. "It's not fair to ask her to stay when I'm leaving."

"Why not take her with you?"

"Ask an unmarried woman to journey west with me? Are you mad?"

"Who said she'd be unmarried?"

"I can't have a wife on the ranch."

"Silas, you have to decide if you want Cora in your life. Put everything else aside, because if you let her go now, you'll never get another chance. I s'pose there's always a possibility things could work out in the future, but if you think she's the woman God has for you, step out and tell her how you feel. There may be a solution for you that you can't think of but she can. What's that verse say about a threefold cord not being broken?"

"Ecclesiastes." Silas sighed. "You're right."

"Naturally. But pray about it first."

"And in the meantime, what of protecting her?"

"From the man who tried to take that statue from her?" David handed Silas his sandpaper. "Adaleigh filled me in this morning after she got the whole story from Mrs. Whittlebush. And a rumor he was released?"

"Yes." Silas breathed deeply. "I can camp on Cora's porch to keep her safe for a couple days, but what happens when I leave?"

"She goes with you."

Silas rolled his eyes, the tangle between the complications and joy at that thought irritated him. "And what of her health? It seemed the strain of learning about Gordon being released triggered an episode for her. She's in no state to travel. And if she stays there's Mrs. Whittlebush and Adaleigh to consider. As long as they're around Cora, they won't be safe either."

"Let's plan for now, then over the next few days, work out a plan for when you leave." David tapped his knuckles on the sanded wood. "I'll take tonight, but I have to be on my boat before dawn."

"I'll see if Nick will take a turn." The help of a friend calmed him. "Thank you for helping me think of a way we can end the threat to Cora."

"Be sure to talk to her. We both love intelligent women, and we'd be wise to listen to them."

Love.

Silas's heart skipped a beat. Did he truly *love* Cora?

David clapped Silas's shoulder. "If you're asking yourself the question, then I'd say the answer is *yes.*"

Cora should have turned the key in her door. Tante respected her request to be left alone. Adaleigh did not. Sure, the first time she knocked and Cora told her to go away, she did as Cora asked. But ten minutes later, she barged right in without so much as a by your leave. She toed the door closed behind her and set a tray on the bed.

Tea and tiny sandwiches.

Cora's lips twitched in a smile.

"Don't tell me I'm going to eat this all by myself." Adaleigh sat on the bed and poured two cups of tea, the spicy scent of ginger wafting in the air. "Grandma Martins always says tea solves everything, and I'm inclined to believe her."

Cora held the steaming cup to her nose. She took a sip. The ginger settled the rest of her nausea. "Thank you."

"I know how it feels to not know when the danger will show itself. How is your sleep?"

"Other than last night, fine. There's something Henry Gordon and I argued about that I wish I could remember. If I could think of that, I feel as though I'd have the missing piece of the puzzle."

Adaleigh chuckled. "I envy you the forgetting. But what has helped you remember so far?"

Cora considered the times the memories returned. Each had occurred during high emotions and usually in the company of Silas. Heat unrelated to the tea flooded her. "Silas. Silas helped me remember."

Adaleigh nodded as if that was the answer she expected, and that it was perfectly normal. "And how did he help you remember?"

"Because even though a storm raged inside, I felt ..." How to describe it?

"Safe? Secure? As though he provided a refuge for you where the uncertainty and turmoil couldn't harm you?"

"Yes." Cora set her half-empty cup on the tray and leaned forward. "That's exactly it! He's seen me at my worst and hasn't judged me or tossed me aside. He—"

"Loves you?"

Cora opened her mouth to protest but stopped herself. Did he? "But he's leaving, which is strange to say. I was the one leaving, and now he is. To provide for his family, so I cannot begrudge his choice. In fact, I support him completely. I just wish—"

"That you could go with him?"

Cora stared at her. "How are you reading my mind?"

Adaleigh laughed. "It's written plain as a book on your face. You love him, too."

Hope tried to sprout, but she shook it away. "I don't know that it matters."

"Of course it matters. I think he's the key to unlocking that last memory. I'm not Dr. Matrone, but I have studied psychology."

"I've had no more memories return, not since—" *his kiss*. And she wasn't repeating that if there wasn't a hope for a future, no matter how amazing it had been. Come to think of it, the first time her memories returned had been when he'd held her in his arms after she nearly tumbled into Lake Michigan. "I don't think he's the answer this time."

Adaleigh sighed. "All right. We'll think of something else. How is your head feeling?"

"The tea calmed my stomach, but my head feels like a weight on my shoulders. At least the dizziness is better. What if ... what if ..." She couldn't finish the thought that had been circling her like a tiger circling its prey.

She took the cup to finish it, but Adaleigh stopped her by refilling it from the teapot. "What if ... the headaches don't go away? What if you have to stay?"

Cora blinked against her tears. Hearing Adaleigh say the words aloud ... "What if I will be better enough to return to my work?"

"Are you considering staying with Mrs. Whittlebush?" Adaleigh lowered her voice in a conspiratorial way that eased the tightness in Cora's chest. "I figured out she's your aunt, by the way. There is a slight family resemblance."

Somehow, Cora wasn't surprised, not after Buck pointed it out. "I wouldn't need to hide our relationship any longer if I resigned from my work in archaeology."

"You'd miss it." The way Adaleigh said it, that it was fact, not question, caused Cora to open up even more.

"I would. I suppose I could help Mrs. Ward and Marian at their shop, but I wouldn't ask them to employ me, which means I would need to find work elsewhere. Tante's sewing work plus the money I sent home made enough for her, but if I stay and people stop buying new clothes, then we'll be in the same position as the Ward family." Cora pressed a hand to the throb in her temple. "I wish we could know whether things would improve or not."

"My lawyer, Mr. Binitari, has been keeping his ear to what has been transpiring in New York and Washington. Buck Wilson has, too. Some are saying it will improve, but others are saying it will only get worse before it gets better. I think we need to plan for today, which means there is not a guarantee for tomorrow's provision. Except for God. His eye is on us no matter what happens. But I think you know this. You're living the uncertainty."

"If I married, my husband would have to take on the care of both me and Tante. I can't do that to Silas."

Adaleigh looked away, but Cora saw her smile.

"What?"

"You're thinking about marrying him."

"Of course I—d" Cora covered her face. "I'm so embarrassed I said that aloud."

Adaleigh grinned. "Don't be. It tells me what I needed to know. You do love him. In fact, you love him enough to let him go so he won't be burdened by your circumstances."

"How is it you can sum up my scattered thoughts so well?"

"I have a degree in rhetoric." Adaleigh shrugged. "I want you to think on another question. What if, by keeping the burden to yourself, you're robbing him of a chance of sharing his burden? And vice versa? Aren't two better than one?"

Cora opened her mouth, though who knew what would have come out if Adaleigh hadn't held up her hand.

"Don't answer right now. Pray about whether you're the person God has to share in Silas's burdens and he in yours."

"What if it doesn't matter? What if Silas doesn't ... want me?" Those dratted tears again.

"Oh, Cora." Adaleigh scrambled to her side and hugged her fiercely. Thank goodness she didn't give platitudes and promises. No false hope either. Because they couldn't be sure what Silas would say. If Cora put her heart before him, he might well reject her.

Chapter Fourteen

Thursday, October 2

Silas stood outside his family's shop and stared at the yellow telegram in his hands. Three days.

"Is that news from your old foreman?" Marian appeared in the double doorway opening to the shop. The stiff wind blew her brown hair loose from its coil.

Silas massaged his neck, a headache growing though it was early morning, and he whispered a prayer for Cora. She dealt with these almost every day. How did she survive? Today Nick had gone to pick up Cora and bring her here to work on Claude's letter while Silas would meet Buck to deliver the money in an hour.

"This means you really are going back west, aren't you?" Marian shook her head. "The girls are going to miss you, but I understand. There just isn't work here in the winter unless you want to go up to the lumber camps, most of which have also moved west."

Silas merely nodded. What else could he say? Marian's parents worked for a lumber camp, so she knew all about that work. He folded the telegram. Anchorman told Silas the job was his and to arrive as soon as possible. He couldn't disappoint Nettie, so he wouldn't leave until after the Harvest Festival Dance on Saturday.

The only hitch in his plan? He didn't have the money to get to the ranch. Not after this seller took the last of their profits. Despite the loan from Buck, there would be no money, even for groceries, if he didn't sell one more piece of furniture or Marian sold something from the shop. And there had been no customers all week.

"What about Cora? Are you leaving her behind too?"

Silas bristled at Marian's accusatory tone. "I don't know that it's any of your business."

"I think it is." Marian crossed her arms. "If she's to be family, you know we'll look after her until you return."

Of course Cora and Marian would look after each other. Mom and Mrs. Whittlebush, too. He'd thought of every angle. The combination of the Ward and Whittlebush gardens would provide enough produce for the winter—and he'd go fishing with David once more before he left to stock the cellar with salted fish. So his family, whether or not that included Cora and Mrs. Whittlebush, shouldn't starve before he could send money home. To assure himself of that, he wouldn't take anything with him when he left, not food, not money. He'd hop a boxcar, like so many others were doing these days. And that was another reason he couldn't bring Cora, nor would he leave her behind with nothing but promises he might not be able to keep.

"There's something to be said for hope, Silas." Marian left her post in the shop doorway to lay a hand on his arm. "I'd suffer years without Zachariah by my side if I knew he'd return one day."

Silas adjusted his Stetson as emotion clogged his throat. Zee would have said the same thing had he been the one to lose Marian. Thankfully, the familiar rumble of the Wards' truck gave him an excuse to end the conversation. Marian patted his arm and left him to greet Cora and Nick alone.

Cora had been quiet the past several days. Even as he finished painting Mrs. Whittlebush's porch, Cora chose to stay inside. Whether she preferred Nick or David's company, he couldn't say, but she didn't want his. She hadn't even been back to look over the letter since the day they learned Gordon was released from jail. Anticipation at seeing her and perhaps spending an hour in her company wrestled with the logic of letting her go.

As for Henry Gordon, they'd heard nothing of him. It was as if the man had disappeared after being released from jail. Just how long should they keep watch over Cora before they assumed Gordon had given up and gone away? Likely, when Silas left in three days, which meant Cora would be on her own. He didn't like it, but what choice did he have?

Take her with you.

It's not fair to her.

He shoved the same old argument away as Cora emerged from the truck.

Nick sauntered around the front. Lifted a hand to Silas. "Mind if I borrow the truck the rest of the morning? I need to pay Dr. Thompson a visit. He wants a second opinion on something."

Not having to share Cora's attention with Nick Matrone? "Take it for the day." Buck would drive them to drop off the money, so he wouldn't need a car for that errand either. And Marian would be here when he left.

"I'll replace the gasoline I use." Nick tipped his bowler and returned to the driver's seat.

Cora narrowed her eyes. "If he's replacing gasoline, just how hard up are you, Silas? I know I shouldn't ask, but after you refused payment for the porch and refused to entertain the idea of me selling the statue, I think I deserve to know."

Silas pinned his lips closed and stalked back through the shop. Cora followed on his heels, barely acknowledging Marian as they marched past her.

"Silas Ward, you stop this instant." She grabbed his arm before he reached the workshop. "You have been closed-mouthed ever since Henry Gordon showed up. You used to tell me what was going on. Am I no longer your friend?"

"Not if I'm leaving." He didn't mean to say the words so harshly. But with her so close, he wanted to hold her, kiss her, and that was the last thing he could do.

"You know that newspaperman is making the most of it, saying you discovered I'm seeing other men, namely Nick, or speculating you're running because I told you I'm with child." Her lovely cheeks turned red, but she barreled on. "Obviously, there's no truth to any of it. You and I promised we'd be honest with each other. We've always spoken the truth, even if we didn't realize the judgment we passed while speaking it. Now all there is around us is hearsay. I want the truth, Silas. Why have you stopped talking with me?"

"Because you—" He spotted Marian peering out the back door of the shop, so he grabbed Cora's hand and tugged her through his workshop, out back, and down to the lake where they could have some semblance of privacy. It also gave him a moment to rethink his words. He wouldn't blame Cora, even if she'd chosen not to keep him company while he painted her aunt's porch.

"Because I ...?" Cora pulled her hand free as their feet hit the old planks. "Because I avoided you all week?"

"Why did you?" The question slipped out.

Cora twirled her fingers in her scarf. Was she as scared as he was? Somehow it infused him with courage.

"The honest truth?" he said, looking out of the choppy water. White caps dotted the wide open blue. Even the horizon was an uneven line. Like the path he was about to tread. "Cora, I hate that I have to leave. I hate that I can't court you properly. I hate that a missing ledger book is costing us every cent we own. I have no choice but to go find work elsewhere. I can't take you with me, not when I have to ride the rails to get there. And I can't leave you here with a promise that someday I might return."

"Riding the rails—are you out of your mind?" Her voice shook ... with anger or fear, he couldn't tell. "You know how dangerous that is! Not to mention illegal. What if you get caught?"

He turned from the water to face her. "You're missing the important part."

She squared her shoulders. "I don't think I am. What if you—"

"What if I ... what? I don't survive the trip?" His voice rose as he took a step toward her. "I'm scared, too. I'm scared I can't provide for my family. I'm scared I can't provide for you. I'm scared I'm going to lose you no matter what I do."

She grabbed his arms, then, and reached up to press her lips to his. The power of it leveled him, and he let all the emotion he'd been holding back since he found her shot in her room pour through his kiss. His control slipped and he tried to rein it in, but the fear that gripped him wouldn't let go. He was leaving her, this woman he loved. And there was no surety he'd survive the trip west. Nor did he know how long he'd be gone, let alone if she'd still be in Crow's Nest, or even alive, if he could return.

"Ward! Cora!" Nick's frantic voice cut through the moment, and Silas broke the kiss. However, he kept Cora tucked close to him as they watched Nick run toward them, his face white. Cora trembled beside him.

"We'll face it together," Silas whispered. Cora nodded and leaned her head against his chest.

"It's Gordon." Nick's chest heaved as he reached them. "He was murdered. In exactly the way my sister found Signora Pimonte."

Cora sucked in a breath as she straightened. "That means Henry didn't kill her. Someone else did, and now they're here in Crow's Nest."

Nick bobbed his head. "And likely tying up loose ends."

Silas's knee bounced as Buck drove them to the meeting place. He hated leaving Cora behind, but what choice did he have? Nick would stay by her side until he returned, and Silas had to pay the seller.

"I know where Greg Alistar will be after we're through here." Buck rested the wrist of his left hand on the steering wheel as he navigated the single bridge that led into and out of Crow's Nest.

Silas nodded. So much he needed to clear up before he left. So many ways to make sure his family, those he cared about, would remain safe while he was half a country away. He glanced at Buck's profile. Could the suave man sway Cora and steal her away? David had thought Buck would win Adaleigh before Adaleigh chose David. Was Cora at risk of being lured away from Silas, especially during his absence?

"You're staring at me Ward. Talk."

Honesty. He could manage that. "Will you look after my mother, sister, and nieces this winter?"

Buck shot him a glance. "You didn't mention Cora. Is she going with you, or are you scared I'll steal her away from you?"

Was he really that transparent? Silas watched out the window at the fields that separated the towns.

"Man, you're smitten. Not sure who's worse, you or Martins. The two of you, mooning over such intelligent women. Should be illegal. A fisherman and a cowboy getting such educated, traveled women like Adaleigh Sirland and Cora Davis. If Nick sticks around, he'll steal the next pretty stranger to visit Crow's Nest."

Silas snorted. "You could pick one of the pretty women who already live here."

Buck rolled his eyes. "Not that there aren't several, your sister-in-law included. Don't get all defensive—I'm not looking for a girl from Crow's Nest. It's too small a place for a guy like me."

Silas crossed his arms. "A guy like you."

"There's a reason Martins's uncle wants to arrest me, and it isn't my charm. Or maybe it is." He chuckled. "But you aren't me. You provide Cora something no one else in Crow's Nest can give her. Not that I've been eyeing her, but since her safety and reputation have been at stake, I've been paying attention. She talks to very few people, and when she does, her expression is closed. With you, she leans closer. She thinks you're safe."

Silas absorbed Buck's observations, the hint of rebuke that laced his words putting him on edge. "Thinks I'm safe?" Was there doubt when he only desired to protect her?

"You're leaving." Buck turned down another country road. "She's begun to trust you and now..."

Silas clamped his mouth shut. Buck Wilson was not the man he wanted to take relationship advice from, but nor could he deny the truth of what he said.

"I'll keep an eye on your family, Ward. And Cora and her aunt. I always have."

Humbled, all Silas could say was, "Thank you."

Five minutes later, Buck turned the car onto a quiet lane leading up to a dark house. "He said he'd meet me out front."

Silas scanned the yard. Golden leaves tumbled along the grass, but nothing else moved. "I think it's deserted."

Buck opened his door. "Let's have a look around."

The house was definitely empty and had been for a while, based on the dust that covered the bare floors. Silas and Buck could only peer through the downstairs windows, but it appeared the family had left nothing behind. The garden out back had been harvested. Not even a stray dog hunkered in the shed behind the house.

A car rumbled to a stop beside their own, and a rotund man stepped out. Buck moved in front of Silas, his shoulder keeping Silas behind him, and his hand went to his back where Silas realized the man kept a gun. Was this a money exchange or a shootout?

"You bring my money?" the large man asked, keeping his trench coat closed and his hat low.

"You're not the owner of this property and therefore not the seller we're meeting." Buck cleared his pistol from the holster but kept it hidden behind his back. "In fact, you, sir, are Robert Cox."

Silas schooled his surprise. Having never gone with his mother on any of her buying trips, he never would have recognized the original owner of the desk. A warning bell sounded in his head, the kind he got right before something spooked a herd, triggering a stampede. Something was off, and they needed to get out of here. Now.

"Buck." He pressed a hand to Buck's shoulder. "We need to—"

"You still owe money." Cox freed a shotgun from the folds of his coat.

"To whom?" Buck leveled his pistol at the man.

"Me." And Cox fired.

"There's something about these horses." Cora tapped Claude's letter. After Silas left, she'd relit her candle and brought the hidden map to life. Now she roved her magnifying lens over top of it, a mildly effective way to keep her from thinking about Henry Gordon and his murder.

"What have you found so far?" Nick sat on the stool beside her, feet crossed at the ankles, arms crossed. He seemed content, but not excited, about being here. Not like Silas, who had infused energy into the search. But Nick would stay glued to her side until Silas returned. Especially now that they suspected Signora Pimonte's killer was here.

Nick had relayed that Mr. Gordon had been found in one of the abandoned buildings on Main Street, one that had been destroyed by the Spring tornado. Chief Sebastian immediately thought Cora a suspect, but with Detective O'Connor present, Nick was able to provide more details. First, that Cora had been in someone's company at all times and therefore could not be the killer. And, second, that the bruising around the neck combined with the location of the gunshot wound in Gordon's back left side would suggest a taller man who could incapacitate from behind before shooting his victim. What he didn't add was that the wound pattern appeared identical to the description his sister gave of

Signora Pimonte's death. That information he shared only with Cora and Silas.

Cora blew out her candle and centered the magnifying glass over the words of Claude's letter. "He says, 'I confess, it will not be long before I join you,' and I can only think that means in the cemetery." She glanced at Nick. "Why would he include a map if not for that meaning? Did he think they would both die? Then why couldn't we find evidence of Martha?"

Nick shrugged. "What if it means that he will literally see her? What if they couldn't be together?"

"Why wouldn't they be able to be together?" She didn't mean to ask it of Nick, but of herself. Yet couldn't keep from asking the question aloud. "It was prior to the Civil War, so if one was white and the other black, even a freedman, they could not be together. Even today, they couldn't marry legally. Why else couldn't they be together?"

"Think of your own situation. Silas has to provide for his family, so you and he will be separated."

Her heart twisted. "If Silas were to write me in that circumstance—"

Nick leaned closer, as if sharing a secret. "*When* he will."

Cora sighed. "*If* he did, he wouldn't write something so cryptic and include a hidden map."

"So you think." Nick rubbed his chin.

"Fine. But what type of treasure would Silas put 'between us'?"

"Treasure could be money or something precious, like that statue. It could also be letters or ..." Nick wagged his finger at her. "Those rumors about you, that Silas is leaving because you're ... uh ... in the family way. Which, by the way, I've been a medical man long enough to know it isn't true, and half the women in Crow's Nest would agree with me."

Cora clenched her teeth as embarrassment washed over her.

"However, if that were the case with the people in your letter, and there was a baby—"

The cemetery. "A baby who died? A baby shunned by the mother's family so that it would have no respected burial?"

Nick uncrossed his legs. "I've seen it many times, but it doesn't answer how he knew where the mother would be buried."

"Nor that Claude was buried at the age of eighty-six." Cora blew out the candle. "I need to see the cemetery again."

He stood, blocking her way to the main door. "Not without Silas."

Cora considered the sun. Silas left only twenty minutes ago, and the ever-shortening day would be spent by the time he returned. She leveled a challenge at Nick. "You don't think you can protect me?"

"I'm scared of Silas, all right?" Nick adjusted his spectacles. "He's got more muscle than me, and if I let something happen to you, he'll pulverize me."

Cora pursed her lips. "I've never been afraid of danger. I make proper precautions and then face it head on."

"I hear a *but* coming from a mile away."

Cora set the candle and glass in her bag of supplies. "But in the past, I've only needed to worry about my own safety. Tante was tucked away here so no one over there could use her against me. Now everyone knows I have a connection to Silas, and Tante, and you, and ... a lot of people."

"So?" Nick prompted.

"So I'll stay put." She smoothed the letter on the table. It was pointless to keep her familial relationship with Tante a secret any longer. Once this was over, she'd let Tante shout the news wherever she'd like. Until then ...

Nick pressed a hand to her shoulder. "I'm glad you're being wise."

"Is it, though?" She looked up at him. "Being wise? Or am I deferring to Silas?"

"They aren't mutually exclusive."

"Maybe. Maybe not. But I—for all my independence, I respect Silas, and that's the reason I won't run off without him." She tapped her forefinger on the letter. "Maybe we can discern something else about this letter. I'm still stumped about Martha. There was no Martha anywhere near Claude's tombstone."

"Marta? The girl he wrote to?" Nick looked over her shoulder.

"Not Marta. Martha." She shifted the letter toward him.

"*Marta* is Italian." Nick scrubbed his lower lip. "I speak almost perfect English, but names trip me up at times."

"Marta." Cora stared at the letter, the implication working its way through her mind. "It's also the translation for *Martha* in German, which was likely Claude's nationality. However, in Swedish, *Marta* is the spelling of a nickname for *Margareta*. And in—"

"And all this means what?"

"Martha means *lady*. Margareta means *pearl*." Cora closed her eyes, picturing the tombstones surrounding Claude's. If his letter was cryptic, did he use code names as well? Did any of the tombstones belong to a lady or a woman named Pearl? Pain sliced through her head as she attempted to concentrate. She pressed the heels of her hands to her temples.

Nick's hand rested on her upper back. "What would Silas do if he were here?"

Heat warmed her cheeks.

"Ah, not something I'm willing to do, then." Nick gave her back a pat. "Maybe let's set the letter aside for a while and investigate the desk itself. It's still in the shop, right?"

"Unless it's been sold." Cora carefully secured the letter for safekeeping, then followed Nick across the yard and into the shop, the fresh air easing her symptoms.

"You have impeccable timing." Marian dashed up to them, looking as frazzled as Cora had ever seen her. "Can you mind the store? Mom is set on making some stew dish for dinner—she insists her husband and mine will be there—and the mother of a fellow student came by to tell me Nettie is beside herself about a project she made for the Festival this weekend. Something about it getting broken, so she won't leave school. I can't—"

"We can manage, Marian." Cora put her hands on Marian's shoulders. Good thing she hadn't followed her whim and dashed to the cemetery. She'd needed to be here for the Wards. "You go on and get Nettie. We'll mind the store and Mrs. Ward."

"I really like you, Cora." Marian sighed. "I wish Silas would ... it's not my place, but either way, I will miss your company when you move on."

Before Cora could react, Marian was gone, Nick calling after her to take the truck. Cora looked around at what she could do to help Marian when she realized Nick was staring out the back door, concern etched into his face. "Nick?"

"Mrs. Ward." He waved toward the house. "I'm concerned she's having an episode. I can't forsake my duty to you, but I'm a doctor and I took an oath."

"You mean she could be in danger?" Danger of dying?

"Most definitely. I have to check on her. What's a few priceless treasures when compared to a human life? Come with me."

Cora wasn't about to argue and followed Nick to the house. He knocked at the back door before pushing it open. The smell of fish and vegetables mingled with fresh bread. Cora's stomach rumbled. Nick waved her ahead of him, always the gentleman. Only, this time, she wished he hadn't been.

There on the floor lay Mrs. Ward.

Silas dodged behind Buck's car as if he dodged the hoof of a bronco. Maybe a wild bull would be more accurate, considering Robert Cox fired another blast into the side of Buck's car.

Beside him, Buck muttered something under his breath as he hauled Silas into the car and squealed the tires as he tried to outrun a third shot. It blew out the back window, spraying glass everywhere.

"What does he want?" Silas braced his hand on the dash as Buck took a curve too wide.

"Who knows, but obviously, he capitalized on the other family's misfortune to line his own pockets. My sources weren't as thorough as I expected. That will be investigated."

"We need a way out of this first." Silas glanced out the broken back window. "He's following us. We can't take him to my house, not with my—"

"Your women. Seriously, Ward. You're surrounded by them."

"I am, and I want to keep each one of them safe. We aren't bringing Cox anywhere near them."

"The Conglomerate Headquarters, then. I have a phone, so we can call my *friend,* Detective O'Connor."

Silas nodded and silently urged Buck to drive faster. Cox was gaining on them in his Buick. Over the bridge, into Crow's Nest, past the western side streets, left onto Main. Cox nosed their rear bumper with the front of his car.

"Does he not understand we'll hit pedestrians?" Buck shouted.

Silas cringed as Buck fought for control of the vehicle, people jumping out of the way of his swerving car. Cox slammed into them again, spinning the car like a top. It slammed into a gaslight pole, and then Cox was yanking Silas out of the car as screams echoed in Silas's ears.

"You're taking me to the desk." Cox shoved Silas into his own car. "We're loading it into your truck, and I'm taking it to a buyer I have lined up. He'll pay me enough to let me keep my house, my standing, and my wife until the banks straighten out."

His wife? "What about the other sellers?" Silas asked. Buck hadn't emerged from his damaged car. Was he unconscious? Dead? Cox accelerated away before Silas could be sure.

"What other sellers? The ones who supposedly had a problem paying your grandmother. Or was it your mother? The old lady. I cut them in on the deal. That last one didn't have the stomach for it and left before I could complete the transaction. Your mother was the checkbook I needed to keep my life together."

Silas was going to be sick. "Did your wife and son agree with you?"

"How dare you bring them into this?" Cox backhanded Silas. "My wife left me. If I can't keep my house, I'll lose her for good. Now we're getting the desk or I'll fire a shotgun blast into that girl you're having the fling with."

Cora? "What have you done with her?"

"Nothing. Yet. And I won't if you do everything I say."

Leverage. And this was exactly why Cora kept her relationship with her aunt a secret. Greedy men would use anything—or anyone—to get what they wanted.

How could he keep Cora safe?

As soon as they turned into the yard, Silas realized his truck was missing. If Cox wanted to drive the desk away in it, then they were stuck.

"I have my shotgun, so mind." Cox urged him out of the car with the muzzle.

Silas walked ahead of him toward the open doors to the store. Empty. Worry twisted in his stomach. What if whoever killed Gordon got to Cora and his family? Who cared about a desk then?

"Ah, there it is." Cox ran a hand over the shiny top. "Load it up."

"I need a hand." Silas stalled. Had Nick taken the truck somewhere? But he'd promised to stay and watch over Cora.

"You have help around here?" Cox peered down an aisle.

"Yes." Silas thumbed toward the rear, not knowing what else to do.

Cox followed with the shotgun. The workshop was empty, and Silas's hands began to shake. None of this was good.

"Where is everyone?" Cox looked around the empty yard. The last thing Silas wanted to do was take Cox near the house, and likely his mother, but he needed to know if everyone was okay. Or at least why the place seemed deserted.

He ran to the house, hoping to get there before Cox could do any damage, but Cox and his gun came directly behind him. Silas leapt up the two stairs in a single bound. Pushed open the back door. And stumbled to a stop as he reached the kitchen.

Nick bent over his mother, who lay unconscious on the floor. And Cora knelt beside them, tears in her eyes.

He latched on to her gaze, the only strength holding him upright. "Is she ..." And where were Marian and his nieces? "Is my mother ...?" Silas attempted the question a second time.

Nick glanced up. "She's breathing, thank God. I need to get her to a clinic or hospital. Your sister has the truck."

"No one is going anywhere until I get my desk." Cox cocked the shotgun.

Nick stood in one smooth motion, putting himself between Cox and everyone else. "You'll get nothing of the kind if I have to start cleaning up bodies. I'm a doctor, sir, and I suggest you stay out of my way."

The man blinked, allowing Silas to kneel beside Cora. "That's Cox. He wants the desk. The money demand was a ploy, a sham, to get money from Mom." He rested a hand on his mother's forehead. How had this happened? Was Cox behind the missing receipts?

His back bowed beneath the questions. Was he nothing but a lost boy playing dress-up in his cowboy hat?

Cora squeezed his arm. "I have an idea."

Silas gave a single nod, Cora's presence beside him strengthened him. He wasn't a kid. He was strong, capable. She made him remember that. He pressed his hand atop hers. How could he let her go? He wanted, no needed, Cora by his side. Not just now, always.

"Mr. Cox." Cora's sweet voice rang in his ear. She'd help him figure out what next step to take in order to appease Cox while Nick got Mom to the hospital. "I think you'd be interested to know that I came across a treasure map in the drawer of your desk."

Wait, what? "Cora, no." They didn't know if there even was a trea-sure.

She pressed her lips to his temple in the gentlest of kisses and whis-pered, "Trust me."

He did. With all his heart.

CHAPTER FIFTEEN

ora's heart—and head—pounded in time to her steps as she led Mr. Cox toward the workshop. She had no idea if this would work, but if it got Mrs. Ward the help she needed in time, then it would be worth it. Hopefully, Silas could see that, too, especially if anything went wrong with this half-baked plan of hers.

"You'll need my help." Silas! She'd left him in the kitchen, planning to distract Mr. Cox on her own.

Cora spun around. "But your mom ..."

"Is in good hands." Silas slowed to match their pace. "Mr. Cox, I'd like to introduce you to my girl, Miss Cora Davis. She's an archaeologist and has uncovered a mystery that you can help us solve."

Cox flatted his mouth, but Cora grabbed hold of her confidence and pushed into the dim interior of the workshop to retrieve the letter.

"This is old paper, so we must handle it with care." She set the letter on the desk, then pulled out her candle and lit it. Cox kept his distance, shotgun aimed at them.

"You sure about this?" Silas muttered at his side.

She nodded as she held the paper over the flame. If they could distract Cox, get him away from the Ward's property, Nick would be able to get Mrs. Ward the help she needed. And Marian and her girls wouldn't stumble on trouble when they returned home.

Cox's gasp as the map was revealed was incredibly satisfying. She exchanged a grin with Silas. He winked.

"We discovered that Claude is buried in our own cemetery," Silas explained. "Would you care to take a ride?"

"By all means." Cox waved them ahead of him. "Just remember, I have the gun, so no funny tricks."

This plan, by its very nature, risked everything.

Mr. Cox made Silas drive and had Cora sit in the front seat so he could keep his shotgun trained on her. Silas drove even more carefully than on their first trip to the cemetery, but the tension tightened the muscles in her neck, worsening her head pain and triggering her nausea. She needed the symptoms to hold off just a bit longer. *Please, God.*

Silas took her hand as they trudged up the hill to the old part of the cemetery where Claude had been buried. The wind whipped her scarf into her face and she shivered. She should have brought her coat. Silas rubbed his thumb across the back of her hand. He knew. He'd protect her, too. Had she made the right gamble? Perhaps appealing to Mr. Cox's greed would get them out of this. But what if—

"Where's the treasure?" the rotund man demanded as they reached Claude's tombstone. Showtime.

"Marta. Marta is the key," Cora whispered to Silas, cluing him into the hunch she'd discovered with Nick.

"Martha, you mean?" Silas stayed close by her side, keeping himself between her and Cox.

"No. Marta." On the other side of a towering stone to the right of Claude's plot stood a small headstone for Helene Marta Falk. Giddiness dampened her fear. She was right. "Look."

"Where's the treasure?" Cox demanded again, cocking his shotgun.

"Somewhere between these two gravestones." Cora waved at both. She had no idea what that meant—yet—but as her mind worked the problem, feeling Silas's protection, her fear melted away.

"This better be worth it," Cox growled.

"Give her a minute to figure it out, all right?" Silas rested his hands on his waistband, not a waver in his voice. "You'll get your money."

Before the tension between the men could escalate, Cora explained the situation. "The letter said the treasure was between Claude and Martha, and this family marker"—she pointed to the tall stone—"is all that's between Claude's and Helene's respective burial plots."

"I've never met a family named Siegel," Silas muttered.

Something sparked in Cora's aching head. "Say that again."

"A family named Siegel?"

"That! Siegel. It has Latin roots, but it's German for *seal*." She grabbed Silas's forearms. "Seal, Silas. Look for the horses!"

"Horses?" Cox's confusion had him lowering the shotgun. Silas shifted toward him, but Cora tightened her grip on his arms.

"Just wait," she whispered. "Don't anger him until I have something to mollify him."

"He could fire at any time," Silas hissed.

"Stop talking!" Cox jabbed the gun into Silas's back, forcing him to his knees. "Look for the horses."

"Don't worry, Mr. Cox." Cora showed him her palms. She'd been watched under armed guard before—most guards were there to protect the artifacts she and her colleagues found, and that included keeping the archaeologists, especially a female one, from absconding with them—so with discovery imminent, his weapon had ceased to faze her.

Silas, however, was primed to attack like a catapult.

"Then get searching." Cox took a step back.

Cora knelt beside Silas. "What money, Cora?" Silas's words were barely audible. "We don't have any treasure."

"Not yet, anyway." The excitement of discovery overtook every other emotion. This is what she lived for.

From the top to the bottom, she ran her hands over every square inch of cold surface. The edges of the wide block letters to the flat bare areas. Then she moved to the blank left side. Nothing but divots and cracks there. The back showcased the Siegel name again, large and centered on the pillar.

She refused to lose hope. Dirt caked her hands as she traced the letters, feeling every dip and ridge. She knelt, running her palms along the rim of the large square base. Grass grew close to the stone, and she pressed it to the ground, out of her way. Again, her fingers traced the bare stone of the base, but this time, she found something. A circle.

She dropped to her stomach, tore the grass away from her view. Within the circle were the two horse heads from the desk that housed the letter and the same as the watermark. If the earth mounded against the stone, they'd vanish to sight. She dug into the ground to see the horses better, not caring for the mud that slipped between her fingernails.

There, fully visible now. The seal. *Siegel*. She'd found it!

"What are you doing?" Mr. Cox demanded.

"I'm looking for your treasure, Mr. Cox." She pressed her thumbs, one situated over the head of each horse, and the seal gave way. Nothing else happened, so she tried turning it, like she did with the desk seal. The horses moved beneath her fingers. A spring snapped inside.

"Over here," Silas said from the other side of the stone. "The front dropped open."

Sure enough. Cora knelt beside him. Despite his shotgun, even Mr. Cox leaned close. The front panel of the bottom stone had fallen forward, revealing a hollow center.

She went to reach her hand inside, but Silas caught her wrist. "Cox, whatever we find in here, you'll take it in exchange for letting us go? No matter what it is?"

"Of course." Greed made his eyes bright. He waved the shotgun. "Hurry it up."

"Let me." Silas's face was mere inches from her own. A face she was beginning to hold so dear.

"I do this for a living, Silas. I'm not afraid." Not even the spiders could keep her from sticking her hand into this cold, dark, unknown space.

Silas moved his thumb along the inside of her wrist, weakening her resolve. "It's the big man I'm concerned about. Let me protect you. Please."

"You have been. Keep your focus on him and let me handle what I do best." She infused assurance into her smile. "Trust me, Silas."

He closed his eyes for a moment, then nodded and released her.

Cora slid her hand into the opening, feeling for whatever treasure Claude buried here. Nothing met her fingers.

"Well?" Mr. Cox demanded.

"Give her a minute," Silas growled.

Whatever was in here either wasn't here or had no height. She dropped her hand, expecting to land on cool marble or even dirt. Instead, her palm rested on paper. Several papers. She carefully drew them out.

"Another map?" Mr. Cox seemed ready to tear them from her hand.

"Let me see what they say." Cora spoke as patiently as she would to a child, hoping to let him know she'd tell him once she figured out the secrets on these pages if he would allow her a minute. "This top page is a letter signed by Claude, Helene, and a judge."

"What does it say?" Silas peered over her shoulder.

"Permission to read it aloud, Mr. Cox?"

At the man's nod, she began:

"Being of sound mind and sound heart, we, the undersigned, Claude Herman and Helene Marta Falk, write this to assure the care of our son. While we were forbidden and unable to wed, we love one another and that love produced a son. Circumstances are such that in order to give our son the best chance at life, we must give him to another family and keep his parentage a secret or risk the deadly revenge of someone close to us. However, we wish our son to know that we will always love him. When the time comes, we charge his new parents with sharing the secret of his birth with him. We sign this on the fifth day of May, in the year of our Lord seventeen hundred and eighty-five."

"Seventeen eighty-five?" Silas pointed to Helene's headstone. "She died two years before Claude, but I wonder how they both ended up here with the papers between them? And so many years later."

"This second paper tells us more. The name of the child was James Alexander. He was given to a Harold and Catherine—" She stopped. Was this information good or bad? How would Mr. Cox respond? Did he already know the truth?

"What is it?" The man aimed the shotgun at her and Silas jumped between.

Cora swallowed before meeting Mr. Cox's gaze over Silas's shoulder. "It says the boy was given to an older couple who could not have children."

"And?"

Cora leaned into Silas's back, receiving the strength she needed to share the rest. "The names of the couple who took in baby James Alexander were Harold and Catherine Cox."

Before Cox could respond to Cora's pronouncement, Silas went on the offensive. He'd had enough of waiting, of seeing the shotgun pointed at Cora. He advanced on the man, pinning the shotgun sideways between them as he grabbed the man's lapels. Cox outweighed him by fifty pounds, but Silas had muscle Cox lacked.

"You lied to me," Silas growled in the man's face. "You said you didn't know anything about the desk, that you didn't inherit it. But you did. From your parents—because it was handed down from James all the way to you. Did you know about Claude too?"

"I knew nothing of the sort." Cox shoved away from Silas, but it gave Silas the opening he needed to grab the gun, twisting and taking possession.

Cora was at Silas's elbow. "What did you think you'd find here?"

"Compensation." Cox's round face turned red. "I'm broke. The bank wants my house, so my wife left me, and my son won't speak to me. Money would have allowed me to keep my house, which would fix everything else."

Silas stared at him. Stealing from a widow to save one's social standing? A wife who left because of reduced circumstances? Silas was desperate to put food on the table for the women in his life, but he'd never resort to extortion. And Cora would never want him to, even if it meant they could never be together.

Cox waved at Silas. "Do you mean to shoot me now that you know the truth? Punish me for having an illegitimate ancestor that will leave a stain on my family? This is no treasure. This is disaster. My wife will never return to me. I'm ruined."

Ruined because of those reasons? Cora was an illegitimate child of an illegitimate child and Silas thought the world of her.

"What now, Mr. Cox?" Cora's question was firm but quiet.

"Now I am nothing." Cox sank in on himself. "I have lost everything. The bank will take my house tomorrow. Worse, if my wife discovers illegitimacy in my family line, she will never return to me."

Cora stared at the papers in her hands. "James's illegitimacy shouldn't matter."

Silas wrapped his arm around Cora's shoulders. He didn't know what to say, but Cora's background would never drive him away, and he wanted her to know that about him. Cox was wrong. It didn't matter because what truly mattered—love—could not be taken away so easily.

"It does matter." Cox dropped to his knees, head bowed. "I have nothing. I am nothing. And I am sorry."

Silas's thoughts echoed in his head as he delivered a subdued Cox to Detective O'Connor twenty minutes later.

They dogged him as he and Cora visited Mom at Dr. Thompson's clinic, where Nick assured them he and Marian would bring Mom home that evening. She'd suffered an apoplectic attack, but because of their quick actions, Nick had been able to get her help in time. Her forgetfulness might increase, but none of her other faculties seemed changed.

Before he took Cora home, he made sure Buck had survived the car crash with nothing more than scrapes and a wrecked car. So many people injured because of Cox's greed and desperation.

Silas's shoulders weighed heavy as he walked Cora to Mrs. Whittle-bush's house. They'd left the truck for Marian and Nick to bring Mom home. His nieces were with Mindy.

Three days—less, now—until he hopped a boxcar to head west.

Just because Cox was in jail and the threat of bleeding money was gone from the Ward family, they still were left with dwindling funds.

Nor was the danger to Cora gone. Whoever had murdered Henry Gordon was still out there. Would they come for Cora? Detective O'Connor hadn't known when Silas asked him upon handing over Cox. They had no clues, but even Chief Sebastian admitted Cora was not a suspect, seeing that she hadn't been alone since Detective O'Connor delivered the news that Gordon had been released.

What would happen to Cora once he left?

"You're distracted," Cora said as they climbed the porch steps. The pain from the afternoon's danger lined her eyes in the evening light.

Not distracted, uncertain. He tugged her hand to lead her toward the side porch where they could watch darkness overtake the lake. Instead of handing her to one of the rocking chairs, however, he stopped them at the railing, keeping hold of her hand.

She rested hers against his shoulder. "Are you going to tell me what's going through your mind?"

He ran a finger from her temple to her chin. "How's the head pain?"

"Better. It began to fade after finding the papers about James, but it lingers."

"And the dizziness?"

"Gone."

"And the nausea?"

She tipped up her chin. "I only get it when the dizziness or pain gets bad."

"Okay, then." He freed his hand from her fingers so he could wrap his arm around her waist and draw her closer. She closed her eyes, and he dropped a kiss on her contented smile. At her sigh, he kissed her again.

"Silas?" She put an inch between them. "What are you trying to say?"

He rested his head against her forehead, both arms wrapped around her waist, hugging her to him. "I don't want to lose you, but I can't stay."

She chuckled. Chuckled! "You know, staying in Crow's Nest isn't my cup of tea."

True. "But I can't take you with me."

A mischievous twinkle lit her blue eyes, like the moon when it glistened off the lake. "Nothing says I won't find myself in the same vicinity as your ranch."

"Cora."

She backed up a step, and he released her. "I'm free to go where I please, Mr. Ward. Maybe I'll stay with the Corinvetter Foundation, maybe I won't. If I don't, then who says I can't work out West? Not in the same capacity as my mother or grandmother, of course, but surely, there are respectable jobs for an unmarried woman. Frankly, being a female archaeologist was controversial, so that doesn't scare me. As long as my morals aren't compromised, I'm not beyond doing most work, even men's work."

"But there are more cowboys than eligible women out West. You'll be snatched up before I can declare any intentions."

"Aren't you declaring them now?"

He rubbed his neck. "I want to. Heavens, how I want to. But I can't provide for you and my family. I can't make promises I might not be able to keep."

She put her fists on her hips. "Why can't you keep them, Silas? Will your feelings change in a year or two or three? If that's the case, then we need to end whatever it is between us, because that doesn't work for me."

She had a point there. "But I can't ask you to wait for me."

"You haven't asked, Silas. That's my point. You haven't asked whether I'd be willing to wait. Or is it that you aren't willing to do so?"

Silas turned toward the lake, planting his palms on the newly painted railing. Was it selfish of him to listen to what his heart wanted? For the last year, everything he'd done was for his family. Nothing he did was for himself. Telling Cora the truth felt like a betrayal of the promises he made in the wake of Zee's death.

"You're not ready." The sadness in Cora's tone bit into his heart. "I'm not sure my heart could belong to anyone else, but I won't follow you to your ranch unless you welcome it."

"Cora, wait." He snagged her hand before she could turn the corner of the porch. "If I could marry you before Sunday so I could take you with me, I would. I want you by my side forever, and I never want to be apart."

"You do?" she breathed.

"More than I can express. But my duty, my responsibilities ..."

She tugged him to her. "Silas, I've been working for as long as I can remember. I can help you."

He brushed a curl from her cheek. "Married women don't work."

"They did during the Great War. Some still do, even if men claim they stole their jobs. It isn't true. There are enough jobs for all of us."

"There isn't, though, Cora. Buck told me the unemployment rate is rising rapidly. I have to take this job while I have a chance to get it. There's no guarantee there will be a job for you nearby. And having you close, but unable to marry you, would be sweet torture. Cora, I can't do it. I can't ask it of you."

"Okay." Cora deflated.

He lifted her knuckles to his lips, knowing this was goodbye.

Saturday, October 4

Cora pinned her up her curls and glanced at Tante in the mirror. "I'm not sure I want to go to the dance tonight."

"I know, my dear." She placed her aging hands on Cora's shoulders. "Seeing that boy dressed up won't do your broken heart any good. But maybe seeing you looking so pretty will remind him of what he's leaving behind."

"Oh, Tante, I don't want to do that to him." He, David, and Nick had been keeping an eye on her, even though there had been no signs of whomever harmed Mr. Gordon. She should be thanking him. "I cannot leave him with bitter memories."

"You're a good girl, but Nick is taking both of us, so make sure you're ready." Tante spun on her Mary Janes and marched from the room. When she was determined, there was no changing her mind.

"It'll be all right," she told the mirrored version of herself. The one that showed dark semi-circles beneath her eyes and pale cheeks. Her darker skin veiled both, but she could tell, and she had no doubt Silas would notice as well.

"Nick is here, Cora!" Tante shouted from the kitchen a few minutes later. "Enough dawdling. Let's go."

Opening her usual blue scarf to use as a wrap over her dress, she hugged it to herself like a shield and descended the stairs. Adaleigh had opted to get ready at the Martins' house, saying that Samantha, David's sister, specifically requested her presence or she wasn't going. Cora hadn't minded, hoping it would allow her to get out of attending, but Tante had other plans.

"You're looking lovely tonight, Miss Davis." Nick bowed from where he stood just inside the front door. "Are you ladies ready?"

Nick drove Tante's car, and the two kept up a steady stream of conversation all the way to the Crow's Nest Social Hall—otherwise known as a well-kept barn near Crow's Nest Creek, just west of the Wards' property. The area was more farmland on this side of town, with high stalks of corn and low fields of soybeans.

Other cars lined the road. Nick offered Cora and Tante both an elbow to help them navigate the uneven ground between where they had to park and the hall. Cora inhaled the cool night air, her exhale visible in a white puff. Lights glittered from inside the barn, and the sounds of people, music, and running water drifted their way. In the darkness beyond the barn ran Crow's Nest Creek, which sounded larger than its name implied.

"It's going to be okay." Nick's quiet words didn't calm her. Had Silas said them, she'd believe him. Nick was nice and all, but he wasn't Silas—that was clear to her—and she wanted Silas. "If your symptoms act up, tell me and I'll take you home."

Could she lie and fake a headache to get out of being here? No one would question her. Then she could escape. One glance at Tante's face, full of anticipation and joy over the night ahead and she discarded that notion. Cora was here for Tante, and she'd stay the course for her.

"You made it!" Adaleigh greeted them just inside the doorway, hugging first Tante, then Cora, before offering her hand to Nick. "I've never been to anything like this. Oh, sure, balls and socials, but this is delightful!" She spread her arms wide and twirled as if she wore a ballgown and not a slim-flitting, sleeveless dress. It was the height of fashion. Cora might not go for that type of thing, but working in antiquities, she'd seen plenty.

"Where's David?" Tante asked.

"Getting us punch." Adaleigh's smile wavered at the corners.

As soon as Cora spotted the punch table, she understood why. Silas. And wow, did he look good. At the Apple Picking Party dance, he'd worn his work clothes. Today, he sported a dark suit that showed off his broad shoulders. A little girl in a pink dress of Tante's creation dashed up to him. He knelt before Nettie, who animatedly explained something, then put her hand into his large one and pulled him away.

"I want to whack him for hurting you," Adaleigh's voice said low in Cora's ear, "but it's hard to be angry at a man who is that devoted to his nieces."

"Precisely my problem." Cora sighed.

"Aw, you need something to take your mind off Silas. How about I give you the first dance with David?"

"I couldn't do that." Cora pulled herself together. "No. I'll be fine. Nick is technically my escort, so I'm sure he'll offer one."

"Either way, you can count on David, too."

"Thank you, Adaleigh. I'm glad we've become friends."

Cora held up the wall of the barn for most of the evening. Nick, David, and Buck each offered her a dance, which she accepted—she declined all others—but Silas never did. Yet she couldn't seem to keep her gaze from finding him. Watching the joy on Nettie's face as Silas spun her warmed her heart. This is what Cora had missed by not attending her own dance with Onkle.

Tears pricking her eyes, she slipped out the door. The creek gurgled just out of the light shining from the back of the barn, so she wandered over to the water, pulling her wrap tight against the cool air. The ground ended at the river bank, then dropped five or six feet to the quickly flowing water. It splashed and bubbled around large rocks, dark masses breaking up the moonlight reflecting off the water.

She'd get Nick to declare her healthy so she could return to archaeology. There was no way she could stay in Crow's Nest without Silas. Returning to Italy was for the best.

"Signora Davis?"

Cora turned and gasped. Signore Camposano, in his black bowler and tailored suit, stood beside her. What was the man doing here, in Crow's Nest, so far from the dig in Italy?

"I apologize for approaching like this." He eased closer and she stepped back, her instincts firing. "I came to find you when I received word about Henry Gordon. He told me about the bucchero accident."

Accident? Pulsing blossomed in her head, and the ringing grew louder in her ears. Henry Gordon had been dead for two days, and that wasn't long enough to arrive from Italy. She needed to get inside, find people to be around.

She spun on her heel, prepared to run, but he dashed out a hand, wrapped his fingers around her upper arm.. "He also told me about the statue. If you hand it over, then we can forget everything."

Like a shock of lightning, she remembered. She remembered everything. The argument before Mr. Gordon knocked her in the head had been about Signore Camposano.

"I have a deal with him, Davis. If I don't deliver an incredible find, he'll fire me. It'll ruin me. What does it matter if I claim the bucchero and you don't? You're a woman. You're here for your pretty face, that's all. If you'll be reasonable, we can discuss a trade. I'm sure you have your...assets. If not, well, I'll just have to take the thing by force."

"Never, Mr. Gordon. I don't care about the credit. Had you asked politely, I may have even given it to you, but now, you—"

She hadn't seen the blow coming, not with how her chest had been churning over the suggestion she turn into her mother or grandmother. Never would she sell herself for a piece of antiquity. And because of her outrage, she'd forgotten the most important part—Henry Gordon had a deal with Signore Camposano.

Now this was the first she'd been alone since Henry Gordon was released from jail. Here in the dark, by the edge of the creek ... if her head hit one of the rocks below, it could render her unconscious. Or worse.

"What did you want with the bucchero?" she demanded of him, trying to shake his grip.

"To sell it." He grabbed her other arm. "And you stole it from me. Then that old woman had to get in the way."

"Signora Pimonte." Camposano had killed her, not Mr. Gordon.

"If only she hadn't sent you that statue before I could get my hands on it. I want it. I deserve it for all I've had to do, thanks to you and Gordon." He shook her. "Take me to it."

She raised her chin. "Never."

"Worthless woman." He smacked her across the cheek, then shoved her, sending her sailing over the bank and into the icy water.

CHAPTER SIXTEEN

Silas led Nettie around the dance floor for the third time, taking small steps to keep his boots from crushing her little toes. He hadn't seen her smile as big, nor laugh as much, since he returned after her father died. It was a balm to his wounded heart and a reminder of why he had to let Cora go. This little girl deserved food in her belly and a roof over her head. If it meant he couldn't be with the woman he loved, he needed to make that sacrifice.

It didn't stop him from casting a glance toward Cora every few minutes, however. Where Nettie was all joy and happiness, Cora had a cloud of sadness wrapped around her like that blue scarf of hers. He'd done that. Because he hadn't been able to keep his priorities straight from the first moment he met her.

The song ended, and Silas laid a kiss on Nettie's head. He needed to be the type of man he prayed his nieces would marry someday, which meant making amends with Cora. Not that it changed the circumstances, but he couldn't bear having crushed her spirit.

He aimed for where he'd seen her last but didn't find her there. A survey around the room didn't locate her either. His pulse picked up. He wasn't convinced she was out of danger. Had she gone for fresh air, or had someone lured her outside? And, if she'd gone of her own free will, had she taken someone with her?

Again, he searched the room. Mom sat comfortably in a corner, still not quite herself, but Mrs. Martins had promised to see to her wellbeing tonight. Marian served snacks to her girls. Nick spoke with Mrs. Whittlebush. Buck and Adaleigh were on the dance floor. David frowned at his sister Samantha, who was gesturing at Kyle as the young man took steps backward. Patrick was surrounded by several young women. Plenty of interesting actions among his friends, but no Cora.

He made for the door, the cold air striking him across the face. The temperature had dropped in the time they'd been inside, and if he wasn't mistaken, they'd awake to a layer of frost in the morning.

His growing sense of urgency had him circling around back, where he heard Cora's voice. Light filtered from the barn, casting the lawn in a halo. Empty. Where was she?

"You stole it from me. Then that old woman had to get in the way." A man's voice. One with an accent he didn't recognize.

Silas stepped out of the light, following Cora's voice toward the creek. The creek! At this point in the year, it might be lower than at the spring thaw, but that just revealed the rocks. And it would be cold. It was always cold. Silas coiled his muscles to dash forward, stop whatever argument was happening. Then he realized how close the man stood to her. Her scarf lay at her feet, and the man had her by the arms.

He shook her. "Take me to where you hid it."

Silas froze. Hid what?

Cora raised her chin. "Never."

Cora, no!

"Worthless woman." The man smacked her across the cheek, and she tumbled into the water.

Silas's feet launched him forward of their own accord. The man turned and Silas plowed into him. With a solid thump, they hit the ground. Silas slammed a fist into the man's face, rendering him uncon-scious. Silas didn't recognize him. Perhaps because the darkness shroud-ed his features. Features that might now include a broken nose. He had no time to deal with him if he aimed to save Cora. He scrambled for the edge of the riverbank.

"Cora!"

The shadows were even deeper with the raised earth blocking any hint of light shining from the barn. Down there, he couldn't tell the difference between rock and the possibility of Cora's body. When no sound reached his ears other than the rushing of water, Silas slid down the bank. Cold water swirled around and into his boots. It threatened to sweep his feet from under him, but he planted them wide and searched the swirling creek.

There!

Three feet downstream, Cora lay face down. He clawed his way over the rocks and pulled her head out of the water. Crouching beside her, he lifted her into his arms and pressed his ear to her mouth. She breathed! Oh, thank God! Then something sticky dripped down his hand. Blood. She'd struck her head. A third blow in nearly as many months.

Before he let himself sink down that worrisome path, he situated her in his arms and navigated the rocks toward the bank. He could just see over it to the barn. The man who'd struck Cora still lay unconscious. Beyond him, no help came searching for them. He would need to get Cora out of this himself.

She stirred, and for a moment, he rested his cheek against her hair. His breath came in ragged. He could have lost her for good. What had he been thinking? Logic. Responsibility. Duty. He tightened his hold as tears pressed his eyes. He loved this woman too much to let her go.

"Silas?" Her voice was quiet.

Her head moved, and he lifted his to look into her eyes. He couldn't see much, but he didn't miss her grimace. And then she pushed away from him, nearly dumping herself into the water.

"Cora. Cora, honey, stop." He dropped her feet so she could feel some semblance of freedom but kept his arm around her so she wouldn't go headfirst into the water again.

And then she emptied her stomach.

He held her steady with one hand and tucked her hair back with the other. She'd worn it up for the dance, but the water had dislodged a good amount of her curls. They stuck to her neck, her cheek, her forehead. In this moment, he knew he could never walk away. He didn't know how he'd reconcile caring for his family. But Cora would forever be his first priority, the one he provided for before any other ... if she'd have him after the mess he'd made the last few days.

"Ready to climb out?" he asked once she'd collected herself. "I'll hoist you up, but if you lose your footing, don't worry, I won't let you fall. I'll keep you safe. Trust me?"

Those beautiful blue eyes stared into his. Of course he couldn't see their color now, but he'd memorized their hue. "Thank you, Silas." Her words were slow, deliberate. Because she was freezing or because of the bump bleeding on her head? At least she remembered who he was.

"I'll be right here." He dashed his lips across her forehead before cupping his hands into a stirrup for her foot. "Just like mounting a horse." The embankment was steep, and ideally, there would be someone up there to receive her. Someone other than the attacker, who hopefully remained unconscious.

How long had he been gone from the party? How long had Cora? Surely, someone had realized they were missing. Or did they assume that because both were missing, they were together, and chose not to interrupt?

"On the count of three." Silas offered a grin, which Cora barely returned. He needed to get her to Nick for his medical expertise. At the count, he used his legs to launch Cora up to the ground above. She gave a soft *oof*, but with the lack of any other scuffle, that should be a good sign.

Now his turn. He shrugged out of his coat and tossed it up, then dug his wet shoes into the embankment, grasping roots and stones to haul himself up. Just as he hooked his stomach on the top of the ledge, he looked up to find a pistol pointed in his face and Cora with the man's right arm around her neck.

The man waved the small muzzle, his left hand easily wrapping around the handle. "Let's walk."

"Signore Camposano, please let him go." Cora's voice held pain. She was strong, but this tested her mettle. Silas hated to see her suffering for him.

"No." Silas circled in front of them, hands raised so Camposano would have no reason to fear him. "Take me and let her go. I'll do as you ask."

"I'm not a fool. My car is there. You drive to where Signorina Davis tells you. We'll sit in the back."

Cora pleaded with her eyes for him to listen, to not push back, and so he complied. Where Cox was desperate, Camposano was calculating. Panic threatened to cloud Silas's judgment. They wouldn't get out of this the same way they had with Cox. If they got away at all.

Cora directed them back to her aunt's house, to the barn where they'd stored all the apples. Then she told him which floor board to lift and there, in a hole in the ground, he found the pinkish-white statue. The gift from a woman who considered Cora a daughter. He couldn't let her give this to a thug if he could help it.

"Hand it over." Camposano waved the pistol. He couldn't take the statue without releasing either Cora or the gun. If he let go of Cora, he'd surely shoot them both since he now had what he wanted. If he let go of the gun, he still had his arm wrapped around Cora's neck. Either way, this wouldn't end well once Silas relinquished the statue.

"Here, Silas, give it to me." Cora held out her hands. "I'm going with Signore Camposano until he deems it safe to let me go."

What?

Camposano stiffened, and Silas bit back what he wanted to say. There was no way he was about to let her go with this man, but the look in her eye ... the one that had told him to listen before told him the same now. She had an idea. A plan. Did he trust her?

Yes, of course, but could he trust her not to sacrifice *her* life for him? He hadn't yet told her he didn't want to lose her. That he might be the provider his family was counting on, but he didn't want to face the future without her. How could he communicate that to her without putting an even larger target on her head?

"Hurry up." Camposano pressed the pistol into Cora's side.

Cora grimaced, her eyelids heavy and pain lines etched her face. Silas set the sculpture in her outstretched hands, keeping his gaze firmly on hers, hoping she could see how much he loved her. He didn't dare say a thing, however, and so stepped back in silence.

"All right." Cora hugged the statue to her chest. "Let's go."

"First ..." Camposano aimed the pistol at Silas's chest.

He was going to die, so what worth was silence? "I love you, Cora." *Please, God, protect her and my family. Provide for them without me.*

Cora's head pounded. Her ears pounded. Her heart pounded.

She wanted to assure Silas, but words tangled on her tongue. The man stared death in the face with a peace that fired her resolve. Nausea threatened to undo her, but she tightened her grip on the statue. *Signora Pimonte, I am sorry.* As Signore Camposano took aim, Cora spun, using the force to slam the marble statue into the side of his head.

A crack resounded throughout the barn, but not a gunshot. No, marble on bone. Had she killed him? The thought had her heaving, though there was nothing left in her stomach. She just wanted him stopped, not dead. She dropped the statue. And then Silas's arms were around her, leading her to a stool.

"Sit, my love." His voice soothed her. Then he knelt beside Signore Camposano. "He's breathing."

Relief swept through her. And then cold. And pain, greater than before.

The next instant, she was in Silas's arms. He carried her into the house, laid her on the sofa where he'd helped her sit when they first met, and covered her with the blanket.

"Rest." He kissed her. Not her cheek. Not her forehead. Her lips. Gently. Sweetly. And she held onto that feeling as he disappeared.

It must have flavored her dreams because instead of rocks and water and blood-stained marble, she dreamt of horses and cowboys. Well, one cowboy. She didn't care what he said about not taking her with him. She was going if she had to ride the rails to get to the town near the ranch where he'd be working. If it meant fending off all the men, she'd wait as long as necessary because she wouldn't give up. She'd win her cowboy. They hadn't survived today just for her to walk away.

And there was no way she was ever going back into archaeology. Not now. Not when *things* were at the center of Mr. Gordon's and Signore Camposano's greed. She would miss the stories. But weren't there plenty of people in Crow's Nest? And people in whatever town Silas was going to who had stories that needed to be told. She'd collect those, preserve the memory of people like Mrs. Ward and Mrs. Martins. Tante and Marian. Adaleigh and Mindy and all the friends she'd made the last couple weeks. Even Nick. It might not be proper for her to write to Nick when he returned home to New York, but she could ask for his sister's address. What better way to preserve Signora Pimonte's memory than to befriend those she held dear?

As if she conjured him by her thoughts, Nick himself entered the room. "Ah, she awakens." Was that an extra measure of relief in his voice?

"She's awake? Thank God." Silas's relief was unmistakable as he elbowed Nick out of the way to get to her. "You slept for nearly twenty-four hours. We were so worried."

"Twenty-four?" What? "You're leaving today." She'd missed spending her last day with him.

"No. I sent a telegram to my foreman, explaining—" He glanced at Nick.

"Give me three minutes." Nick pointed his head toward the door. Silas squeezed Cora's hand, then left them alone.

"What is going on?" Cora tried to sit up, but the room spun and her head ached.

"Shh. Rest. You've had another hit to the head. Not as hard as the one you gave Camposano, who will be fine to face his trial, by the way. You and Silas were missed at the party, and David came upon your scarf and the coat Silas left on the riverbank. We immediately started a search for you, and when someone recalled seeing you get in the car with another man, I suspected what happened. David, his uncle, and I arrived in time to see you in action."

"I don't remember you there."

"I don't doubt it. Silas carried you to the house, and you were unconscious moments later. It was quite the ordeal for you. Now, allow me to be your doctor for a moment? I won't be able to keep Silas out for long."

This time, all Cora's memories remained intact. Other than her pounding head, dizziness, and nausea, which she'd had before she was sent into the river—again—Nick said she appeared perfectly fine. He tended the scratch on her head from where she landed on a stone in the river. Maybe she was back at the beginning of healing. Maybe she would never be rid of these symptoms. But right now, it didn't matter. Silas cared about her regardless, and she cared about him. That's what mattered. Just as they'd tried to explain to Mr. Cox.

So she was particularly glad that Silas was as impatient to return to her as she was to see him. Nick gave them both a smile, and she got the impression he knew something that she—or both of them—didn't know. She'd puzzle it out later when her head didn't hurt so much. For now, she wanted to enjoy Silas's company for as long as she could.

"When do you have to leave?" She held Silas's hands as tightly as he held hers.

"That depends on the answer to a question. See, I told my foreman something that I'm hoping wasn't a lie." Silas shifted uncomfortably as he knelt beside her on the sofa. "When I sent the telegram, I asked for a week."

"A week?" Joy and dread jockeyed for dominance. She was thrilled to have longer with him but couldn't imagine traveling just now to follow him. Not with the drums beating in her head.

"When I told him why I needed the extra time, I told him there was an attack on someone I cared about." Silas rubbed his neck, then reached into the pocket of his denim trousers. "I told him there was an attack on my fiancé, and I couldn't bear to leave until I knew she was okay."

Cora blinked. Fiancé? Had she heard him right?

"This was my grandmother's." Silas pulled out a ring. A simple gold band. Nothing fancy about it, but it glistened in the electric light. "I don't know how long I'll be gone or if you're willing to wait for me, and maybe you'd even be willing to go with me, but—"

"With you." *Please God, let this not be a dream.* "Oh Silas, I decided I was going to follow you, whether you approved of the idea or not."

"Really?" He brightened as if his very dreams had come true. Then he shook himself. "Let me finish."

Cora grinned, and the corners of Silas's mouth slipped up.

"Cora Davis, would you do me the great honor of marrying me and becoming my wife?"

Cora's smile surrendered to quivering lips. Her eyes filled, but she forced her head up and down so Silas wouldn't doubt her answer for even a second. She wanted to marry this man more than anything in the world.

Silas's eyes developed a particular sheen. "I take it that's a yes?"

"Most assuredly, yes."

Silas wrapped her to his chest, then tipped up her chin and kissed any other words away.

Silas was speechless. When he'd sent the telegram to Anchorman that morning, he had to convey the necessity of his request, the urgency. Saying Cora was his fiancé just made sense. He would have asked her last night had she not slept the whole night through. And when she didn't awake in the morning, there was no way he'd be able to leave her side until he was sure she was all right.

And he knew then that whether it would be as soon as she woke, he would ask her to marry him. And would ask again as many times as it took for her to either send him away forever or say yes.

Thank heavens she said yes on the first try.

Remembering her condition, he eased back on their kiss but kept her in his arms. He wasn't sure he'd ever be able to let go. "I thought I was going to lose you or you lose me."

"I'm going with you." The firmness in her voice had him shifting so he could see her face. "I don't care about all the reasons why I shouldn't. I'm not letting you travel across a country without me at your side."

"You're my fiancé, but we're not—" He cocked his head as a ridiculous plan entered his brain.

"We're not married. I know, but we will be and I want to be close by. I'll wait for you, Silas, no matter how many cowboys throw themselves at me. There is only one cowboy for me."

The words did funny things to his chest. Most of all, gave him boldness to ask ... "What if we *were* married?"

She frowned. "But when you arrive at the ranch, what will your foreman say? I can't live on the ranch with you."

"Even if you have to live in town, then I could stay with you on my days off." Heat slashed through him at the implications. "I mean—"

"Then we'd have to marry within the week, right?"

Silas nodded, unable to release the air trapped in his lungs. She didn't say no. Or push him away. She was helping him work through the obstacles so they could remove them. His heart pounded. Was she going to agree to his crazy scheme?

Did she read his thoughts? Because she bracketed his face in her callused hands. "If we know we want to spend our lives together, why would we wait?"

"You mean it?" He blinked. He needed to think this all the way through. "It will get tongues wagging if we marry so quickly, especially after the rumors already circulating."

She shrugged. "We won't be in Crow's Nest to hear them."

"No, no, we certainly won't." Silas laughed—he couldn't help it—then grew serious again. "Tante won't mind if you leave? I assume she wouldn't join us."

"She's content here while I spread my wings. In fact, I suspect she'll worry for me a lot less, knowing I have a handsome cowboy by my side."

Handsome cowboy? *Yes, ma'am, always by your side!* He captured her lips in a kiss, and Cora's hands left his face to slide around his neck. He might not be able to see her every day at the ranch, but he'd know she was waiting for him to come home to her as often as he could slip away.

He cupped her cheek and ran his thumb over her lips. "A week won't be long enough for any elaborate wedding plans."

"Do I look like a girl who wants a big, fancy wedding? I dig up long-buried pots and unearth forgotten lives. This is where our stories entwine, and I can't wait to witness every moment of it with you."

"I love you, Cora Davis." And he kissed her again.

CHAPTER SEVENTEEN

Saturday, October 11

Cora stood before the mirror in Tante's studio. The blue fabric of the dress Tante had created for her draped over her curves. After today, the outfit would be repurposed to her Sunday dress, but right now, she would be married in it.

Married to a cowboy.

She pressed a hand to her chest, another to her stomach. No nausea or dizziness today, just a subtle throb in her head. Her scratches and bruises had faded and had been easily covered by Adaleigh's magic touch.

Cora turned to face her audience. "What do you think?"

The ladies before her clapped, and Cora took a moment to smile at each one. Her new friends, Adaleigh and Marian, even Mindy and Samantha. And the older ladies—Mrs. Ward, whose health had improved each day though she didn't seem to realize Cora would be her new daughter-in-law, and Mrs. Martins. Then her aunt. Tears sparkled in Tante's eyes as she clasped her hands beneath her chin.

"You look like an angel, my dear." Tante blinked. "If only your mother and grandmother could see you today. They'd be so proud of what you've made of your life."

Cora nodded, for that's all she could do with the emotion crowding her throat. These women had not only been incredibly supportive of the idea of Cora and Silas getting married within a week of their engagement, they had made sure it happened.

Of course that newspaperman spread rumors, but Mindy and Buck had made it their mission to set the rest of the town straight. Not that Cora cared all that much about the rumors. She didn't like that Silas's reputation could be tarnished because of her. Then again, Silas had said the same thing about her. Sweet man kept melting her heart.

"Goodness, my dear, I'm going to miss you." Tante took her hands. "But I know this is the next adventure God has for you."

She was going to be Silas's wife! Her melted heart was swept up in a wave of giddiness.

"Just know"—Tante shook her hands, drawing her thoughts away from her soon-to-be husband—"you can always find a home here. If ever you're in need, don't hesitate to run back here where you can sort things out in a safe place. Ya hear me?"

"Yes, Tante."

At the moment, she didn't want to think of what danger or trouble could await her in the future. The past few months had held more than she wished for in a lifetime. She wanted to ride off into the sunset with Silas and begin a new life. However, it wouldn't be an easy start for them. They'd likely be apart more than they were together. Frugality and hard work lay ahead, but they would be pulling together, like a team of horses.

Tante patted her cheek. "Remember, God will always be your refuge. People—even husbands—will come and go, but in Him you can always trust."

Cora wrapped her arms around Tante's frail body. If only Onkle were here to walk her down the aisle. They both missed him, in different ways, of course. But somehow, on days of celebration like this, his presence was missed most of all.

"Goodness me, I'm going to ruin your dress." Tante pulled away, smoothing Cora's skirt before wiping her eyes. "I couldn't be happier that you and Silas will have each other now. A good man is hard to find, and he's one of the good ones. Even if he is a cowboy." Tante winked.

Cora laughed. "Especially because he's a cowboy."

"Knock, knock," Nick called as he entered the house. "May I enter safely?"

"Come in!" Tante gave Cora's hand one last squeeze.

"*Mamma Mia!*" Nick whistled as he stepped into Tante's studio. "You are looking mighty fine, Signorina Davis. Are you ready? If you want to back out, just say the word, and I'll smuggle you away to wherever you want to go. No questions."

"I'm ready." Then Cora bit her lip.

Nick was by her side in a few long strides. "What is it?"

"I wish Signora Pimonte could be here."

Nick bent to look directly into her eyes. "You know she'd love Silas, right? She'd pinch his cheek and declare him a most handsome man. Then she'd bake your entire wedding feast. Flour would cover her house. Dough would overflow the windows. And she'd declare your wedding day a holiday the whole town would be invited to celebrate."

Bittersweet joy, that. "It's exactly what she'd do."

"And don't you doubt it." Nick straightened. "Now, how's your head? Any symptoms?"

"I'm in relatively good health today, Dr. Matrone."

"Wonderful. Once you're out West, have the doctor there write to me so I can make sure he understands your medical history. I leave Monday to return to my practice in New York, so he can reach me there."

"I have all the information, Nick. Thank you."

Nick nodded. "I feel like I'm sending my little chick out into the big, bad world. You've become a little sister to me, Cora. I'll miss you."

"You can always visit us, or Tante."

Nick cast a glance toward the other women. Did his eye snag on one of them? "I may do that one day. But now it's time to get you married off. I was sent to retrieve all of you and here I am, caught talking."

"Nick, thank you for walking me down the aisle."

"It's my honor." Nick kissed her cheek. "You and Silas make a wonderful couple, and I trust him to take care of you. For you to take care of each other. Ready?"

Cora took a huge breath. "All right. Let's have a wedding!"

"You promise you'll keep an eye on them?" Silas gave Buck his most intimidating glare. He was especially worried for his mother, who seemed not to realize she was the mother of the groom at today's festivities. "I'm trusting you to make sure my mother, sister-in-law, and nieces, and Tante, all won't starve until I send money home."

"Do not worry." Buck pushed off the apple tree he'd been leaning against.

They'd decided to have the wedding on Tante's property, and they couldn't have asked for more perfect weather. While it had frosted earlier in the week, warmth had returned for a last gasp yesterday. Today the sun shone brightly in a blue sky, the lake lay like glass, and a gentle breeze stirred the tree branches. Brightly colored leaves danced along the ground, hinting at the gorgeous display of color that would cover the area in only a couple weeks.

He hated to miss the fall transformation, but he and Cora planned to catch an early train in the morning.

"Did you hear me, or is your mind already on your bride?" Buck punched his shoulder. "You're a sap, Ward. But Cora is a catch."

Silas scowled. "Do I have your promise to watch out for my women?"

"My word." Buck held out a hand to shake on it. "I know it isn't worth much, but I watch out for the widows. You have three of them under your care, and I won't let you down."

"I'll hold you to that."

"Good. Because David just claimed the same promise from me. He leaves next week for the lumber camps, and Adaleigh is returning to Chicago to meet with her lawyer. We're hoping he can get us more information about what's happening in New York and Washington."

"You don't think things will improve?" Silas stuffed his hands into his trouser pockets, worry climbing his back.

"I hate to add a damper to your celebration today, but yes. I think life is about to get much harder before it gets better. Plenty disagree with me, and I hope I'm wrong, but ..."

"We have to prepare." Silas toed the ground. "You're not such a bad guy. You should make it right with Detective O'Connor."

"I wish it were that easy. But thanks."

An awkward silence passed between them, broken by David's arrival. "The preacher man is here. Nick has gone to get your bride. You ready, Silas?"

"The question, Martins, is how did Ward beat you to the altar?" Buck slapped his shoulder and made a quick exit.

Silas laughed at the color rising in David's face. "He's right, you know."

"I'd have asked her already, but—" David shook his head. "I won't say more. It's between us."

Silas sobered and nodded. "You be careful up at the lumber camp."

"Marian's parents got us into theirs, so we'll have them looking out for us. Patrick decided to come along. Not sure how I feel about that."

"He's not a boy, David. He has to grow up sometime."

"Then he needs to be more responsible. In the camps, he could kill someone. I'm already worried about keeping an eye on Kyle. If something happened to him, Sam would never forgive me. She already frets with Kyle and me out on the lake after my boat sank this spring."

"Danger comes with our jobs." Silas couldn't count the number of close calls he'd had as a ranch hand.

"Enough gloom for today." David squared his shoulders. "It's time to get you married. Cora seems like an amazing woman. Adaleigh adores her."

Silas grinned.

"Speaking of my girl..." David nodded toward the house where Adaleigh and a host of other females exited. All except the one Silas couldn't wait to see. He adjusted his Stetson, nerves firing to every limb.

David tugged his arm, and though Silas's gaze was pinned on the door, somehow David got him positioned where a groom was supposed to stand. Silas's heart beat to the rhythm of a galloping horse. Where was she?

The back door opened, and Nick emerged. Their gazes connected, and Nick grinned. This was it.

Nick stepped aside and offered his arm. A tanned hand took it, then a dress as blue as Lake Michigan followed, and finally, they cleared the shadows to reveal the most beautiful face Silas had ever seen.

David, Nick, and Buck would give him a hearty wallop if they realized just how smitten he truly was. This was the woman to whom he was about to pledge the rest of his life. Their meeting and courtship happened in a whirlwind, but the only regret he had was the pain Cora had to suffer to bring her to him. He prayed the hardships they'd face would pale in comparison, especially since they would face them together, side by side, for as long as they both shall live.

Continue the series in …
Escape with the Prodigal
Read on for an excerpt.

Escape with the Prodigal

Northern Wisconsin
Thursday, December 18, 1930

Still a week until Christmas and Patrick Martins's gloved fingers were nearly frozen. He flexed them on the handle of the crosscut saw he shared with his sister's friend, Kyle Docherty. Kyle's stocking cap hid his shaggy strawberry-blond hair but not his wind-burned ears.

They'd already notched one side of the hardwood tree to control the direction of its descent. Now they bit the teeth of the saw into the tree's opposite side. Back and forth they drew the saw. Sweat gathered on Patrick's back. His arm muscles burned, the pain the only feeling that reminded him he was alive.

"Timber!" The voice of his brother, David, had Patrick and Kyle pausing their work.

The tall tree Patrick's brother had cut with his lumber partner teetered before cleanly crashing to the ground. Kyle tugged their saw to get it moving again, but while they worked, Patrick watched as a handful of men attacked the felled tree. They would trim the branches until only the trunk was left. Then they'd drag it over to the sled wagon where a pulley system lifted the log to the top of the horse-drawn sleigh that would take the towering load down the icy road to the rail line.

Their foreman, Emyr Hughes, directed the loading. He owned the team of four draft horses that pulled the sleigh. Stories told how he and the owner of the Alaric Lumber Company, Arthur Alaric, grew up together. While Alaric founded the lumber company, Hughes kept it running. He swore like a taskmaster, drank like Patrick's father, and had a beautiful daughter Patrick—and every other lumberman, except saintly David—had a difficult time keeping his eyes off of.

"Put yer mind back on the tree, Martins," Kyle grouched, his Scottish brogue accentuated by his grumpiness. "You're going to get us killed."

Patrick rolled his eyes. Yes, lumbering was dangerous. Yes, a lumberman needed to keep focused so he didn't get hurt. But, frankly, Patrick liked the danger, the thrill. It reached past the numbness that had calloused his heart since his mother died when he was a kid.

"I aim to get home to Sam," Kyle muttered. Usually, he had an easy smile on that freckled face of his, but not today.

"What was that?" Patrick shoved the saw back at Kyle, causing him to *oomph*.

Kyle sent the saw back just as hard. "You know how I feel about her."

Just now, Patrick didn't care. He wasn't about to let another man destroy his sister's life, as their father continued to do. "You stay away from her, you understand? Samantha deserves better than you."

The man was a fisherman, working in the lumber camps to earn a living during the offseason. Like David. But Patrick didn't need the money, not really. He had no needs. Only a quest to stay occupied. However, Kyle and David, risking life and limb out here, showed how a girl could turn a man's head.

Women made a man do things he regretted. Not to mention the responsibility they required. Patrick shivered. Never would he tie himself to someone who needed that of him. No duty meant no reason to fail. As his father did. Because he would never be like his father.

"Martins!"

A crack brought Patrick's head around faster than Kyle's shout. When had they cut through the trunk?

"Timber!" Kyle yanked the saw from Patrick's hands and they dodged the falling tree.

The tall giant of the forest tipped, tipped, caught. Its wide-reaching branches tangled with those around it. Then it snapped, dropping the trunk to the ground and leaving the large crown caught in the treetops. A widowmaker.

Historical Note

In this story, Cora suffers from a Traumatic Brain Injury (or TBI) after surviving an earthquake. Not all post-concussive disorders end in a TBI, but for Cora, it did. Sometimes TBIs develop Migraine, a neurological disorder. Again, in Cora's case, her TBI caused her to experience what is now called Vascular Migraine, sometimes called Silent Migraine because it doesn't always occur with head pain. One of the hallmarks of Silent Migraine is the vertigo. Losing consciousness is not common, but it can happen.

Migraine is more than a headache. How do I know? I battle Chronic Migraine. Migraine is different for every person. Not only are there different symptoms, which range from debilitating head pain, to sensory (all five senses) sensitivity, to temporary paralysis or stroke-like symptoms, but the triggers are different as well. In Cora's case, emotional stress is her main trigger. If you battle TBI or Migraine, know you are not alone. If you would like to find out more, visit The American Migraine Foundation website.

The earthquake Cora survived is a real, historical event that occurred on July 23, 1930 in Provincia di Avellino, Campania, Italy. According to the *Reuters* article, "Timeline: Major earthquakes in Italy in past century," the 6.4 magnitude earthquake killed around 1,400 people. The region is also near the Accesa Etruscan settlement, where archaeological research was conducted beginning in 1930.

Women were just being allowed into the field of archaeology in the 1930s thanks in large part to the pioneering efforts of women like Dorothy Garrod, who worked on archaeological digs in the Mediterranean region beginning in the 1920s. This inspired me to make Cora an archaeologist. And for more about how someone like Cora would have authenticated Claude's letter, visit the Raab Collection online.

Lastly, the Crow's Nest Harvest Festival is inspired by the one in Monroe County, Michigan. You can read more about the festival that took place there for about ten years in the 1920s in the archives of the *Monroe News*. Apples were also a boon in the early days of the Great Depression, so I enjoyed adding that aspect to this story. Find out more at *History.com*.

From the Author

Dear Reader,

Thank you for joining me for Silas and Cora's journey together. I had great fun creating the mystery Cora discovers in the secret drawer of the old Chippendale desk and watching the love between her and Silas grow.

A year into the Great Depression and the financial challenges, and the desperation they caused, were exploding. Men often had to leave home to find work to feed their families, or became so desperate they resorted to crime or took their own lives. Many face similar challenges today, whether with finances or health or other difficulties, and I pray within the pages of this story, you might find hope. God doesn't magically take away our troubles; however, I believe He will walk beside us through the hardships that come our way.

Many thanks to the people who helped bring Silas and Cora's story to you. My friend and critique partner, historical romance author Ann Elizabeth Fryer. My second reader, Sarah Hinkle. My editor, Denise Weimer. My cover designer, historical romance author Roseanna White. My Early Reader Team and all the amazing readers who have encouraged me throughout this process. My husband, Gabriel, who reads every one of my stories before they release. And my boys, who keep Mama company as she writes her books.

There are many more names I could list, people who offered encouragement and readers whose excitement encourages me to keep sharing stories. I thank God for each of you.

For the characters in Crow's Nest, more danger—and romance—are in their future! Discover how David, Kyle, and Patrick survive the lumber camp, especially when Patrick's impulsive irresponsibility collides with a woman in need of rescue. Visit daniellegrandinetti.com/escape-with-the-prodigal for more information.

Then in Book 4, we return to Crow's Nest as Marian Ward faces off with winter's cold, ruffians, and the appearance of an enemy she's forced to rely on. Visit daniellegrandinetti.com/relying-on-the-enemy for more information.

Curious about the origin of Crooked Tooth Ranch? Then don't miss my Beauty and the Beast retelling in *Heart of Beauty*, A Tale of Tenacity, Romance, and Peace.

If you enjoyed *Refuge for the Archaeologist*, would you consider leaving an honest review on your preferred retail site? Reviews are a great way to help support your favorite authors and their books. In the meantime, I'd love to keep in touch. The best way is via my weekly Fireside News email. As a thank-you, new subscribers receive a complimentary ebook. Sign up here: daniellegrandinetti.com/fsn.

Thank you again for reading *Refuge for the Archaeologist*. I'm grateful to have readers like you.

Danielle Grandinetti

Join My Fireside News

Grab a spot on my virtual hearth and receive a weekly email filled with bookish content. As a thank you for subscribing, you'll receive a digital copy of my historical romance novelette: *Fire and Water*.

Subscribe Here

Harbored in Crow's Nest

Welcome to Crow's Nest,
where danger and romance meet at the water's edge.
danellegrandinetti.com/harbored-in-crows-nest

Confessions to a Stranger

Harbored in Crow's Nest, #1
She's lost her future. He's sacrificed his.
Now they have a chance to reclaim it—together.

Refuge for the Archaeologist

Harbored in Crow's Nest, #2
Will uncovering the truth set them free
or destroy what they hold most dear?

Escape with the Prodigal

Harbored in Crow's Nest, #3
Only a Christmas miracle will save
an unwed mother and the lumberjack protecting her.

Relying on the Enemy

HARBORED IN CROW'S NEST, #4
She's protecting her children.
He's redeeming his past.

Sheltered by the Doctor

HARBORED IN CROW'S NEST, #5
A fake relationship might keep her safe,
but will it break their hearts?

Investigation of a Journalist

HARBORED IN CROW'S NEST, #6
A second chance to set the record straight,
and rekindle a lost love.

Fairytale Retellings

Heart of Beauty

stand-alone origin novella

Discover the origin of Crooked Tooth Ranch in this 1870s western retelling of Beauty and the Beast.

daniellegrandinetti.com/heart-of-beauty

His Boss's Little Sister

stand-alone novella in the Apron Strings Tea Tale multi-author series

A touch of fairy tale, a spoonful of history, and a teacup of hope ... a 1930s historical romance retelling of Hansel and Gretel.

daniellegrandinetti.com/his-bosss-little-sister

UNDERCOVER WISH
stand-alone novella, part of the Di Stasio Giornaliste
Agency series

*A Di Stasio Giornaliste Agency origin story and a retelling of Aladdin
and the Magic Lamp.*

daniellegrandinetti.com/heart-of-beauty

OUR HOUSE NOVELLAS

As the world marches toward what will become WWII, visit Our House as we join the resistance.

The Italian Musician's Sanctuary

Romance, history and intrigue at Our House on
Sycamore Street.

Hunted by one man, can she open her heart to another?

Eden Cove, England, 1931—Margherita Vicienzo flees Italy pursued by her former fiancé, a member of Mussolini's Blackshirt. Smuggled illegally into England, Margherita is a foreigner at the mercy of strangers. Her limp from an improperly healed broken leg means she has nothing to offer the Ferryman family, who offer her sanctuary, and nothing to appease their son who resents her presence.

Luke Ferryman needs a wife. He wants to marry for love, but carries the weight of his family's generations-old expectations on his shoulders. Though he inherited the role of both baker and ferryman, he knows he can't fulfill both needs once his aging grandparents retire. A wife would help, but not an illegal one like the refugee his matchmaking grandmother is harboring.

As opposite as night and day, Luke and Margherita forge a tentative friendship that grows despite the constant threat of Margherita's discovery. But when strangers appear in the close-knit seaside town, threatening Luke's livelihood and Margherita's safety, the choice between justice and mercy becomes harder. And sacrifice proves the only answer.

The Recluse's Vindication

Rumors, Monsters, and Second Chances at Our House
on Heather Wynd

The Loch Ness Monster isn't the only recluse seeking a Scottish haven.
Bieldfell, Scotland, 1933—Falsely accused of murder sixteen years ago, American cowboy Benjamin Ford has chosen to hide out in the Scottish Highlands. Reclusive and not afraid to die, he rescues children out of an increasingly dangerous Germany. When his childhood best friend appears at his door, he's not the boy she remembers.

Eleanor Finch's life ended sixteen years ago. In one horrible day, she lost her dreams, her reputation, and her heart. However, she never gives up the hope of finding her friend, so when she learns of Ben's whereabouts, she leaves all that is familiar to convince him to return home.

But Eleanor isn't the only person searching for Ben. Hunters follow her trail. The thin veil of gossip and rumor may be their only chance of a future ... unless the Loch Ness Monster is real after all.

daniellegrandinetti.com/our-house

DI STASIO GIORNALISTE AGENCY

La Verità con Integrità. Truth with Integrity.
The Legacy of a (Girl) Stunt Reporter.
daniellegrandinetti.com/di-stasio-giornaliste-agency

Undercover Wish

DI STASIO GIORNALISTE AGENCY, #0
Alessandra Di Stasio
Chicago World's Fair: World's Columbian Exposition

Eyewitness Sketch

DI STASIO GIORNALISTE AGENCY, #1
Gabriella Salatino
Prohibition

Sabotage Games

DI STASIO GIORNALISTE AGENCY, #2
Emma Hancock
Summer & Winter Olympics: Lake Placid & L.A.

Shrouded Trail

Fraudulent Progress

Pursuing Dust

Hostile Ally

About the Author

Danielle Grandinetti is an award-winning author of 1930s historical romance, where mystery and suspense intertwine with hope. Her work has received recognition including a Distinguished Faith in Writing Award, two National Excellence in Storytelling Awards, and finalist honors in the FHLCW Reader's Choice, Selah, and Daphne du Maurier contests.

A second-generation Italian-American rooted in Midwest traditions, Danielle draws inspiration from tea, books, and the creative beauty of nature. Holding a master's in communication and culture, and driven by a lifelong love of stories, she crafts tales that celebrate resilience, diversity, and belonging. Danielle lives along Wisconsin's Lake Michigan shoreline with her husband and two sons. Find her online at daniellegrandinetti .com.